CHAMELEON GAMES

The Crossing Trilogy Book 2

JUNE V. BOURGO

OTHER BOOKS BY JUNE V. BOURGO

The Crossing Trilogy

Magnolia Tree, Book 1

The Georgia Series

Missing Thread, Book 3

Chasing Georgia, Book 2

Winter's Captive, Book 1

To my twin sister, Janice Sheila Rogers…
I wish we'd had more time together in this realm.
See you in a parallel universe.

ACKNOWLEDGMENTS

With this trilogy, I adopted a different style of writing. I chose to bring a secondary character from the first book, Magnolia Tree, into the forefront of this story. Sydney still maintains a character role in Chameleon Games, as does her grandmother, but the main protagonist in this tale is her mother, Chelsea Grey. I hope you enjoy the transition.

The town of Stoney Creek, Emerald Lake and Tallulah Falls are fictitious names, but the rest of the areas mentioned are real locations in the Okanagan area of this beautiful province of British Columbia.

No story can be its best without some team work. I am fortunate to have a group of people who help me in a supportive and nurturing way; pushing a point when needed, but never to the point of losing the original concept. To my Beta Readers, Anne Marsh, Heidi Frank, and Ronald Bagliere, your diverse creative insights and skills are always appreciated.

And to my husband, Dennis, for his constant support, creatively and personally. I can always count on his patience when I disappear into my world of characters and plots.

A big thank you to Patti Roberts of Paradox Book Covers Design and the team at Creativia for the beautiful cover.

To Creativia, thank you to the whole team for helping to make Chameleon Games the best it can be. And to Miika Hannila, your understanding of the digital marketing field and your dedication to helping your authors is truly amazing, and I am grateful.

❧ I ❧

Loneliness is the poverty of self;
 Solitude is the richness of self.

— MAY SARTON

✣ I ✤

KELOWNA

Chelsea Grey pushed her pounding head upwards, bending her neck back so her face caught the full force of the hot, steamy water. Still a little inebriated, her legs wobbled, knocking her off balance. *Oops!* She locked her knees and threw her hands forward to steady herself firmly against the shower stall wall. She would have giggled if the facial images of her mother and daughter weren't still fresh in her mind.

The night before, she'd gone to a night club and danced until closing. *What's wrong with that? It made me feel free.* She'd left with some joker and his friends and partied all night at his house. She frowned. *Okay, so things got a little out of hand.* She couldn't recall every-thing…too much booze and pills. Her stomach rolled over, and she took in deep breaths of moist steam until the nausea passed.

Chelsea had returned home moments ago and immediately headed to the shower. Faces of people she didn't know flashed through her mind. Chelsea winced. For the life of her, she couldn't put names to them…mostly she envisioned bodies intertwined around a room. Shame overwhelmed her. She placed her face against the marble wall and let the water pound down her back. *What was I thinking? The problem isn't my lack of thinking, that's just the cause and effect of the real problem—booze and pills.*

Chelsea stepped out of the shower stall. She wiped the mirror with a towel and stared at her image. The face that reflected back shocked her. Her blue eyes were red and glassy, her cheeks blotchy. Her long, blond hair hung wet and stringy down the sides of her face. *Not a pretty sight.* She watched water droplets find their way down her forehead and follow the length of her nose to the tip. Her eyes focused on the drip, drip, drip as they left her face and fell to the counter. In that moment, Chelsea saw the face of her future; all that it could mean and what it could cost her.

You just turned forty years old. Keep up this lifestyle and the looks you still have won't last long.

She made her way to the bed, dropped the towel from her body and climbed under the covers. Her thoughts returned to her mother and daughter eating breakfast when she'd arrived home. Her heart felt heavy. It wasn't that they said anything. *Not a word from either one.* It was their expressions. That said it all —the pain and worry on her mother's face; the anger and disappointment in the eyes of her daughter. Chelsea felt pained. One thought came to mind just before she passed out.

I'm so messed up.

THE MOTOR SOUND got louder and louder. *What the hell?* Chelsea tried to ignore it and pulled the pillow next to her over her head to drown out the annoying noise. It didn't work. She tossed the pillow off the bed in a fit of temper.

"Aargh…trying to sleep here!" she shouted.

Forcing her eyes open, she focused on the alarm clock on the side table. "Omigod…" The digital numbers read three in the afternoon. She'd slept through most of the day. Chelsea pushed the covers back and sat on the edge of the bed. The pounding in her head, worsened by the constant drone of the neighbour's chainsaw, brought back the memory of her exploits the night before. A groan escaped her lips and she crossed the room to close the window and at least muffle the grating racket.

Chelsea padded to the bathroom to relieve herself. She filled the sink with water and used her hands to splash it on her face and neck. The sting of the cold water jolted her back into the land of the living, however painful. She grabbed the bottle of mouthwash to gargle and rinse away the horrid taste and rancid breath exuding from her mouth. Only then did she look at herself in the mirror. Her face mirrored the pain she was feeling inside; physical effects of course, to be expected after her indulgences the night before— but there was something else looking back at her from the reflection. It was something that had been well hidden in the past but now stared back at her from deep in her eyes. An awareness of mental and emotional pain slapped her so hard across the face, like the sting of the cold water moments before, that she reeled backwards. The words she'd thought this morning before passing out came back to her: *I'm so messed up.*

A brushing of her long, blonde hair, some blush and pink lip gloss helped to normalize her otherwise stressed face. She added some concealer under her eyes and eyeliner. *Much better.* Skinny jeans and an oversized sweatshirt suited her mood, and Chelsea dressed, adding a pair of rainbow-striped woolly socks. She went to the kitchen. *Thank God, it seems no one's home.*

A thermos of hot coffee sat on the counter with a clean cup beside it. A daily gesture of her mother's that evoked a feeling of guilt. Chelsea poured herself a cup. The neighbour had finished his wood cutting chore, and assured of peace and quiet, she slipped through an all-glass door to the enclosed sun room and curled up on the loveseat.

The sun shone through the large panels of glass. It was a beautiful April day. Chelsea found it hard to believe she was living in her mother's bungalow in Kelowna. *Where did the time go?*

She'd been held captive by Arne Jensen for twenty years. He'd abducted her at the age of nineteen and locked her up on his farm, across the road from her parents' place. Her daughter, Sydney, was a year old at the time. Four years later, Chelsea's father died of a sudden heart attack and her mother, Elizabeth, had left the farm with Sydney and moved to Kelowna. They returned years later when Sydney was twenty-one. Sydney found her mother's journals, and through a series of events, dream sequences, and visitations from spirits, and a set of lost keys, Sydney and Elizabeth discovered her existence at Arne's and rescued her.

She shuddered at the thought of Arne. He'd died that fateful day that Chelsea found her freedom. One swift blow to his skull with a cast-iron fry pan delivered by her mother, and all of their lives changed forever. Chelsea sighed and put her head back against the back of the loveseat. She closed her eyes and felt the hot rays of the sun reflecting off the glass panes onto her face. There had been times that she'd missed him. After all, he'd been her only companion and provider for all that time. And she'd learned how to be what he wanted and bend to his rules to avoid punishment. *Not that it worked all the time.* He could be unpredictable and unreadable. Sometimes his demons surfaced for no apparent reason, and Chelsea bore the brunt of it. *But still, he was my only connection to the outside world and within the confines of my prison; the only one who could take care of my needs.*

Nine months of freedom. Why don't I feel free?

A broken ankle had brought Sydney's grandmother back to the farm to recuperate, and Sydney had renovated the farmhouse and started a home-based business. When Chelsea was freed, the three of them lived at the farm for two months. Her mother, Elizabeth Grey, returned to her home in Kelowna once her ankle was on the mend to her hairdressing business. Chelsea came with her. Living across from Arne's property wasn't an option. She needed to find a life for herself and heal. For six months she'd attended counselling and tried to fit into a world she didn't know or understand. Then at New Year's she discovered night clubs and dancing, reconnected to music which she'd always loved…and found alcohol. The pills were a new addition. And Chelsea was forced to face the fact that she was on a reckless course that spelled disaster.

The door to the sunroom opened. Chelsea turned her head and watched Sydney cross the room and pick up a sweater from a chair. A pretty girl, she had her mother's blue eyes and blond hair, only she wore hers in a razor-cut shag that fell around her face. Chelsea watched her daughter hold the sweater against her chest and stare out the windows, oblivious of her presence. "Hey."

Sydney jumped. "Uhh…" She turned towards her. "Chelsea…I didn't see you sitting there."

A pang of disappointment passed through her. *Chelsea…not Mom.* "Sorry, I didn't mean to startle you."

"No problem." Sydney started towards the door.

"Please…sit with me for a minute. I haven't seen much of you since we went out with Mom to celebrate our birthdays."

Sydney stiffened. "I'm packing. I have to be back in Stoney Creek for a yoga group session. The residence is full this weekend."

Chelsea felt awkward. She knew Sydney was angry with her. "Just for a few minutes. Talk to me."

Sydney sat rigidly in one of the wicker chairs facing her.

"I know you're upset with me." Chelsea paused to gauge her daughter. "We need to discuss it."

The girl stared at the floor. "I don't know if this is the right time."

"Somehow I think if I left it up to you, the time would never be right. You're angry with me, I know."

Sydney raised her eyes and looked at her mother. "Yes…I'm angry. About a lot of things."

"Well then, let's start with the first thing."

Sydney's eye's narrowed. "If you insist. I'm angry that you came on to Jax. What mother does that? Comes on to her daughter's boyfriend?"

Chelsea's face reddened. "I did, and I'm sorry. But I was drunk at the time."

Her daughter leaned forward towards her. "Nuh-uh…you don't get to write it off like being drunk is the excuse and that makes it okay."

"That wasn't my intent, just an explanation. He had flattered me, and I needed that. As lame as it sounds, I forgot for the moment that he was with you. Of course, it was totally wrong, and I feel terrible about it. It won't happen again."

The young woman sat back in her chair. "Until the next time you're drunk. It hurts for me to say this, but how can I trust you? And I don't mean just about Jax."

It was Chelsea's turn to stare at the floor as she weighed her next words. "Today, I realized how messed up I am, and I…"

Sydney interjected. "Yes, you are. It saddens me, disappoints me, and completely disgusts me." She stood and paced the room. "I thought I'd found a mother…*my* mother. But you don't act like a mother. You dress like me, you listen to the same music as me, and you act like we're best friends or something. Chelsea, you're forty years old; I'm twenty-two. I just don't know how to absorb that."

Tears filled Chelsea's eyes. "I was a good mother to you when you were a baby. Ask your Nan, she'll tell you. But you've come back to me two years older than I was when I was abducted. I just…I just don't know how to be a mother to an adult because I don't even know how to be an adult myself."

Sydney sat back down. "And do you think you'll find that out in the bottom of a bottle? Oh…and that's number two on my angry list. Yes, you were victimized for twenty years. I can't even begin to imagine how that affected you and what it cost you. God knows I've tried. I've been patient, tried to understand the stages, and I've gone to counselling. But you…you've given up."

Chelsea eyes flashed with anger. "I have not."

Her daughter leaned her arms across her knees and stared across at her mother. "Oh, really? You moved to Kelowna for a new start six months ago. You were going to go back to school. Instead you've become a drinker and partier and stopped going to therapy." Sydney stood and grabbed her sweater. "And that brings me to the thing I'm angry about the most."

Staring up at her daughter, Chelsea said nothing. There was so much she wanted to say but knew it was best to let Sydney get out all the anger she'd been holding back. "Tell me."

"My Nan. She spent twenty years in silent pain, wondering if you were dead or alive." Sydney paused. "It was easier for her to handle your disappearance by believing that maybe you ran off and were alive somewhere living a happy life, even if you didn't want her in it. When we found you, do know how guilty she felt carrying that anger towards you for all those years, when you were right across the road the whole time locked up by her neighbour?"

"There was no way she could know that," Chelsea whispered.

"No, there wasn't. And then she got you back and instead of building on the time the two of you could spend together, you're throwing it all away." Sydney was worked up now, and her voice had risen to a fever pitch. "It's one thing to deal with all of this, but watching Nan suffer—it sets my blood boiling. You lost twenty years of your life. There's nothing you can do to change that. But you could have three times those years in your future to make up for them. But if you choose to remain a victim and follow the path you're on, you're going to self-destruct, and you'll take Nan along with you. And if that happens, then I wish we'd never found you."

Sydney turned and ran out of the room.

Chelsea was blinded by her tears. She wanted to chase after Sydney, but she couldn't move. She stared ahead through the windows into the garden. Everything her daughter had said was true. This morning she'd faced her inner demons, seen herself as the person she'd become. She'd wanted to explain it to her daughter but knew in Sydney's current emotional state she wouldn't have believed her. It was better to say nothing.

The front door opened and closed. A few minutes later a car engine could be heard, and Chelsea knew her daughter had left. *I wish we'd never found you.* The words hurt. They cut deep into Chelsea's psyche. She let the tears flow, buried her face in her hands and cried. She cried for the pain she was causing her mother and daughter; she cried for all that she'd lost; but most of all she cried for her own weakness.

E lizabeth Grey studied her granddaughter. She knew her facial expressions and body language well. *Something's wrong,* she thought.

The two had met for an early dinner at their favourite Greek restaurant before Sydney was to head home to Stoney Creek. All through their meal, her granddaughter was distracted, and her conversation was vague. Sydney was picking at her gluten-free lemon tart, while Elizabeth sipped her coffee. "Okay…what's going on?"

"What? What do you mean?"

"You've been distant throughout the whole meal."

Sydney smiled. "You know me too well."

"Yes, I do. And I know you're upset about something." Elizabeth reached across the table and squeezed her hand.

"Oh, Nan. I had words with Chelsea before I left the house. I said some horrible things to her. I didn't mean to, but once I started I couldn't shut up."

The thought of her daughter brought a look of pain across Elizabeth's face. "I can't say that I'm surprised. It's been a long time coming. The two of you have been at odds for months. Even our dinner out the other day to celebrate you and your mother's birthday was obviously tense."

Sydney's brow went up. "I was hoping you hadn't noticed. Do you know why?"

Elizabeth shrugged. "I assumed because, like me, you're disappointed in how she's handling her problems."

"That's part of it, yes. But it's more complicated than that. I've been really angry at her. She wanted to talk about it, and I let loose. Remember when Jax and I came up to celebrate your birthday?"

"Yes, it was a fun night."

"Most of it. You went home ahead of us with your friends and Chelsea got drunk...per usual. I went to the ladies' room, and when I got back, she was all over Jax. He was embarrassed, and I was disgusted."

Elizabeth shook her head. "I'm so sorry. But perhaps it's for the best that you talked it out with her."

"Nan, I was really mean. I said her lifestyle was hurting everyone, especially you. And if it continues, I wish we'd never found her.

Her grandmother cringed. Her chest hurt. "Oh, Sydney."

"I'm sorry. I feel terrible, but sometimes that's how I feel. I understand why she's struggling, but it's hard when she acts out and does things like coming on to my boyfriend."

"I'm not condoning her actions of late, but it's only been nine months. Chelsea has a lot to overcome."

"I know. But this sudden drinking and partying path she's on can only hurt her. I want to understand her battle, but to me it's like she's given up."

Elizabeth put her cup down. She absent-mindedly wrung her hands together. "She's definitely in a self-destruct mode. I talked to Dr. Sauvé about it. I was hoping she could do something in this type of situation, but her hands are tied."

Sydney gave up on her lemon tart and covered it with her napkin. "Do something like what?"

"I don't know…maybe put her in a hospital for thirty days observation where she'd get counselling more intensively, send her to rehab…something. Dr. Sauvé says she's an adult and unless she tries to harm herself or others, she doesn't have the authority under the law to do anything about it. And Chelsea hasn't returned her calls since she stopped going to her sessions, so she doesn't really know what's going on with her."

Sydney reached over and placed her hand over her Nan's to stop her from rubbing her fingers raw. "It's a worry, Nan. But I don't know what we can do. Chelsea has to figure this out on her own. My main concern is really the effect it's having on you."

"It is hard, but I'm hopeful she'll heal. We've both given her lots of space, even when we haven't agreed with her behavior. It's time I try to talk to her. I'm sorry your talk went badly, but give her some space and time."

The waiter brought their bill and Elizabeth insisted on paying. The two women left the restaurant and walked towards their cars.

Sydney linked her arm through her Nan's. "You know, I suggested she read her journals months ago because I thought she might reconnect with that strong, independent person she was before all this happened to her."

Elizabeth stopped beside her car. "I get why she didn't want to go there. It would have made her feel like a failure now. I'm hoping that the free spirit she has hidden somewhere inside her will fight its way to the surface."

"Let's hope so. I'd best get going, Nan. Give me a hug." The two embraced.

"Drive safe and text me when you get home," Elizabeth said.

"I will."

Not ready to return home, Elizabeth called a friend and arranged a visit with her for coffee. Three hours later she drove into her driveway. There were no lights on in the house as she unlocked the door and let herself in. She knocked on Chelsea's bedroom door. With no answer, she opened it, confirming that she was home alone. *Out again.* She walked over to her daughter's unmade bed and straightened it out, an unconscious effort that gave her little comfort. Not wanting to imagine where her daughter was or with whom, she retired to her own bed early. A favourite series on Netflix with new episodes caught her attention. When she couldn't keep her eyes open any longer, she turned it off and fell asleep.

A short time later, she awoke to hear the front door open and close. Chelsea passed her door and entered her own bedroom. The clock read 10:30 p.m. Elizabeth was surprised.

An early night for once. At least I know she's home and safe.

❧ 3 ❧

SEVEN HOURS EARLIER...

C helsea used the sleeves of her sweatshirt to wipe the tears on her face. A calmness enveloped her as she stared through the window pane, focusing on the antics of a black squirrel running up the bark of a tree. The sun disappeared around the corner of the house and the room chilled. Goose bumps rose on her skin. She ran her hands up and down her arms over her sweatshirt to warm them while reliving the confrontation with her daughter. Sydney's hurtful words forced Chelsea to assess the past nine months, to re-evaluate her actions and face her failures. She tried to imagine it all from her mother and daughter's perspective.

A burst of jumbled ideas assaulted her mind. One word rose to the surface above the quick succession of thoughts that opened her to an awareness—victim. Sydney had used the word in her anger towards her.

I was a victim; I AM a victim...because I still think of myself as one.

Chelsea gave this a lot of thought. She'd talked through all the stages of her recovery with Dr. Sauvé and experienced all of them; shock, anxiety, guilt, depression, anger, loss, and loneliness. But understanding them didn't seem to be helping her. *Why? I want to feel normal—be normal.*

In that moment, Chelsea knew what she had to do. She returned to the kitchen with her empty coffee cup. A glance at the clock told her it was 4:00 p.m. *Hmm…better get a move on. It's getting late in the day.* She retrieved the telephone book and searched until she found the number she wanted. She punched in the number and waited.

A voice answered. "Rhyder Developments, Mr. Rhyder's office."

"Hello. Is Mr. Rhyder available?" Chelsea asked.

"He is in, but I'm not sure he's taking calls at the moment. Can I ask who's calling?"

"Yes, please tell him Chelsea Grey would like to talk to him. It's important."

"One moment, please," the voice said.

Chelsea paced the kitchen, tapping her fingers nervously on the cell phone to the beat of the music playing in her ear. She didn't have to wait long.

"Chelsea? Wes here. I'm so glad you called. How are you?"

Wow, he sounds the same as he did at eighteen. A nervous laugh escaped her lips. "Well…that's a loaded question. Let's just say I'm getting there, or trying to. Listen, Chaz…" The nickname she'd always called him slipped out. Another snicker. "…or should I call you Wes?

It was Wes's turn to laugh. "No one's called me that in years. You can call me Chaz if you like, either way is fine. It's good to hear your voice."

He sounds as nervous as me. "I'd like to thank you for the flowers and card. I should have called months ago, but I wasn't…" Chelsea faltered, searching for

17

the right words. "I wasn't ready to talk to people from my past."

"Hey, I get that. I really do. And now…here you are."

Chelsea decided to get to the point. "Listen, there's something I'd like to run by you, but I'd rather not do it over the phone. Do you think we could meet for coffee?"

"Sure. When did you want to get together?"

"As soon as possible. I need to make a decision, and our meeting might have an effect on that."

"Wow, intriguing. Look, I'm finishing up here for the day. If you're available now, why don't you come to my office? Everyone will be gone in thirty minutes and we'll be free to talk."

She let out a sigh. *Step one.* "I'll be there."

"Third floor, turn left when you leave the elevator. How do you like your coffee? I'll order some in from downstairs."

"Black, thanks."

"Easy. Okay, see you soon."

Chelsea raced to her room and pulled off her sweatshirt and replaced it with a black silk blouse with a cowl neckline. She redid her make-up and pulled her hair up and tucked it into a wool cap, leaving a partial bang and wisps of hair soft around her face. Black leather knee-high boots over her skinny jeans and a black leather bomber jacket finished her apparel. A glance in a full-length mirror revealed a haggard face with tired eyes. *That's as good as it gets, girl.*

As she drove to meet him, she thought about their teenage relationship and all that had happened over the past twenty years. She had grown up and gone to school with Chaz in Stoney Creek. Wes 'Chaz' Rhyder had been her only teenage boyfriend.

They'd been in love. But after he'd left Stoney Creek to go to university, she never heard from him again. At least that's what she thought. Chaz had written letters and called, all intercepted by her father, who didn't like his family. After her father had passed, her mother found the letters and put them away. Chelsea had gone missing by that time, and Chaz had married another. When Chelsea was found and freed after twenty years, her mother gave her the letters.

After his marriage had failed, Chaz returned to Stoney Creek to set up his own construction and renovation company and recently moved to Kelowna to go into commercial development. He was also the father of Jax Rhyder, her daughter's boyfriend. Jax had stayed behind in Stoney Creek to run his own residential development and renovation company. When Sydney moved back to the family farm in Stoney Creek, she hired Jax to renovate the buildings on the property, and their business relationship became personal.

Chelsea arrived at Chaz's building right on time. She took an elevator up and found his offices easily. She took a deep breath to steady her nerves, opened the door and entered.

Chaz came out of an inner office right on cue. "Chelsea. Please, come in."

Chelsea was taken back. He looked almost the same at forty as he had at nineteen. His blond hair was a little shorter than in those days, his blue eyes still sparkling. A few lines at the corners of his mouth and eyes added a mature look. A mature, handsome man stood before her, no longer a boy. *A damn handsome man.*

He led her into his office. "Let's sit here in the armchairs." He handed her a cup. "One large, black coffee."

"Thank you."

She took in his office. Dark heavy furniture with winter colours of rich browns and olive green. "Nice office. You've done well, Chaz. You must be proud of what you've accomplished."

"I am, and proud of Jax. He's doing well in Stoney Creek."

There was an uncomfortable silence. Chaz changed the subject. "It's so good to see you."

"And you." Chelsea dropped her eyes to the floor. It had been twenty-two years since she'd last seen him. "This...this is really weird."

Chaz nodded and ran his fingers through his hair. "It is that. Look, one day, if you are up to it, maybe we can talk about what happened back then —I mean...not about Arne, but with you and me. Somehow, I don't think this is the time. Why don't you tell me about this decision you need to make and how I can help you?"

Chelsea nodded. "We'll talk—one day. A couple of months ago, I had a conversation with Jax about your grandparents' cottage at Emerald Lake. He reminisced about summers he spent at the lake in his childhood and how you rarely get to go there anymore. I told him about the one trip you and I made to visit your grandparents the month before you left Stoney Creek. He mentioned that you had considered selling it, but your heart wasn't in it because it held so many memories from your own childhood." She paused to take a sip of her coffee.

"No, I can't bring myself to sell it. But it's a shame no one gets to use it. I try to go to the lake a couple of times a year to check on things."

"I'd like to address that. I was wondering if you'd be willing to lease it to me."

Chaz's eyebrows rose. "Really? Are you planning to live there full-time?"

"For a while anyway. Let me be honest here. I'm sure you've heard from within the family that I've been having my struggles of late. Some of my choices have been...let's just say not helpful to my healing."

Chaz studied her for a moment. "I always ask after you. Although Sydney and Jax have expressed concern for you, they've not elaborated on anything specific."

If he'd heard anything, he chose not to say so. She appreciated his discretion. Chelsea decided that this was a good place to leave that part of the conversation. "I need to make some changes, and to do that I need to live alone. And I need to have some space. The cottage is perfect. There are neighbours close by, but they won't be in my face."

"Can I ask how Elizabeth and Sydney feel about you distancing yourself? They've just got you back into their lives."

"I haven't told them yet. Hopefully, they'll understand my motives. They do want what's best for me. And Emerald Lake is halfway between Kelowna and Stoney Creek, so they can visit whenever they want."

"Hmm...two questions. Did you want it furnished, and when did you want to move in?"

"Furnished would be great to start, and as soon as possible. I've received victim compensation monies from the province and a monthly living allowance until my doctor deems me able to work and be a productive citizen. I'd planned on going back to school, but I'm just not ready to integrate with people. I'm thinking of taking online courses from home."

"That's a great idea." Chaz looked at his watch. "I haven't been to the lake since October, and it's due to be checked. The hydro is always on. The electric heat kept low. There is a pellet stove if you like fires. Are you up to taking a run there right now?"

Chelsea's face lit up. "Now? Absolutely."

Forty minutes later, they reached Emerald Lake, southwest of Penticton. Chelsea couldn't believe the changes in the area. "Omigod…is that a subdivision on the north side of the lake?"

"Yup."

"Wasn't that part of the Double T Ranch?" she asked.

"It was. They sold out to a developer and moved into Penticton. But on our side of the lake, the south end, the Desert Hills Ranch worked hard to have the land designated an environmental grasslands protection area. So all the properties on the south side back onto the grasslands. They'll never be developed. Sure pissed off the developers."

"That's impressive and so right. I'm happy your cottage is on the south side. There's some beautiful hiking trails back there."

"There are. But don't forget the rock cropping half a kilometre back. Rattlesnake Bluff—aptly named for its deep crevices full of rattlers."

"Ewww…I forgot about that place. A beautiful spot from a distance."

They reached the driveway and turned in, pulling up beside the cottage. Chelsea got out and looked out at the lake. She instantly felt a sense of peace. "Our timing is great. With daylight savings last weekend, we have another hour of daylight."

"I was thinking that, too, when I suggested we come right away. I'd forgotten how tranquil this place makes me feel," Chaz said.

Chelsea looked from east to west. "What I love is that I can sit on the deck in the early morning with my coffee and watch the sun rise in the east and sit out here again in the cool of the evening and watch it go down in the west. Beautiful."

"Let's go inside and check the mouse traps."

Once inside the sprawling open-style Pan-abode, Chaz checked all the traps. "Wow...no mice this year. Guess I found all the holes last year."

"Good to know."

They walked the three-bedroom cottage, searching for anything that might need repair. "I was planning to repaint the trim and modernize the doors, and replace the curtains with wooden shutters. It needs a good cleaning, too."

"I don't mind doing the work. I'd enjoy it. It'll be fun and keep me busy when I'm not doing studies."

Chaz studied her. "Okay. How does this sound? You do what you want to the place—cleaning, painting, new whatever—and I'll pay for the materials and throw in the first month's rent free."

"So whatever I decide, do you want me to run it past you first?"

"No, I trust your judgement. If you're going to live here, I want you to be comfortable." His eyes scoped the living room. "Whatever you choose will be an improvement over this old tried look. And I'm sure your choices would be better than mine."

Chelsea laughed. "Come on. You're an architect."

Jax scoffed. "I design exterior structures, not interior design. Well, I could, but it's not what I like to do. Feel free to do what you like. You can use my commercial account in Kelowna to charge materials. Now that I see the old furniture, if you want to put your own furniture in, I'll take this stuff away. Most of it will be tossed, but there's some memories attached to some of it, and Jax and I might want to keep some of it. I'll give you a list of my suppliers and let them know you can use my accounts."

She crossed her arms across her body and walked in a circle around the room. Chelsea turned to the expansive living room window and stared out at the lake. "It's perfect. When can I move in?"

"I'll be out of town tomorrow, but the day after I'll get some keys cut. I'll drop them off at your mother's that night if that works. And the cottage is yours."

Chelsea grinned from ear to ear. "Oh, Chaz, thank you. I'm going to love it here. Will you bring a lease with you? How do you want to set up payments?"

"We don't need a lease. You can stay as long as you need to and leave when you are ready. As for rent, I'll give you my account info and you can set up auto-pay if you want."

She nodded her head. "Okay. We're doing this." She put out her hand and they shook on it.

They left the cottage and Chaz locked up. "See that shed? It's filled with bags of pellets. Should last you for a couple of months anyway…" He stopped mid-sentence. "I should have shown you how to use the wood stove. Let's go back."

"No need. It's the same model as Sydney's in Stoney Creek. I know how it works."

Chaz laughed. "Of course, a Rhyder Construction special."

It was dark when they reached Penticton. Chaz broke through her thoughts about what she would say to her mother about moving out on her own. "Are you hungry? We could stop here for some dinner."

"I'm starving. Let's stop."

Settled at their table, they studied the menu. The

waiter asked if they'd like some drinks first. Chaz looked up at Chelsea. "Would you like some wine?"

"Um...no. Nothing for me, thanks."

Chaz was a good companion. He kept up the conversation throughout their meal with stories about raising Jax on his own, and his business dealings, never once asking her anything personal. Chelsea felt at ease, just an evening out sharing a meal with an old friend. *Almost normal...almost.*

He dropped her off about 10:30 p.m. back in Kelowna. "Thanks, Chaz...for the cottage and for dinner. See you day after tomorrow." She watched him drive off, and as she let herself into the house, she noted her mother must have retired early. She smiled to herself.

I guess I am, too. It's been awhile since I was home this early...and sober.

❧ 4 ❧

Dr. Sauvé sat back in her chair and crossed her legs. "I'm so glad you called this morning. It's good to see you again, Chelsea."

"Thank you for fitting me in on such short notice."

"If you've decided to continue our work together, I'm grateful that I had a cancellation."

Chelsea shifted in her seat. "Well…that is something we need to discuss."

"Okay. I'm listening."

"In recent months, my life has kind of fallen apart. I've made some bad choices. I've come to recognize that changes are needed."

"Recognizing that is a healthy sign. But I'd like to talk about the bad choices you say you've made for a moment. Do you understand why you chose them?"

"Maybe not entirely…yet. But I do know they're destructive and won't help me heal."

"That's a positive step."

Chelsea leaned forward towards Dr. Sauvé. "The most important trigger for me is that I'm still feeling like a victim."

"This is something we've discussed as you've

moved through the stages of healing. Intellectually, you know you aren't a victim anymore. But you're still emotionally tied to the victim cycle. But why? This is something we need to continue our sessions on."

Chelsea frowned. "I think I've figured out part of the reason why."

Dr. Sauvé wrote something in her notebook, but her expression remained stoic. She looked back up at her patient. "Continue."

"Because all the people around me see me as a victim. They express it through their facial expressions, their eyes, their hesitant verbal interactions with me, or their blatant curiosity and infuriating questions."

"You aren't responsible for what other people think or say to you."

"I know that...but every day they remind me that I'm different...not normal. And then I come here and we talk about it all over and over again, which just reinforces it."

"You need to separate your perception of yourself from theirs."

Chelsea jumped up. "Exactly." She paced back and forth in front of her doctor. "There's only one way I know how to do that."

"Please, sit down and tell me."

She sat down and tried to relax. "I'm moving out of Kelowna. In order for me to become introspective and figure this all out, I need to be away from people."

"And where would you go to be away from people?"

"Jax Rhyder's father, Chaz, is willing to rent me his grandparents' cottage at Emerald Lake. It's right on the lake, and there are hiking trails through the

27

grasslands. A peaceful hit of nature." Chelsea looked expectantly at Dr. Sauvé.

The doctor looked concerned. "And what about our sessions? Will you continue them?"

"Doctor, we've talked all this out over and over for months. I don't want to keep talking about what happened to me. I need to move forward. It's the only way I see me growing."

"My concern is that you may be thinking that a change of location will make it all go away. That's just running away. There are no geographical cures."

"That's not my plan. I don't want to stop thinking about it, I can't. But I just don't want to talk about it anymore."

"What do you plan on doing with yourself all day, alone and hidden away in a lakeside cabin?"

Chelsea chuckled. "It's a beautiful, bright and open-plan Pan-abode cottage with three bedrooms, not a cabin. I do have neighbours around the lake. There's the small town of Tallulah Falls close by, and I'm only forty minutes away from my mother and you, and thirty minutes away from my daughter. And I plan on taking online university courses."

"Are you still taking your anti-depressants?"

Chelsea squirmed in her chair. "No. We've tried a couple of different ones, and the side-effects make me worse. I'd rather not at this point. And if I'm being honest, I've been drinking too much, and dabbling in other pills, and didn't want to mix them." She placed her elbows on her knees and leaned forward. "It's been a long time since I've felt excited and right about doing something. I not only want this; I need it."

The doctor smiled. "I can see how excited you are. As your doctor, though, I do have concerns that over time, the bloom will wear off the rose, and I worry about you dealing with that all alone without a support system."

"Maybe I can alleviate your fears. I know that I couldn't have gotten through these initial months without your help and that of my family. I do recognize the value of your work, Doctor, as well as family support. And I'm appreciative. But I think it's time I stood on my own two feet and figured this out on my own without everyone else trying to do my thinking for me."

"I will say that is a positive second step. I'm just not sure about cutting you loose all together yet."

"You're only a phone call away. If I think I'm slipping, I'll call, I promise." Chelsea paused and reached into her bag for a bottle of water. She drank down half of it while the doctor studied her and wrote more notes.

"And the partying and drinking, are they something you intend on changing?"

Chelsea shrugged. "I think they were a coping mechanism to avoid feeling like a victim."

Dr. Sauvé studied her face but didn't say anything.

Chelsea sat back in her chair. "I have a suggestion. When I was a kid, you know I always kept journals. Thank God I did, since they were a big part of what helped my family find me. I want to start keeping a journal again. Writing down my daily thoughts and feelings could help me."

"Now that is a good idea. One I strongly encourage. And if you let me check in with you by phone… and if you come in once a month…I'll be happy to support your move."

Chelsea beamed. "Done."

"Have you told your mother yet?"

"Not yet." Chelsea hesitated. "I wanted your

blessing first. She's booked solid with clients today and will be out tonight. I'll tell her tomorrow morning. Chaz is bringing the keys over tomorrow night."

"If she has concerns, ask her to call me."

When she returned home late that afternoon, she stayed in her room until after her mother had left for the evening. She needed more time to think about how to approach the subject with her mother.

THE SMELL of fresh coffee and bacon permeated the house. Sounds of running water and doors opening and closing from upstairs made Chelsea smile. Her mother was up. Soon her footsteps could be heard coming down the stairs.

Elizabeth appeared in the kitchen. "It smells awfully good around here. Who can sleep through the smell of cooking bacon?"

"That's how you used to get me up on school mornings when I was being lazy. Remember?"

Her mother laughed. "That's so true."

"There's a cup of coffee for you at the table. Breakfast will be ready shortly." Chelsea tested the heat in the second fry pan and poured four rounds of pancake batter into the hot avocado oil. She turned to see her mother sitting at the table, studying her.

"You're up early this morning," Elizabeth said. "This is nice, having breakfast together. And having someone else make it."

Chelsea flipped the pancakes, and while they finished, she took the bacon to the table. She glanced at her mother nervously. "I had an early night last night, and I wanted to catch you before your first client arrives."

Elizabeth had a home-based hairdressing business. She'd turned the garage of the home into a salon. On summer days, she opened the garage door and let the warmth of the sun in, along with the view of the lake across the street.

"That won't be for a couple of hours. My first client cancelled."

Adding the finished pancakes to the previous pile kept warm in the oven, Chelsea took the tray to the table and sat down. They served their plates and Chelsea poured syrup from the ceramic jug in front of her, then passed it to her mother. One bite and she licked her lips. "Oh yum…real Canadian maple syrup. There's nothing like it."

The two chatted while they ate, keeping the conversation light. When they finished, Chelsea cleared the table and returned with two filled coffee cups. Her nerves were back, but it was time. "I saw Dr. Sauvé yesterday."

Elizabeth's eyebrows shot up. "Oh? Are you resuming sessions with her?"

"Not on a weekly basis. I'll be talking with her on the phone and checking in once a month." Chelsea hesitated. "I want to tell you that I've appreciated being able to stay here with you. I know it's been hard on you these past few months. I haven't exactly been the ideal daughter."

Her mother was silent for a moment. "No, but you have a lot to deal with. I'm trying to be understanding and put myself in your shoes."

"I appreciate you saying that. Look, as I told the doctor, I've made some bad choices, and I've come to realize some changes are in order. Mom, I'm ready to go out on my own and take responsibility for my life."

Elizabeth looked frightened. "How does Dr. Sauvé feel about that?"

"She supports my decision. The night before last I met with Chaz Rhyder. He's going to lease me his cottage on Emerald Lake."

"Emerald Lake? But you'll be all alone out there."

"Yes, Mom, and that's exactly what I need. Arne took away my youth and my identity. I don't know who I am anymore. That's why I haven't been able to read my journals. That strong, unafraid, ready-for-anything girl that I was disappeared. I knew reading about myself back then would make me feel like more of a victim. Being independent is the only way for me to reconnect with who I really am."

"I guess that makes some sense. But I just got you back into my life, and I don't want to lose you again."

Chelsea reached out to her mother and squeezed her arm. "You aren't going to lose me. I'm close enough for you to visit."

"I suppose that's true. What'll you do with yourself all day?"

"Take online college courses, read, hike, and canoe. And do some renos that Chaz will pay for. Lots of things. It's time, Mom."

"And what about the lifestyle you've been living?"

"I need to remove myself from people who make me feel like a victim in order to stop acting like one. That's what this change is about."

Elizabeth didn't look too convinced. "Maybe. But when people realize who you are, they're always going to see you as a victim."

"That may be true. But once I feel strong enough, it won't matter what they think. Dr. Sauvé said if you're troubled with my decision to call her. I'm sure she can help you understand this better than I can."

"If this is what you want, of course you should do it. I have to accept that you aren't the teenager who disappeared twenty years ago but a grown woman."

Chelsea shook her head. "It's hard to believe that I just turned forty."

"When are you moving in?"

"This weekend. The cottage is furnished, so there's not much I need to supply. Chaz is coming by tonight to drop off the keys. Tomorrow I'll go shopping for the extras I need and some groceries. Would you like to follow me out on Saturday and help me settle in?"

Elizabeth visibly relaxed and smiled for the first time since Chelsea had opened the conversation. "I'd love to."

❧ 5 ❧

STONEY CREEK

Sydney studied the weekend schedule she was working on. She held daily yoga classes in her studio, but she also held weekend retreats of yoga sessions, massage therapy, and meditation. People travelled to the Okanagan for two nights and days of workouts and relaxation at her spa. The sound of a vehicle crunching on the gravel driveway pulled her attention away from her work. *That must be Jax.* A hurried walk to the living room window confirmed her assumption, and a wide smile spread across her face. Jax Rhyder was Chaz's son and Sydney's boyfriend…a handsome, lanky young man that made her heart race. She watched him exit the pickup. His blond hair fell across his face as he leaned into the back of the truck. He stood tall with a box in his arms and threw his head back, clearing his hair from his eyes. When he saw her in the window, his smile matched hers, reaching his blue eyes and making them sparkle.

Sydney raced to the front door and threw it open. "Hey, cowboy. Need some help?"

"Nah. Everything you wanted is in this one box."

Jax strode up to the doorway and stepped into the hall.

Sydney leaned forward to plant a kiss on his lips. What was intended to be a quick peck turned into a series of deep kisses. She ran her hands down his back and squeezed his buttocks.

"Hey, mind if I drop this heavy box? You're taking advantage of an unarmed man." Jax headed to the living room and put the box down on the couch. He turned and lifted his freed arms above his head. Wiggling his fingers, he let loose with a wicked laugh. "I have a better use for my arms. These fingers know all those ticklish spots you try to hide." Jax lunged towards her.

Sydney screamed and ran into the kitchen and Jax followed, chasing her around the island until he was close enough to throw his arms around her. "Gotcha."

"I let you catch me." She struggled and giggled as his fingers found their mark.

"All the better for me." He spun her around and leaned his forehead against hers, staring into her eyes. They stared in silence until Jax led her by the hand to the master bedroom. Sydney let Jax undress her, her eyes never leaving his. When he was finished, she removed his clothes. No words were necessary. Their locked eyes spoke volumes. Under the covers, their hands roamed the familiar recesses of each other's bodies, building them to a fever pitch. They came together as one, and the silence was replaced with sounds of pleasure and murmurings of love until their frenzy reached a mutual climax.

Jax held her to his chest until their breathing returned to normal and they rolled onto their sides to face each other.

"Are you ready for tonight?" he asked.

"Uh-huh. The first clients should arrive in about four hours. I love these yoga retreats. Everyone is so excited to be here for the weekend. It's rewarding."

"You've had a successful first season, I'd say. You deserve it. You've worked hard for this."

"Thanks."

"So did you call your Mom yet?"

Sydney frowned. "No. I don't even know how to start a conversation with her. I said some nasty things."

"Perhaps she needed to hear them."

"Maybe. But I lost control of my emotions. I'm not proud of the mean things I said."

Jax gently pushed some strands of hair falling across her face behind one ear. "Then start with an apology and see where it goes."

"Easy to say. I need to think on this for a bit."

"Then let's change the subject. I hate it when either of us goes away...even for a few days. I really missed you this time."

"I missed you, too. At least we don't have time to take each other for granted."

Jax snickered. "Never. Do you realize we've been seeing each other exclusively for a year now?"

"It certainly went fast, didn't it? We've both been so busy with our business start-ups." Sydney attempted to sit up, but Jax put his arm across her shoulders. "Wait. There's something I want to discuss with you. It's been on my mind."

She studied Jax and found his expression hard to read. He appeared tense. This wasn't the man she normally saw. "Okay, cowboy. Give it up. What's on your mind?"

"I think we should take our relationship to the next step."

One eyebrow rose. "Next step? What does that mean exactly?"

"Let's move in together."

Both eyebrows rose and Sydney gasped. "Wow… that is a big step." This time she did manage to sit up.

Jax stared at her. "So that's it? Wow?" His face dropped. "Not exactly what I wanted to hear."

"Hey, I didn't say no. I'm just…surprised. Given your past reputation, and that's not a criticism, I only mean that you never had serious relationships before…"

Jax jumped out of the bed. "I didn't have serious relationships because I never found anyone I wanted to be serious with until you. And I wasn't a playboy. I was always upfront with women I dated. But obviously you aren't as excited about this as I thought you'd be, so forget it."

Sydney smiled and patted the bed. "Sit and stop acting indignant. Can we talk about it first before I answer?" Jax sat and Sydney took his hand. "Let's talk logistics. You'd have to move in here with me. My business is here. What about your Dad's house?"

"He never comes home to Stoney Creek anymore. It's more of an investment than a home. Perhaps he can lease it. I'll talk to him about it when I tell him." Jax was smiling again. "And we should have papers drawn up. The farm and your business is yours, and my business is mine. I don't want you to worry that I'd lay claim to what's yours because I moved in."

"Oh, Jax. It's not very romantic to plan on moving in together and at the same time make plans in case we separate."

"Okay, just trying to cover any concerns. You will

have to share that beautiful kitchen I designed for you."

"No problem here. You're still a better cook than me. But the en suite is mine. You can have the main bathroom."

"Done."

Sydney sighed. "It would be nice to spend more time together, even if running our businesses has us passing each other in and out the door."

"In your case, up the stairs to the attic. But think, the nights will belong to us." Jax leaned forward to stroke her face with his fingers and kissed her gently. "How's that for romantic?"

She melted under his touch. "So when are you moving in?"

They stared at each other and started to laugh.

"We're doing this then?" Jax asked, his eyes big and expectant.

A flutter inside her stomach moved into her chest and up into her throat. With equally large eyes, full of excitement, Sydney nodded. "There's no backing out now, cowboy."

❧ 6 ❧

EMERALD LAKE

The lake was like glass. The sunlight glittering off the surface of the water blinded the two women who stood in the living room of the cottage staring out the large picture window.

"I can't believe I've never been to this lake before. It's such a beautiful spot," Elizabeth said.

"Isn't it? And this side will never be developed, as it falls in the grasslands preservation habitat."

"It will be peaceful then; no ATVs allowed."

Chelsea smiled. "No, but lots of hiking trails are available for public use."

Elizabeth studied her daughter. "You're looking well. Are you happy here?"

"Yes. I am. And thank you for coming." Chelsea turned and looked around the room. "These past few weeks flew by with the renos. Mostly painting, that's finished. Still a bit of work in the bathroom with new tiling. Soon I'll be able to replace the old furniture and window coverings."

"I love the color scheme."

"Everything will pull together when I get the rugs and accessories in. Are you hungry?"

"Starving." Elizabeth followed Chelsea to the kitchen. "What can I do?"

"You can wash up and have a seat. The table's set and everything's ready and waiting in the fridge."

Chelsea placed some cold chicken and Caesar salad on the table, followed by hot biscuits fresh out of the oven, mixed pickles, and potato salad. She poured two glasses of homemade lemonade into tall glasses and they sat down.

"Looks delicious," Elizabeth said.

"So you mentioned Gord was paying you a visit. How are things with him?

"He's fully retired from the wildfire service and looking to move from Kamloops to the Kelowna area."

"That's wonderful, Mom. You'll be closer together."

"Well...maybe closer than you think..." Elizabeth trailed off.

Chelsea's hand, holding a hot buttered biscuit, stopped halfway to her mouth. "Oooh?"

Her mother turned red and held up her left hand. "Gord's asked me to marry him, and I said yes."

Chelsea's jaw dropped. She put the bun down and took hold of her mother's hand, pulling it closer. Her ring finger sported a white-gold band with a round diamond in the centre, surrounded with a ring of smaller ones. "It's beautiful. Mom, I'm so happy for you.'

"I'm still in shock. Marriage was never something I thought I'd do again. But life is full of surprises, isn't it?"

Chelsea smiled at her mother. "It certainly is. When is the wedding?"

Elizabeth shrugged. "We're not sure yet. Gord

wants me to sell the Kelowna house and retire to a cottage in Naramata on Okanagan Lake. The wedding won't be anything fancy, a small family affair."

"That sounds lovely, and Naramata is only thirty minutes from here. You'll be closer to me."

Her mother paused. "I told him I would marry him, but some things needed to fall into place first. You're one of them."

Chelsea helped herself to more potato salad. "Me? How so?"

"First, you've only just moved out on your own, and I told you the door was always open if you felt the need to move back. It's only been a few weeks, and I feel like I'm abandoning you."

"Mom, no…"

Elizabeth cut her off. "Let me finish. I need to feel you are okay and making your way on your own before I can move forward with my life."

"I appreciate that you are that concerned for my well-being, but believe me when I say this, life is too short to not embrace opportunity. If anyone should know that, it's me. I'm a work in progress for sure, but I'm forty years old, Mom. You can't put your life on hold while I figure out mine. Thank goodness I did move out. As long as I was under your roof, you would never have said yes to Gord."

"You're probably right. Our situation is a unique one. It's important to me that you know that I'll always be there for you, and Gord says our door will always be open."

"That's very comforting to know, Mom, but you deserve someone like Gord in your life. I like him, he's a good man. God knows you've given your life to other people, and you took on the role of raising Sydney. This is your time. Do whatever makes you happy."

Chelsea watched her mother relax, and the worried expression on Elizabeth's face disappeared. "Now, eat your lunch, Mom. You haven't touched your plate."

"One more thing regarding the house. I had left the farm for Sydney in my will but gave it to her early because she wanted to return to Stoney Creek and open a business. Of course, that was before we found that you were still alive. I know you didn't want to remain on the farm. I told Sydney that the Kelowna house would go to you, and she agreed it was the right thing to do. So you have two choices; one, you move back to Kelowna and the house is yours, or two, I sell the house and the money is yours to do with as you wish."

Chelsea was stunned. "Uh…that's generous, but don't you need that money to put towards the new house in Naramata?"

"No, because Gord and I have both agreed that we are coming together late in life and his house that he sold in Kamloops was to go to his daughters and mine was go to you. So he'll buy the Naramata house and leave it in a will to his girls. If Gord passes before me, our will is going to stipulate that I get to live in it until my passing, then it will go to his daughters."

"One thing I do know is that I love it here. I don't think I could live in Kelowna around all those people. So do sell the house, but it's your money. You should keep it. Will me whatever's left if you want, but I don't feel right about taking it now."

"Okay, then I'll sell it. But the house will sell for about seven hundred thousand. I can't believe an old bungalow because it has access to the lake is worth that much. Do you know how much I paid for it? Sixty-two thousand, so understand something, you'll get a big chunk of that now. It will give me peace of mind knowing that whatever adjustments you are going through, at least you'll have financial stability."

Chelsea felt overwhelmed with emotion. She reached out and grabbed her mother's hand. "I'm so glad you're in my life again, Mom. Not because of the money, but because your love and support is so important to me and my re-entry into society."

Elizabeth squeezed her hand. "You'll always have it. Good. Now that's settled, I can eat."

They fell silent while they dug into their lunch. Chelsea cleared the table and brought out some brownies and poured them each a coffee. "Try these. They're sugar free and so good."

Her mother took a bite of one. "Wow. You're right. You must give me the recipe."

"I've been practicing my cooking skills since moving here. Trying out healthy dishes."

Chelsea looked up at her mother under hooded eyes. "So…how's Sydney doing?"

Elizabeth put down her coffee cup. "She hasn't called?"

Chelsea swallowed hard. "No."

"Look, she told me about what she said to you. I wasn't going to say anything unless you did. She feels terrible about it but hasn't been able to bring herself to call and apologize."

Chelsea shrugged. "I won't say it didn't hurt… but I deserved it. She was concerned and upset. I'd call her, but if she isn't ready, I'd only put her on the spot."

"Give her some time. It's only been a few weeks. I'm sure she'll come around."

"Okay." Chelsea popped a piece of brownie in her mouth, glad to end the conversation.

"She's been busy, and since you haven't talked to

her, I do have some news. Jax has moved in with her."

Chelsea grinned. "Really? That's wonderful. I'm happy for them."

"It seems like we're all moving on with our lives, doesn't it?"

"Just as we should. Are you up for a walk around the lake?"

"Absolutely. I need to walk off this lunch. Let's go."

They walked into town and visited a few of the gift shops before turning back towards the lake. They walked with their arms linked in silence, each of them lost in thought.

Elizabeth spoke first. "When Gord and I do get married, I'm only going to have one person stand up for me, no bridesmaids. I would love for you to be my maid-of-honour. What do you say?"

Chelsea stopped in the road. Her heart skipped a beat. "Oh, Mom. I'd love to. Thank you for asking me."

The evening air cooled fast once the sun disappeared, as was the way in the Okanagan spring. Chelsea zipped up her jacket and put her hands in her pockets. The walk into town was a pleasant one if you kept moving. Tallulah Falls was a ten-minute walk at best. She had been at the cottage almost a month now, and her renovations were complete. A couple of her closest neighbours had come by to welcome her, but other than a visit from her mother, she'd been alone the whole time. *And loved it.* She smiled to herself. Some thought living alone was a punishment, but she'd learned that she liked her own company and enjoyed not having to answer to anyone else's schedule or needs. Her pocketed fingers of her right hand wrapped around a canister she carried with her everywhere she went. She pulled it out and studied it. The can of bear spray gave her the confidence to walk by herself into town and hike around the grasslands. She really wasn't concerned about four-legged animals; it was the two-legged males that left her edgy.

The road wound around the south end of the lake to the west. There wasn't any traffic at this time of year; only a few neighbours were out on the lake in canoes or kayaks. A few sat on their decks. She waved as she walked by. That much she could handle. As the road curved and grew from a dirt road to a paved one, she saw the main street of the small village of Tallulah Falls. At this time of year, there were only about five hundred permanent residents; in summer, two thousand inhabited the vast empty homes and camps and empty marinas.

She hit the main street and instantly heard music playing. She'd ventured into the village on this Friday night because she needed a change of scenery. There were about a dozen people out and about. Her intention was to go to a restaurant for dinner instead of cooking. But the music drew her attention towards the venue housing it. She stopped before a pub and listened. *Pub food is usually tasty. I could eat there and enjoy the music.* She continued down the street to the drug store to pick up some needed items. She pushed her way through the entranceway. Before she let go of the door, she felt a hard shove against her back, and she flew forward off balance. A pair of arms grabbed a hold of her shoulders and pulled her back. Chelsea screamed and pulled herself free.

She turned quickly to face the culprit, her right hand already inside her pocket, wrapped around the pepper-spray canister. A man in his fifties stood before her red-faced.

"I'm so sorry. I wasn't paying attention and tripped on the metal lip. Are you okay?"

Chelsea relaxed but felt rattled. "I'm fine. How about you?"

"Other than feeling stupid, I'm good."

She gave him a thin smile and hurried away, feeling embarrassed herself for yelling out. Seeing a cashier, she rushed to the counter to ask where she could find the items she needed.

"Hi, you're the lady staying at the Rhyder cabin on the lake, right?"

"Yes, I am."

The matronly woman smiled broadly. "Welcome to Tallulah Falls."

"Thank you."

The woman nodded behind her. "He scared the wits out of you, didn't he?"

"That he did."

"Well, you needn't worry about Wenner. He's a stand-up citizen around here."

Chelsea turned and watched the man disappear down an aisle. He was wearing some sort of uniform, but he was gone before she could identify it.

"Good to know," she said to the woman.

The cashier directed her to the products she was purchasing. Five minutes later, she was back outside heading to the pub for dinner. Chelsea entered the drinking house. It was still packed with the after-work crowd, and the band had only just set up. She found a quiet table in a corner near the games end of the pub. A waitress approached her.

"What can I get you to drink?"

Chelsea paused. *Why not? I haven't had a drink in a month. I deserve to celebrate the end of my renovations.* "A bottle of Heineken, please."

"Would you like a menu?"

"Yes, please."

She ordered a basket of wings and some deep-fried zucchini. All great pub fare. The band played country rock. The synergy in the room was electrifying. She was quite happy to sit alone in the back corner and soak up the energy.

When she finished eating, the waitress arrived

with another bottle of beer. "Compliments of the two playing pool beside you." Chelsea looked towards the two men. They were much younger than her. An unease moved from her stomach and into her chest. Her body stiffened. She wasn't sure how to handle it without embarrassing them or herself. She held up the bottle and nodded to them, mouthing a thank-you. One of them approached her table.

"You're new here."

"I am. Thanks for the beer."

"We just wanted to be friendly and make you feel welcome, especially since you're here alone."

"That's very thoughtful of you."

"Would you like to join us and play a little pool? We have a third and need a fourth to make up two teams."

Chelsea was about to say no. After all, they were much younger than her, and she wasn't looking for new friends.

"Please say yes, you'd be doing us a big favour. There's money on the table and we intend to win it." He glanced over his shoulder to see who was listening and leaned towards her. "That third fellow is a braggart, but he's not a very good player."

Chelsea chortled. "And you think if I'm his partner, you'll win for sure? How do you know if I can play or not?"

His face reddened, and he laughed. "We don't. But we want to teach our arrogant friend a lesson. If we win, we'll share the pot with you."

She studied the other two young men. *Harmless enough in here with this crowd.* Something inside of Chelsea came to life. *If only you knew.* "Sure. Why not?"

Chelsea joined the other two at their table. The one who'd invited her introduced himself. He was tall and thin, with long black hair. "I'm Tommy. This is my partner, Cliff, and your partner, Adam."

"Hi, guys. I'm Chelsea."

Cliff was shorter but stocky with short hair, puffed out on top in today's latest style for men. Her partner was shorter still with a beer belly. She nodded to Adam. "So...you ready to wipe these boys off the table?"

Adam snickered. "You bet." The other two laughed and hooted. "She's as cocky as you are, Adam," Tommy said.

"Good partnering, then. I haven't played for a while, but I know the game," Chelsea said with a chuckle. "How much is my bet?"

What the young men didn't know was that Arne, her captor, had a pool table in the basement. It was the only form of recreation he allowed her. They played for years, and when he allowed her to, she played by herself for hours, perfecting her play.

"We'll toss to see who starts," Cliff added, taking a coin out of his pocket.

Chelsea put her money on the table, and Cliff tossed a coin. "Chelsea and Adam start. Who's up first?"

"Mind if I break?" Chelsea asked Adam.

He looked surprised but shrugged. "Ladies first."

Tommy stood. "Do you want me to rack the balls?"

"No, thanks. Got it."

Chelsea placed the fifteen balls in the rack and moved them into place. She walked to the other end of the table, noting it was a regulation-sized table. She placed the white cue ball on the table and weighted the sticks, choosing the one that felt most comfortable. She placed it on the table and rolled it to check for bowing and balance. A quick glance at the opposing team made her smile. They'd been watching her intently and exchanged glances with raised eyebrows. Chelsea rolled the white ball with the stick, placing it at an angle to the balls at the end of the table. She prepped her shot. She hit low and hard on the cue ball, and it raced across the table, scattering the balls in all directions. Two balls were made, one stripe and one solid, giving her the preference to choose which balls to play. "We'll take solids."

"Nice break, partner," Adam yelled.

The three men stood to see what her next move would be. Chelsea turned to their table and grabbed her beer. She took swigs of beer as she walked slowly around the table and examined her options. She took her time, well aware that the young men were watching her every move. She decided where she was going next and put her bottle down. Each move she took was calculated to make sure her next move was protected and available. One by one, she made the balls in numerical order until she was left with the last ball and the 8-ball.

"Holy shit," Tommy said. "Where did you come from, lady?"

By now, other patrons in the bar had joined their section to watch the stranger…and a woman…clear the table. Chelsea picked up her beer and studied her options. *Damn.* The 8-ball blocked her shot.

Adam stood beside her examining the table. "Tough break. Maybe tap this one to open up the last ball and block their access to their first."

"That's a good call, Adam, but I think I've got this."

"What's your call?"

"I can hit the cue ball into the side cushion, angle it down to the end. It'll bounce back, hit the final ball and shoot it into the side pocket. Meanwhile, the cue ball will bounce back and knock the 8-ball to the cushion at this end, shoot back and set itself for the final shot."

Adam let out a whistle. "That's a calibrated shot that could work, but there are things that could go wrong. Namely the cue ball could end up in the end pocket and the 8-ball could follow your last ball into the side pocket."

"Okay, well, give me some room and I'll think on it." Chelsea had done this shot once before, and she was banking on it working now. It was all in the amount of force, more or less. She lowered her head to the edge of the table and measured her shot from all angles. She called her shot out, and a murmur went out around the group watching. Waiting for them to settle down, her eyes never left the table; her complete focus was on her shot.

As if in slow motion, the cue ball moved forward, bouncing off the side cushion. The banked ball projected towards the end cushion. The cue ball raced back up the centre of the table and connected with the final ball, knocking it into the side pocket. The white ball bounced back and ricocheted off the 8-ball, raced towards the end pocket, hit the corner and came back a couple of inches and stopped. Meanwhile, the 8-ball banked off the end cushion at an angle and raced back towards the same side hole that just pocketed the last ball. There was a gasp in the crowd. The black ball stopped right in front of the side pocket.

Not realizing she'd been holding her breath, Chelsea let it out amidst the whistles and murmurs. She walked around the end of the table and smiled. The cue ball was perfectly set up a few inches from the 8-ball, and she easily made her last shot, clearing the table in one full uninterrupted round.

The crowd erupted into applause and cheers. Chelsea walked to her table. Adam was hooting and pounded her on the shoulder for their win. He picked up the money and gave her half. As she sat, she looked at Tommy and Cliff, who stared at her, shaking their heads.

She gave them a crooked smile. "Sorry, boys. I guess I got lucky."

"Like hell you did. Where did you learn to play like that?" Tommy asked.

"Let's just say there was a period in my life where I had nothing but time on my hands. Pool filled that time."

Adam beamed. "Have you done that shot before? It was amazing."

"Once before. But I practiced it a lot."

People sent her free beer, and before long their table was covered with bottles. The music got louder, and soon Chelsea forgot she'd intended to stop in for some dinner and one drink.

❈ 8 ❈

A loud ruckus of Canada geese flying overhead drew Chelsea from sleep and back into the world of wakefulness. She rolled over and groaned. It was still early, and it would have been nice to sink lower into the bed and pull the covers up over her head. But the ache of a full bladder forced her out of bed, and she headed to the en suite, noting she was still fully dressed and had slept on top of the covers. By the time she relieved herself, a force-ten headache replaced the bladder ache. A splash of cold water over her face and a capful of mouthwash made her feel human of sorts. She pulled her hair back with one hand, leaned under the facet and washed down a couple of aspirins. Chelsea padded back to the bedroom and removed her clothes. She donned a fresh pair of underwear and pulled an oversized t-shirt over the top. Picking up a brush on the dresser, she stared at her reflection in the dresser mirror. Her thoughts were lost to the previous evening...at least what she could remember of it. She concentrated on the slow, methodical brush strokes as she worked through the tangled mess of hair.

A reflection of a face peering over her right

shoulder caught her eye in the mirror. She froze. *Okay, now this is too weird.* Chelsea stared at the face, mesmerized by its presence. Anyone else would have been frightened to suddenly find another face reflected in the mirror, but she remained calm. The reason was that the face was hers. *Maybe I'm still drunk and seeing double.* She blinked a couple of times to see if the double image would disappear. *Nope, still there.*

Chelsea spun around, expecting to find nothing behind her. To her surprise, she found herself staring at a woman…a woman who looked exactly like her. "Uh…" she gasped and backed into the dresser, dropping the brush to the floor.

The woman smiled. "Good morning, Chelsea. Sorry if I startled you."

Chelsea opened her mouth to speak, but words failed her. She slipped past the woman and backed towards the bedroom door. The two women stared at each other in silence while she tried to sort out the thoughts that were banging around inside her aching head. Finally, Chelsea spoke. "Okay, if I thought you were real, and I don't, I should be scared and ask you who the hell you are." She sucked in her lips and looked the woman up and down. "But you are me, and that means that I must be having a psychotic episode or something…and why am I talking to you?" She took a deep breath and let it out. "Wow." Chelsea walked towards the bed and sat down, blocking her view of the woman she didn't believe was there.

The woman walked around the end of the bed and settled into the armchair facing her.

Chelsea looked up in surprise. "You're still here."

"Yes, I am. And I'm not going anywhere until we have a chat."

"Oh, really? If I sit here talking with you like

you're real, I might as well check myself into the psych ward."

The woman sat back, crossed her legs and held her hands out, palms up. "Why would you do that? You don't need them. You've got me."

Chelsea shook her head. "So which dualistic voice in my psyche do you represent?"

The woman frowned. "I don't understand the question."

"You know—good angel, bad angel. One pushes me into doing bad deeds, and the other tells me to smarten up. Which part of me are you?"

The woman laughed. "Ahh...I get it now. I'm not your conscience talking. Nor am I a part of you."

"Then why do you look like me?"

"Because I'm your sister, Chloe."

Chelsea's jaw dropped. "What are you talking about? I'm an only child. I don't have a sister, let alone a twin sister."

The woman looked chastised and squirmed in her seat. "Oh, dear. So you were never told about me. I'm sorry to spring it on you like this, but I am your sister. I died a couple of days after we were born."

Chelsea swallowed hard. "This is nuts. I'm nuts. Why wouldn't my parents tell me I had a sister, especially an identical twin?"

The woman shook her head. "Nuh-uh. You and I were identical twins, same egg...split. But we had a brother too, Cameron, who was stillborn. He was fraternal. We were triplets."

Chelsea blinked. "I must be hallucinating. Chelsea, Chloe and Cameron?"

"That's right."

"So if you are really the spirit of my deceased sister, why are you here looking like...me...now? I mean, you were only two days old when you passed."

A chuckle escaped Chloe's lips. "If I appeared as a baby, how would we converse?" Chloe looked herself up and down. "Besides…I kind of like this look."

Chelsea stood and paced the room. "True enough." She stopped and faced the woman. "You realize I'm humouring you, right? I find it very difficult to buy into this triplet thing. I still think I'm having an episode of some kind."

"Understandable, but you'll come to believe me."

"So why now? Why after all these years would you suddenly appear in my life?"

"Because you need me."

Chelsea fell over her words. "You're kidding, right? Where were you when I got pregnant at seventeen? Where were you when Arne kidnapped me and held me hostage for twenty years? And now you think I need you?"

Chloe shrugged. "You had Mom when you got pregnant, and Dad's spirit stayed with you after he was killed for the whole time Arne locked you up. And after you were freed, you had your mother and your daughter."

Chelsea stared hard at the woman claiming to be her sister, Chloe. "This is all bullshit. I'm imagining you. And I need coffee." She pointed to the door. "So, I'm going to the kitchen and make a pot of coffee and when I return, you'll be gone." She turned and headed to the door.

"Don't you think you should put some pants on?"

Chelsea turned around and put her hands on her hips. "Why? Do my undies offend you?"

Chloe stood. "Of course not. You and I have the same bits. But I suggest you check out the living room before you go marching out there."

Turning back to the door, Chelsea opened it and peered into the living room. "Omigod…" A young man lay on his stomach on the couch with his head and one arm hanging over the edge. Another man was sprawled over the armchair. Both were still sleeping, and the one in the chair was snoring. There were empty beer cans covering the coffee table. Chelsea closed the door softly. She looked at Chloe in horror. "Who are they?"

"You're asking me? How would I know? You're the one who dragged them home with you last night."

Chelsea headed to the closet in numbed silence and pulled out a clean pair of jeans.

"You don't remember," Chloe said flatly.

"Hey, don't judge me."

Chloe sat back down in the chair. "Now you know why I'm here. You need help, sister. Sit down and tell me what you do remember."

"I walked into town and heard the music in the bar. I decided to go and have dinner and a drink. I remember playing pool with some guys and dancing…I…that's it. I don't remember how I got home."

"Sounds like you had more than 'a' drink." Chloe nodded towards the door. "Are they the two you played pool with?"

"I don't know. I couldn't see their faces. Probably."

"Jesus…you could have been raped, girl, or murdered and your stuff stolen. You really need to get your shit together."

Chelsea glared at Chloe. "Well, I wasn't." She marched over to a chair and picked up the jacket she was wearing the night before. She reached into the pocket and pulled out the bear spray. "See? I can protect myself. You're awfully blunt and mean for a spirit who came to help me. Maybe you should go back where you came from."

Chloe shrugged. "If you were so drunk you had a blackout, I doubt the pepper spray would have helped you. Come to think of it, if you don't remember them bringing you home, how do you know they didn't take advantage of you?"

"Because I obviously passed out on top of my bed, fully clothed…and so are they. I think I'd know if they'd taken liberties with my body. Putting it delicately, there would be signs."

"Humph…well, you got lucky. You need to hear some truths. And not false truths. I'm not here to enable you or pity you. Isn't that what you told your shrink you needed to get away from?"

Chelsea hesitated. "I certainly don't want your pity." She frowned. "Wait, you know my doctor?"

"Not personally. Look, I'll leave if you really want me to. But if I stay, what you see is what you get."

A deep sigh escaped from Chelsea's lungs. "You can stay, even if you are mean-spirited."

The two women stared at each other and laughed aloud at Chelsea's unintentional joke.

"Shhh…" Chloe put her finger up to her lips and nodded towards the living room. "They'll think you're crazy in here laughing by yourself."

Chelsea cut her laugh off and snickered. "They might be right. I better go wake them up and send them home."

She went to the kitchen and prepped the coffee. The couch guy woke up and she recognized him as the young man called Tommy. He sat up, rubbing his eyes. *At least I know his name.*

"What time is it?" Tommy asked.

"8:30 a.m. I've got coffee on. Then you'll both have to go. I've got some appointments today."

"Man, it's Saturday. Do you always get up this early?" Tommy asked.

"Pretty much. What do you take in your coffee?"

Tommy stretched and headed to the main bathroom. "Some cream, please." When he returned, he shook Cliff. "Come on, buddy. Time to get up." Tommy joined Chelsea at the table with his coffee, while Cliff headed to the bathroom.

"Last night was fun. Even if you did wax us at pool."

Chelsea chuckled. "I'm afraid I don't remember much towards the end of the evening."

"Yea! You were pretty wasted by the time we left the bar. We brought beer with us, and Cliff and I got into it, too. We appreciate you letting us crash here. We were too drunk to chance driving home."

She sized him up and decided to push him on the details of the night before. "I wouldn't want to see you out on the road in that condition. So tell me, what happened when we got here?"

"We listened to some great music on Galaxy, drank more beer, and had a few laughs about nothing important. Then you told us we could sleep in the living room. You said good-night and made your way to the bedroom."

Chelsea felt relief that she hadn't done anything more with these two besides getting drunk. "Thank you for seeing me home safely."

"You're welcome."

Cliff returned from the bathroom and walked to the fridge. "Any beer left?" His eyes searched the shelves.

"Beer's all gone." Chelsea stood. "Coffee?"

"No, thanks. How about I go buy some more beer? It's the weekend. Party time."

Okay, time to get them to leave. "Sorry, guys. Last night was fun, but I've got things to do today." She walked around the island and across the living room to the door. She opened it and walked out onto the porch. The two men followed her.

"You have a great spot here on the lake," Cliff said.

"I like it."

"What if we come back tonight? We could have a BBQ and a bonfire. We could bring some friends," Tommy asked.

Chelsea smiled. "Not tonight. We had a good time, but I'm not much of a partier. Last night was a rare thing." She noted their pickup parked beside her car.

"Some other time then?" Tommy said.

"Some other time. Thanks for giving me a ride home."

"Any time," Cliff said.

She went back inside and closed the door, turned the lock and breathed a sigh of relief. *You're lucky they were okay guys who just like to drink beer and party.* She heard them drive away, poured herself coffee and returned to the bedroom. Chloe was gone. Chelsea wrapped a blanket around her shoulders and headed back to the deck. She curled up in the chaise lounge and stared out at the lake. A mist was dissipating over the water, revealing patches of blue sky. *It's going to be a beautiful day.* Sipping her coffee, she tried to remember the events from the night before. Chloe's words came back to her and stung: *'You don't remember.'*

No, I don't. And that's a problem. I've got a problem. There's no denying the fact. Chelsea thought back to her teen years. *Sure, I did my share of partying like other kids my age.* Of course, while in captivity with Arne, there was no alcohol. He touted the evils of alcohol his whole life.

And when I was free, I found it again. And to what gain? It was alcohol that got me pregnant when I pined over Chaz; got me into trouble with my own daughter when I made a pass at Jax; and now I'm having blackouts.

Chelsea cringed as she remembered the conversation with her doctor. *Am I thinking a geographical change will solve my problems?* Another thought crossed her mind. *And what of Chloe? Is she an alcoholic hallucination? Or maybe I'm crazy. After my incarceration, some people think I am.*

She stood and leaned against a post. *Or maybe she's a real spirit. Am I really a surviving triplet?* She rolled the names off her tongue out loud.

"Chelsea, Chloe and Cameron!"

❧ 9 ❧

PENTICTON

The parking lot contained about a dozen vehicles. Chelsea parked close to the group and checked her watch. It read 6:55 p.m. The meeting was at 7:00 p.m. She stepped out of the car and checked out the building she was about to enter. It was a union hall, closed for the day. That meant the occupants of the parked vehicles were all there for the same reason she was. She took a deep breath and headed to the door. She entered the hallway to find a set of stairs, and she climbed them slowly. At the top, an open conference room sat on the left. She hesitated for a moment, threw her head back and walked into the room.

The other people were taking their seats, and Chelsea slipped into one in the last row, shrinking into the back of the chair in the hopes that no one noticed her. *No such luck.* The leader welcomed them all to the meeting and looked directly at her. "If you want some coffee, help yourself." A few of the audience members turned to look at her. They all smiled and nodded to the newcomer. Chelsea felt her face go hot as she mumbled a thank-you.

The moderator made a few announcements; a

little housekeeping, he called it. This was what was called an open meeting for people who wanted to check out Alcoholics Anonymous. The closed meetings were for alcoholics who entered the 12-step program. Chelsea had done some research on the internet and decided she would attend the open meeting. There were meetings in towns closer to Emerald Lake, but Chelsea didn't want to attend any where people might recognize her as a neighbour.

Their leader proceeded to read the twelve steps followed by the twelve traditions of Alcoholics Anonymous. He then opened up the floor to the audience. Some of the attendees raised their hands and were picked one by one to come forward to the front of the group. They each introduced themselves by their first name, told stories of their own sobriety, their struggles, or words of hope. The last one to speak was a gentleman who looked to be in his fifties. He spoke with an Eastern European accent.

"My name is Janos, and I am alcoholic."

"Welcome, Janos."

"I been sober twenty-five year. In first couple of year, I have slip. I give reason for them but come to see reason as excuse. Was loss of job and almost loss of family that wake me up. Stopping the drink not easy, it take willpower. People ask how I go twenty-five year now with no drink. I tell you what I learn. Is simple but yes, hard." He leaned forward towards the group. "If you want be sober…don't drink it."

Wow. Blunt or what? Chelsea placed a hand over her mouth. She wanted to chuckle but knew it wasn't appropriate. She realized with his accent he may not have intended to sound so harsh, but his words struck a chord. Janos sat down. The leader thanked them all for attending and ended the meeting, inviting them to socialize over coffee, cake and cookies.

Chelsea skirted around people and headed to the table for coffee. She found herself standing beside Jonas.

"You new here. First meeting?" he asked.

"Yes."

"Your first name?"

"Chelsea."

"Welcome, Chelsea. First meeting always hardest. If you have questions, I happy to talk with you."

"Thank you. Congratulations on your sobriety."

"Is mind over matter. Shall we sit?"

Chelsea hesitated and then shrugged. "Sure."

Janos led them away from the others and turned a chair to face another one, and they sat.

"So why you come tonight?"

Chelsea liked his to-the-point attitude in spite of the fact that it made her uncomfortable. "I'm not sure I should even be here…" She paused and rolled her eyes. "I suppose everyone says that."

"You would not come if you not concerned, even with doubt. May I ask question?"

Chelsea squirmed. "Why not? Shoot."

"Have you answered twelve questions we all asked before coming?"

"Yes, I found them online. It said if you answer yes to four or more, you may have a problem. I tried to be as honest as I could. I said yes to four."

Jonas nodded. "Hmm…how long you drink?"

"Four months."

He looked perplexed. "Pardon me, Chelsea. You look…say, late thirties? You not drink until four month ago?"

Chelsea dropped her head. *What am I doing sitting here with this stranger? Now he's asking about my past. If I'm less than honest, I shouldn't be here.* She shook her head and raised her eyes. "Got an hour?"

She explained to Jonas her captivity for twenty years, her release, and her past year of re-entry into society. He listened intently, never once interrupting. When she finished, she explained how drinking had affected her life the past four months.

"I read of your confinement in paper. Thank you for sharing with me. Another question. You crave alcohol?"

Chelsea frowned. "No, never. But if I have a drink, it seems I keep drinking. The past few times, I haven't remembered much of the night before. That is a problem to me."

"Maybe not alcoholic. But could be binge-drinker problem." Jonas flipped his hands out into the air. "Binge-drinker not necessarily alcoholic but if out of control, affects life socially and personally just like alcoholic. Trouble just the same. And if continued, could progress to alcoholic."

"That makes sense."

"Drink is mask for underlying issue. Only you determine the issue, but to me because of past, you dealing with emotion issue, social acceptance issue and more. Drink give you freedom. Deal with issue and you control drink or not want drink."

Chelsea smiled and quoted Jonas. "It's simple, but hard. Thank you for your input."

"Will you come again?"

Chelsea glanced around the room. "I'm not very comfortable around strangers, which might seem odd since I opened up with you. But I couldn't stand up in front and talk about myself like you do. My healing has been contingent on being away from people. You've no idea what it took to make myself come tonight."

"I understand."

"When I was in captivity, I learned to be whatever he wanted me to be and do what was expected of me. It happened subconsciously over a long period of time. Figuring out who I am has just begun. Talking honestly and openly to this group? It's scary."

"You not ready, yea? I give you card. I can be sponsor, and you call anytime you like if need to talk. We talk on phone or we meet for coffee in town. Okay?"

Chelsea breathed a sigh of relief. She took his card and put it in her pocket. "Thank you. You're very kind."

The leader approached them. "We're closing up in five minutes." He greeted Chelsea and handed her a package of literature. He gave her a schedule of future meetings and invited her to rejoin them any time. She thanked him, said her goodbyes, and left.

She drove home mulling over all that she'd heard at the meeting. Chelsea felt better after leaving the meeting knowing that this was one aspect of her life where she really wasn't alone. There were lots of people, for whatever the reason, who suffered from alcoholism. *Binge-drinker. If I had never been kidnapped would I have still become a binge-drinker? Who knows? And what does it matter? The problem exists now, and I'm the only one who can do something about it.*

❧ 10 ❧

EMERALD LAKE

Rain pelted on the tin roof, a much-needed downpour that had lasted all day. It was a sound that Chelsea found comforting, and she'd happily spent the day inside. A homemade stew in the slow cooker permeated throughout the cottage. The past hour had been spent on the computer studying online program studies from an area university. She gave up in frustration and sat back in her chair. The day Chelsea had been kidnapped by Arne Jensen, she'd planned to relocate to Kelowna with her infant daughter, Sydney, where she'd been registered to take a Lab Technician Program. Twenty years later, she was aware that continuing along that vein, she'd be working with people on a daily basis. She wasn't ready to work with people that closely at this point… maybe never. Finding a new path of interest wasn't as easy as she thought it would be. A course of action eluded her. *What am I going to do with the rest of my life?*

A noise on the porch cut through her muse. Her eyes turned to the door and she listened. *Nothing.* Chelsea stood, stretched her taut muscles, and headed to the counter to check on her stew. Halfway across the floor, she heard the noise again. She froze.

The pelting rain overpowered all other sounds, and Chelsea strained to hear a scratching noise. She approached the door cautiously. It could be any kind of critter out there, so she flipped on the outside porch light and moved to the picture window to inspect the deck. A quick scan of the deck revealed nothing. *Humph…must have scared it away with the light.*

Another sound joined the scratching…a whimper. Unable to see anything on the deck, Chelsea moved to the door and opened it. She stepped out and immediately jumped back. Underneath one of the deck chairs, a movement caught her eye peripherally.

"Grrr…" A distinct growl came from the corner of the deck. Chelsea bent down and peered across the deck. A dog lay shivering under the chair. It was soaked to the skin and so muddy, she couldn't decipher the breed. It was medium-sized and very skinny.

"Aww, you poor thing. Look at you." She spoke in a soft tone to calm the frightened animal. Chelsea inched closer to the dog and the dog backed away into the corner of the deck. "Okay, I'm not going to come any closer. I've got you cornered, and you might come out biting." She backed away and cocked her head so she could stare into the animal's eyes. "Who are you, sweetheart? Where'd you come from? By the looks of you, you've been living outside a long time."

Chelsea weighed her options. "I bet you're thirsty and hungry, eh? How about I get you something? Don't you leave now." She stood halfway up with her knees bent and backed into the cabin so not to scare the dog further. In the kitchen, she scooped a bowl of stew from the slow-cooker, threw in a couple of ice cubes to cool it down quickly and filled a bowl with water. The dog was still cowering in the corner on her return. She placed the water bowl in the centre of the deck about halfway between the dog and the doorway; retreating back to the stoop, Chelsea sat on the floor just inside the door and placed the stew bowl on the deck in front of her.

"There you go, sweetie." She nodded at the water bowl. The dog slowly inched forward down on all fours towards the bowl. Her cell phone inside the cabin rang, startling them both. "Damn." The dog stopped and stared at her. She sat perfectly still and let the phone ring until it went to voicemail. All that could be heard once again was the falling rain. The animal inched forward, never taking its eyes off of her. With a sudden thrust of its head into the bowl, the dog slurped the water loudly and frantically. Chelsea suppressed a laugh. The swigging didn't stop until the bowl was empty. "So you were thirsty. How about some stew?" She pushed the bowl forward a few inches, picked out a cube of beef and popped it into her mouth. "Mmm…so good."

The animal lifted its nose towards her and sniffed the air, its nostrils flaring in and out. Chelsea never moved but continued to coax the dog in comforting tones until the dog's hunger overcame its fear. It stood and approached the bowl, its nose sniffing the whole time. If she thought the water slurping was loud, the gulping down of the meat and vegetables in the bowl surpassed it. "Wow…you haven't eaten for a while, poor baby." The dog licked the bowl so hard it moved around the deck. Finally, realizing there was no more to be had, the dog sat down and stared at her. It gave a little whine and put its head down on its paws.

Chelsea stood and backed away from the open door. "Do you want to come in? It's warm and dry in

69

here." The dog stared down the porch stairs into the darkness and continuous downpour. As if he knew what she was saying, he stood and slowly walked to the doorway. He looked around the inner room and stepped into the cottage. She shut the door. Chelsea walked slowly to the armchair and picked up the comforter off the back and placed it on the floor in front of the woodstove. She patted the blanket. "Here you go, right in front of a hot, roaring fire." The dog moved towards the stove, dripping muddy water as it went. It settled on the blanket and lay stretched out, watching her every move. Chelsea retrieved a couple of towels from the bathroom vanity; one she used to wipe up the dirty water from the wood floor. She got down on her knees and inched towards the dog with the other towel. "How about I rub you down? You'll feel so much better." Chelsea placed her hand in front of the dog's nose so it could smell her fingers. The dog gave her fingers a lick. She lifted one finger and stroked his nose. Their eyes locked together, and she spoke in barely a whisper while stroking his nose with her whole hand, slowly moving it to the top of the animal's head. Light strokes at first, then longer ones down its side. The dog shuddered and let out a deep sigh. Chelsea could see the muscles in the animal's neck and shoulders relax. She began to rub it down with the large bath towel, noting that the dog appeared to have beige-coloured fur that was long and matted. "You know what? You look like you might be a golden retriever. Hard to tell with all this dirt. But I can see that you're a female. Maybe tomorrow, if you stick around, I'll give you a bath and brushing. Would you like that, sweetie?" As she wiped her down, she felt around for any obvious injuries and found none. "All done for tonight." Chelsea stood and left the dog alone while she retrieved a bowl of stew for herself. By the time she'd settled at the table to eat, the dog had closed her eyes and fallen into a deep sleep.

Remembering the phone ringing earlier, she checked her missed calls. "Oh." It was from Sydney. *She didn't leave a message, but what if something was wrong? Maybe I should call back.* Hesitation crept in. If something was wrong, she would have left a message. But then, she may not know what to say in a message. *Come on, Chelsea, you're supposed to be the adult here, call her.* She picked up the phone and hit redial.

"Hi," Sydney answered.

"Hi. I missed your call earlier. Is everything okay?"

"Yes, fine. Nan told me about the renos at the cottage and how nice it looks. She said you seem happy there."

"I am, hon. And isn't it wonderful about Mom and Gord? I couldn't be happier for them…and for you and Jax."

"Thank you." There was an awkward silence. "Umm…Mom, I'm really sorry for what I said. I was horrible to you."

"It's okay. My life was out of control, and you were upset. I'm sorry I put you through so much stress."

"I should have handled it better."

Chelsea heard a doorbell ring in the background.

"Hang on," Sydney said. Voices could be heard in the background. "Mom, I'm so sorry, I've got company at the door so I have to ring off. We'll continue this later, okay? I'm happy you called me back."

"Me too. Bye for now."

Chelsea hung up feeling a lot better about the situation with her daughter. *At least we broke the ice.* She spent the evening in her armchair reading a book and watching the dog, who whimpered every once in a while from an obvious dream. She smiled. *It's kind of comforting having an animal in the house. Maybe I need a pet.* Arne had never allowed animals in the house, so she hadn't had a pet since childhood. "Maybe you can stay here with me." She frowned. 'But first I guess I'd better try to find your owners."

While banking the fire for overnight, the animal opened her eyes and watched her, but never moved. Chelsea bent down and rubbed her ears. "I think I'll make up a bed on the couch and sleep in here with you. Would you like that? I know I would." She made up the couch and settled down for the night. The flames behind the glass door of the stove reflected a soft red hue across the room that included the image of the dog sprawled in front. Chelsea fell asleep quickly, lulled into contentment by the homey scene.

Sometime during the night, Chelsea woke. Her eyes scanned the comforter in front of the stove. *No dog.* She pushed up on one elbow and scanned the room looking for the animal. *Where'd you go?*

She stretched out her legs to get up and search. Her feet hit something at the other end of the couch. One glance confirmed that the object she'd bumped was the dog, curled into a tight ball, with her head tucked into her side. "Aw…' Chelsea lay down, comforted by the heat emanating from the dog into her exposed feet. She dropped off to sleep with a smile on her face. *Today was a good day.*

❧ 11 ❧

EMERALD LAKE

Wenner Gibb's smile grew wider. "Ewww… aggressive thing, aren't you? I knew you'd be a biter." He gently ran his hand up her leg, stopping at just the right places to apply pressure with his fingers. She fought him, but he held her down with a gloved hand and continued. He spoke to her in a quiet tone. "Come on, Red, let me finish. You'll come to appreciate what I'm doing…I promise."

Once satisfied, he planned his next move. He held onto Red and stretched forward to grab the surgical tape on the table, a pair of scissors and a stick. He worked quickly, and when he finished, Wenner covered Red with a cut-up sheet. Slipping his free hand into a matching leather glove, he picked her up and put her into a cage. Red tried to stand but gave up and settled in the corner of the cage. Her unblinking stare studied him fearfully. Wenner placed some water in the cage and left the building, making sure to lock the door behind him. Some of the cabins around the lake with absentee owners were broken into this past winter. *Don't want anyone snooping around my place or interfering with my work.*

It was a beautiful spring day, and he wanted to enjoy the warmth of the sun before it disappeared behind Snowy Mountain. He packed some snacks and water in a backpack and set out on Apache Trail through the grasslands. Newly sprouted foliage confirmed the return of the season with a promise that summer was on its way. The trail wound upwards away from the lake, and the spicy smell of sagebrush permeated the air. A rain had fallen overnight, and now with the day's warmth, it drew the poignant aroma to its fullest. He lost himself to the desert landscape, still in its green bloom, and trudged on. Once the season changed and the rains became scarce, the grasslands would become arid and brown, but still very much alive and beautiful. Reaching an open area that overlooked the lake below, Wenner stopped to enjoy the view.

A throaty growl behind him broke through his muse and he turned slowly. A golden retriever stood on the path above him, baring her teeth. He noted the dog was on a flexible extended leash, which pleased him for two reasons. First, if the dog was aggressive, it was under control. And second, too many people allowed their dogs to roam free through the protected grasslands; a flagrant abuse of the laws that governed protected areas.

CHELSEA PAUSED as she approached the crest of the hill. Sage was ahead of her on a lead, having topped the hill first. She was crouched low and growling. Chelsea proceeded cautiously, and the dog moved closer to her in a protective stance. Her free hand was in her jacket pocket, feeling for the pepper spray can. As she passed over the crest, she noticed a man standing off the path in the lookout.

He nodded to her. "Hi. That's a beautiful dog you have there."

She sized him up. He looked familiar to her. "She is. Her name is Sage."

Wenner smiled. "Sage…what a lovely name." He bent down and called to the dog. She approached him cautiously, sniffed his outstretched hand and let him stroke her fur.

Chelsea noted he was wearing a jacket with a patch on it that read Emerald Lake Wildlife Recovery Centre.

Wenner glanced up at her. "I'm on my way down to the valley. Mind if I walk with you?"

She felt annoyed at the interruption but shrugged her shoulders. "Sure." The path was wide enough for them to walk side-by-side. Sage, who'd decided the man was harmless, bounded ahead of them. The man appeared to struggle to converse with her.

"I'm Wenner Gibb, by the way. I'm sorry if I spoiled your walk."

"Not at all. I'm Chelsea." Her memory kicked in and she realized who the man was. "We met once before in town."

He looked perplexed.

She gave him a half-smile. "You fell into me in the drug store entranceway a couple of weeks ago."

"Right. Totally embarrassed myself."

Sage spotted a marmot sunning itself on a rock, barked and pulled on the leash in its direction. Chelsea spoke firmly to her. "No, Sage. Sit." The dog obeyed immediately and Chelsea retracted the leash as they got closer to her. "Good dog." She bent down and patted her.

"She's well-trained. You've done a good job with her," Wenner said.

"Sage is definitely well-trained and smart, but I can't take credit. She's a stray. I've only had her a few weeks. I advertised online everywhere with no response. Considering the condition she was in when she decided to adopt me, she'd been out on her own a long time. How she survived the winter is beyond me."

"A lot of domestic animals bolted last summer during the fires. Sage could be one of them."

"That's what I thought, but the owners may have moved away or were passing through."

"Are you going to keep her?"

"I am. She's great company for someone like..." Chelsea cut herself off.

"You were saying?"

Chelsea stiffened and shook her head. "Nothing."

"She looks pretty healthy, although a bit underweight. Did you have a vet check her out? I could do that for you. I'm qualified."

"Thanks, but I took her into Penticton to a local vet there. She's fine other than the weight loss." Chelsea chuckled. "Let me assure you she's making up for lost time. She's become a big eater."

They continued their walk with Sage on a shorter leash.

Wenner waved a hand around. "I love these grasslands and walk them every day. I've never seen you here before."

"That's because it's my first time."

"Okay. I'm the last property on the south end of the lake. You would have passed it to reach this trail."

"The Wildlife Recovery Centre. I figured because

of your jacket. I'm living about five cottages away. At the Rhyder place."

"Oh, that's you? Driving by, I noticed the wood stove smoke. How long are you staying?"

Chelsea shrugged. "Indefinitely. For now, it's home. Tell me about your work. It sounds interesting. Do you have on-site staff that stay with you?"

"No, just me. Volunteer staff help out. But they are getting harder to find. I usually have local high-school students, but this summer they all seem to be scattering off elsewhere. Spring and summer are my busiest time."

They followed the trail down to the road leading around the lake. They stopped at Wenner's gated driveway.

"Would you like to see the Centre?" he asked. He opened the gate and pushed it open. "Come on. I'd love to show you around."

Chelsea backed away into the road, and her right hand pushed into her pocket to the pepper spray.

Wenner appeared to notice her hesitation. "Hey, I don't bite, and I promise I'm not a serial killer."

Chelsea's body tensed. His attempt at humour made her back away further.

"I'm sorry. That wasn't funny. I get it. We're strangers." He gave her a warm smile. "It's just that I get overzealous when I talk about my work and expect others to hang on my every word. Maybe another time." He started to close the gate.

Chelsea remembered what the cashier had said the night he'd barrelled into her. *You needn't worry about Wenner. He's a stand-up citizen around here.* She relaxed. "No, I'd love to see the Centre."

Wenner led her down the driveway to a large tin building. He unlocked the door and turned to Chelsea. "Sage will have to wait outside."

Chelsea tied the leash to the fencing. Wenner held the door open and ushered her into a room filled with various sized cages. But the cage in the far corner drew her full attention, only because the occupant, startled by their sudden entrance, began to scream. The screams grew in a crescendo until they became a shrill screech.

The door closed behind them with a loud thud.

🎋 12 🎋

EMERALD LAKE

"U h..." Chelsea jumped back, startled by the loud screaming. She turned to Wenner with her hand on her chest.

"Sorry...I should have warned you about Red. Come and meet her."

She followed Wenner to the last cage cautiously. Red became quiet but eyed them suspiciously. She was striking-looking with cocoa-coloured black feathers, a pale underbelly, and a reddish tail. "What is she?" Chelsea whispered.

"A red-tailed hawk. She has a broken leg. I found her on my walk this morning, so she's a little skittish."

"Aw...poor thing. Will it heal enough for her to go back into the wild?"

"Yes, but she'll be here about a month. Time to see if she'll eat."

Chelsea followed Wenner into a side room that looked like a kitchen. Opening the fridge, he pulled out an ice cream bucket full of raw cut-up chicken. He cut some of it up into smaller morsels and put them into a metal dish. "I'm just going to add some antibiotics to the meat. Would you like to feed her?"

Chelsea looked surprised he offered. "Yes...I would."

He handed her the bowl. "Okay, let's go. I'll get you a raptor glove."

Wenner placed the leather glove on her right hand. It came up to the middle of her arm. "Open the lower slot and slide the bowl in. Place it to the right of Red so she doesn't feel trapped. Then take a piece out of the bowl and move your hand slowly towards her and gently throw it in front of her. Watch her body language. She's leaning into the corner right now because she can't balance on her injured leg. But if her head and body are held high and the feathers on her head, neck, and breast become erect, she's displaying aggression. Drop the morsel and slowly back your arm out."

Chelsea moved in front of the cage and followed Wenner's instructions. All the while, she spoke in a whisper to the frightened bird of prey. "Hey, Red. I'm Chelsea. I've got some food for you." As soon as she moved the bowl into the cage, Red's body language changed.

"Careful, move the bowl over to the side and leave it at that," Wenner said.

She placed the bowl to the side, her eyes never leaving Red's. She rested her gloved hand on the bottom of the cage and continued cooing and talking to the bird in soft tones. To her surprise the raptor settled in the corner, allowing its body to relax. Red's head moved from side to side, listening to Chelsea's words. Chelsea slowly reached into the bowl and picked up a morsel of meat and tossed it to Red. Then backed her arm out of the cage and latched the slot shut.

Red stared at her for a moment and quick as a

flash reached forward and grabbed the food, swallowing it in one gulp.

"Great job. I'm impressed. You didn't at all seem nervous, and Red sensed your calmness," Wenner said.

Chelsea beamed. She felt elated. "That was awesome. How do you know she's a female?"

"Normally, you can't tell by just looking at a hawk. You need an ultrasonographic scanning probe, which I don't have. But this hawk has been living here with her mate since before I moved here. The female is usually larger than the male, which Red is. And having watched them for the past two seasons, the female protects the nest and the male usually protects their territory. I've observed this behaviour with Red and her mate."

They spent the next twenty minutes feeding a coyote pup and various rodents, and bottle fed some baby rabbits that'd lost their mother.

"You're a natural with animals. I've been watching how you interact with them. Your natural ease with them rubs off, and they sense you mean them no harm."

"I think maybe I'm more comfortable with animals then I am with people."

Wenner studied her for a moment. "If you're interested, I'd like to discuss your working here with me part-time."

"Really? As a volunteer? I think I'd like that."

"How about a cup of tea at the house? We can talk about it some more."

"Okay."

Chelsea sat at the kitchen table and watched Wenner make the tea. She listened as he prattled on about all the different types he loved…they'd settled on a ginger lemon herbal tea.

A comfortable familiarity had settled between the two new acquaintances, and Chelsea knew they were to be friends...and perhaps fellow workers.

Finally, Wenner sat down with their tea and a plate of homemade chocolate chip cookies.

"And you bake, as well," Chelsea teased.

"I'm a do-it-all kind of guy." Wenner chuckled. "I have to since I live alone."

Chelsea laughed. "I hear you."

"So you mentioned volunteering, but what I'm offering is a part-time paid position."

Her eyebrows shot up. "Oh? I thought you only used volunteers."

"Up until this year, yes. But there are groups in town that do fundraisers for me, and I received a government grant this year, so I can afford a part-timer to share some of the responsibility. The volunteers clean the cages, help feed, but I'm looking for someone I can train to help out as an assistant. I hadn't really looked as yet, and now you've sort of been dropped in my lap, and I think you're just what I'm looking for."

Chelsea frowned. "Wow. Umm...this opportunity has dropped into my lap, so to speak, too. I really think it's something I could enjoy...and perhaps handle right about now." She hesitated. "Look, you need to know a couple of things about me..." Suddenly, Chelsea felt overwhelmed and unsure of how to explain her situation. Instead, she let her eyes drop to the table, and she sipped her tea in silence.

Wenner interrupted her scrambled thoughts. "I sense you're struggling a little here to tell me about yourself...and perhaps with reluctance. If it helps, as soon as you told me your name up on the trail, I knew who you were. We live in a small town, and word travelled fast that the Stoney Creek teenager who'd been abducted and held captive for twenty years was staying in the Emerald Lake area."

She gave him a wry smile. "So much for anonymity."

"You and I have more in common than you know. Once upon a time, I tried to hide who I was, too, but I soon found out that as painful as it was, I had to stand strong and be myself."

Chelsea gave him a puzzled look. "How so?"

"Remember when I made that tasteless joke at the gate about not being a serial killer? I can't believe I was that insensitive. Well, if I was one, you'd be very safe, my dear, because you're of the wrong persuasion."

Chelsea stared at Wenner for a moment. "Oh?" Then the light bulb went off. "Ohh...I didn't know. I mean you're soooo..." She stopped at a loss for the right word.

"Masculine?"

Chelsea blushed and felt mortified. "Oh, God, I'm so sorry. I didn't mean to stereotype gay people."

Wenner laughed. "It's okay. A gay man would have recognized it right away, but you're a woman who was sheltered from the world for a long time. My point is that I recognize your struggle about feeling different around people, and I understand it because I've been there. I'm a bit of a loner, and I sense at the moment that you are, too. That puts us on common ground."

"You're right there. My plan when I came to the cottage was to get away from people who were either uncomfortable in my presence or treated me like a victim. I planned to take some online college courses, but so far I haven't found any I want to pursue.

Which brings me to something else about working for you. I'm on a disability pension until such time as I'm able to work full-time and, as my therapist says, able to rejoin society as a productive citizen. In the meantime, it restricts how much I'm able to earn in additional cash."

"How much additional allowance can you earn?"

"No more than a thousand per month."

"Perfect. Then consider a flat rate of a thousand per month and we'll work out the hours so you can do your studies as well. How does that sound?"

"Umm…sounds great."

Wenner reached for the teapot. "More tea?" He didn't wait for her to answer and filled her cup. "I'm excited about this. I think you have what is needed here. No fear of the animals, an almost spiritual connection to them and calmness. I'm pleased that I'll get some time away and not worry about leaving them alone. I'd still like to have a couple of volunteers, but we'll see what happens as we get closer to the end of the school year."

"So are you trained in wildlife care or a veterinarian?"

"I started as a licensed vet, and I now have my certification in wildlife medicine and rehabilitation. I had my own business in Vancouver. Of course, I dealt mostly with dogs and cats there. This property was a summer home for my husband and I. We were partners for five years and got married in 2003 when British Columbia passed same-sex marriage into law. Brian was my partner in business, as well. He was an accountant and took care of the staff and business side of the practice." A sad look came over his face, and he stopped talking.

"And since you live alone here, I take it the marriage didn't last? I'm sorry."

Wenner brightened up and smiled. "Oh, no, we had a wonderful marriage. He was taken from me two years ago in a car accident."

Chelsea reached out and touched his hand that rested on the table. "Oh, Wenner, how awful. I'm so sorry to hear that."

"Thank you. I'm really not a very good business man, and my practice on the coast meant nothing without Brian. I sold it and moved here full-time. The Wildlife Centre just happened. Once people around here knew I was a vet, they started bringing me injured wildlife. They knew I was in grief, and I think at first they were trying to keep me busy. It's been a learning curve, I'll tell you, but here we are."

"A new calling."

"Yup. I'm still lousy at business, but I'm learning. By the way, you mentioned you didn't know what courses you wanted to take online. First off, maybe a few business courses wouldn't hurt. If things work out for you here, maybe you could help me with the books. And there's a new semester starting online through Thompson Rivers University, Animal Welfare Technology. Two semesters, six months each. I know the professor, and I'm sure on my recommendation, he'll take you on. Why don't you check it out online and let me know what you think?"

"I…will," Chelsea blustered. "I'm going to check on it as soon as I get back to the cottage." She handed Wenner her cell phone. "Here, put your number in my contacts and I'll call back later today."

Wenner did as she asked and then walked her up to the gate. "I always keep it closed, and at night I lock it, just in case some silly kids think it's cool to come around and cause trouble for the animals."

A cry of a bird drew their attention to the sky above them. It sounded like a steam whistle.

"That's Red's mate," Wenner said. "Our properties are all a part of their territory, and I'm sure he knows I have Red inside. He's looking for her." Wenner cocked his head towards the animal house. "Listen. She's answering him."

❧ 13 ❧

Chelsea floated home, her head swimming with excitement, fear, and a million questions.

Sage ran ahead of her. The hawk followed above, soaring over her head, watching her every move. When she got to her back deck, the hawk landed on a tree branch beside the shed.

"Don't worry, Red will be back soon. She's doing well, honest. You need a name, too." At that moment the hawk lifted one leg and started to groom, stretching out his talons. "How about Talon? Do you like that?"

A voice sounded behind her. "A perfect name."

Chelsea spun around. Chloe, her spirit sister, was sitting in one of the lawn chairs. "Jesus. You have to stop scaring me."

"Sorry."

Sage ran up the steps and sat down in front of Chloe, cocking her head from side to side.

"She can see you?" Chelsea asked.

"All animals can." Chloe glanced up at the tree and nodded. "So can Talon. So where did the dog come from?"

"She adopted me a couple of weeks ago during a

thunderstorm. I've had her picture up on the internet, but no one's claimed her. Her name is Sage, and I guess she's mine now."

Chelsea headed into the cabin, and Chloe and Sage followed her. "Come on, Sage. You must be starving."

While Chelsea fed the dog, Chloe stood by the window staring out. "Talon is still out there."

"His mate is at the Wildfire Centre down the road with a broken leg. I think he knows I was with her."

"I'm sure of it. You're his connection to her. You know…seeing a hawk is an omen in Celtic worlds. They believe hawks carry messages from the other side."

Chelsea began prepping her own dinner. "What kind of messages?"

"Did Talon circle above you?"

"He did and then followed me home."

"Hawks don't usually pay attention to humans; circling indicates a message of success or death."

Chelsea stopped and stared at her. "Death? Are you saying I'm going to die? Thanks for that negative piece of news."

"No need for sarcasm. Death doesn't necessarily mean a physical death. It can represent the coming of positive change, which in turn means examining your life and seeking only the positive."

"Hmm…sounds like you're using the bird to give me another lecture."

"Hey, you don't have to take my word for it. You have a computer, see what the internet tells you. Honestly, Chelsea, you are soooo annoying. Do you know what it takes energy-wise for me to come into your realm? I'm not here to fight with you."

Chastised, Chelsea backed down. "Sorry."

"Do look up the symbolism of the hawk. We were born on April 1st, which makes the Hawk our Celtic spirit animal sign. When a hawk connects to someone, that person is intuitive, idealistic, and a leader. Pay attention to Talon and Red. Your life was interrupted by Arne, but before he abducted you, you were strong, confident, and ready to take on the world for you and Sydney. You were destined to come to Emerald Lake, sis. This place is where you'll redefine your power."

Chelsea stared out the window at Talon. The bird stared right back. Perhaps Chloe was right. After all, things were changing for the positive already.

Chloe broke through her muse. "So what were you doing at the Wildlife Centre?"

Chelsea smiled and sat down at the table. "I went for a hike in the grasslands and met the Vet who runs the Centre. He invited me to see it, and I helped feed the animals, and Red, the female hawk. And he offered me a part-time job."

"That's great news."

Chelsea opened her laptop. "He's even willing to go to bat for me if I register for online courses on animal care." She found the website for the university and brought up the courses. Chloe stood over her shoulder and watched while Chelsea read through the course modules and requirements. "I like what I see here. Scary…but I'm going for this."

"Good girl," Chloe said.

After Chelsea filled out the registration, she called Wenner. She gave him a list of the courses she'd signed up for. She turned to Chloe. "Wow… he's calling his contact at the university right now. She put her hands over her face. "What a day it's been."

"I'm so proud of you. You can do this. You know that."

"What makes it feel right is that I don't have to deal with people, and the work can be so rewarding."

"Your new boss is people. You don't seem to mind working with him. What's he like?"

"Very compassionate, obviously, by definition of his work. I think he's in his fifties. He's a widower. A bit at odds with himself, I think, and a loner like me. That's why I believe this job will work for me. We have a lot in common." Chelsea smiled. "I like him. He's…comfortable."

Chloe frowned. "That's good…I think."

"You think?"

Chloe blushed. "Well…I mean…remember he's your boss. Don't get too personal, okay?"

Chelsea stood and placed her hands on her hips. "You mean, don't sleep with him? I don't sleep with every man I meet, you know. That last party in Kelowna was a one-time thing…and the reason I've been trying to work on my life." She paced back and forth. "God…I don't know why you even bother to be here when you have such a low opinion about me."

"Calm down. I'm concerned and not about your morals. There are other things to worry about too, like STDs? My biggest concern is that you are vulnerable right now. You know, I've helped a lot of people over the years, but none of them were as frustrating and combative as you."

Chelsea studied her sister. A slight smile played at her lips. "Perhaps my defiance is because I'm getting stronger. And maybe it's because we're siblings. If you hadn't left me as a baby, we probably would have had many sister fights by now. I am glad you're here, you know."

The two women stared at each other. "I am, too."

Chelsea went to the stove to check on her meal. Bent over to look in the oven, she said to Chloe: "By the way, you don't have to worry about me and Wenner sleeping together. He's gay."

❧ 14 ❧

STONEY CREEK

Sydney sat down at the table with her best friend, Jessie. "It's been too long, my friend."

"We've both been so busy, it's crazy," Jessie said.

"I know I have. Every weekend has been booked for the past six weeks. I'm thrilled, of course."

Jessie grinned. "And of course, living with Jax has added to it all. How's it going? Must be an adjustment, living with someone."

"It's…good." Sydney giggled. "A big change to being independent, but I like it so far. I do most of the cooking during the week because I work from home. And weekends we've had Bea there for the clients, so I get a break there. He says he'll cook on the weekends when we don't need Bea. He lived long enough on his own that he can run a mean vacuum and use a feather duster."

They laughed. The waiter came over with a menu. "Would you ladies care for drinks before dinner?"

Jessie ordered a bottle of white wine and two glasses. Sydney hesitated. "Not for me, thanks. Could I have a glass of lemonade?"

Jessie's eyebrows shot up. "What? No wine?"

Sydney shook her head. "Not tonight. I've got an early morning start tomorrow."

Jessie caught the waiter before he left. "Can I change that bottle to one glass?"

"Certainly."

"So what's been happening in your life?" Sydney asked.

Jessie blushed. "I've met someone."

"Omigod…who?"

"He's a doctor at the hospital, we…"

"Why didn't you tell me? How long have you been seeing him?"

"Hang on, I'm telling you now. We've been dating about six weeks. He started at the hospital about three months ago. He's a little older than me but a slow bloomer. He decided he didn't want any involvements while he went through medical school and his internship."

"Oh, Jess. I'm so happy for you. I've been feeling guilty because since Jax moved in, we've had to cut back on our time together."

"And so you should. That's what happens when you're in a relationship."

"You should have shared this with me sooner, bad girl."

"I wanted to be sure we were a 'thing.' Now it seems we are."

The waiter returned with their drinks and took their orders.

"So when do I get to meet this doctor of yours? Soon, I hope. I'll tell you what. One week night when you're both off duty, you have to come for dinner. I'd love to entertain."

Jessie laughed. "Couple friends. Has a nice ring to it."

The waiter brought their plates of food and left

them alone.

"How's your mom doing?"

"She seems to be happy at Emerald Lake. We finally spoke to each other, and I apologized to her. She was very forgiving, which surprised me considering how horrible I was to her."

"Even the best of families have disagreements, but family is family. I'm glad you're talking again."

"Well, our conversation ended too quickly because someone came to my door. I'm still a bit uneasy with the whole thing."

"But the ice was broken, that's the main thing."

Sydney nodded as she felt what was becoming an all-too-familiar nauseous feeling in her stomach.

Jessie was staring at her. "Are you alright? You've turned white."

"Excuse me a minute." Sydney went to the ladies' room and promptly threw up. She sat in the stall with her head between her knees for a few minutes. When she came out, Jessie was leaning against the counter.

"What's up? Do you have the stomach flu?" Jessie asked.

Sydney stared at her friend a moment. "I…no… oh, Jess." She burst into tears and raced into her friend's arms.

"Okay, now you've got me scared. What is it? What's wrong?" Jessie pushed her back and stroked Sydney's face, pushing her hair back from her eyes.

Sydney gulped. "I…I…think I'm pregnant."

Jessie's mouth dropped open. "Omigod…and I'm a nurse. I should have known this, right?"

"You haven't seen much of me lately. Don't knock yourself down about it."

Sydney moved to the sink and splashed cold water on her face. "I'm feeling better now. I don't think the spices in that dish agreed with me."

"Okay, you said you think, not you are pregnant. Have you seen a doctor yet?"

"No."

"Did you take any drugstore tests?"

"No. I hoped I was just late. But then the nausea started, and I've been too scared to face it."

Jessie looked puzzled. "Scared? Why?"

"Because Jax and I have only been living together a couple of months. Having a baby wasn't part of the plan. It'll change things a lot."

"Babies have a way of doing that, especially surprise ones. But before you start stressing over it all, we need to find out if you really are pregnant. Let's get back to our table before the waiter thinks we've skipped out on the bill."

Sydney smiled. "Good plan."

"She's smiling again. And her colour is back." Jessie linked her arm through Sydney's and led her out of the bathroom. They paid the bill and left the restaurant. They had arrived together in Sydney's car. Jessie insisted on driving in case the nausea returned.

"I'm not an invalid. And if I am pregnant, pregnant women do drive, you know."

"Indulge me, okay? I'm driving...and we're heading to the drugstore for a pregnancy test."

Jessie took charge of the situation and told Sydney to relax in the car while she went in the pharmacy. She came back with a bag and tossed it to her friend. Jessie got in the driver's seat and headed to the farm. "Good thing Jax is away in Kelowna for a few days. Gives you a chance to figure this out."

Sydney opened the bag and looked inside. "Good grief, Jess. How many did you buy? It only takes one test."

"Never hurts to confirm in case one is faulty. And

I got different brands, some may be better than others. I don't know, just being cautious."

Sydney laughed. "So if they're all positive, we know that I'm really pregnant."

"That's right. No more denials."

They reached the farm and went inside. Jessie read the instructions. "You're supposed to pee in a cup."

"Okay." Sydney got a cup and went into the bathroom while Jessie paced outside in the hallway. A few minutes later she called Jessie in. "I dipped them all in the cup and lined them up on the counter. It takes around one minute to five minutes depending on the kit. I can't look. You do it."

Jessie stood by counter and watched the test windows on each stick. Sydney sat on the toilet cover and stared at the floor. It seemed like forever as they waited.

"Just waiting on the last one," Jessie said. "You ready?"

Sydney took a deep breath. "Hit me."

One by one Jessie picked up a stick and read it. "This one? A blue line. This one has a red plus sign, Third one a pink line. And the fourth has a word on it."

Sydney looked up her friend expectantly. "And they mean?"

"You're pregnant."

"No." Sydney stood and looked at the four tests. The one with the word was clearly marked 'pregnant.' "I guess I'm pregnant."

The two women stared for the longest time at the four test windows, each lost to their own thoughts. Jessie came alive first. "Oh, oh…" she yelled.

Sydney jumped. "What? You scared me."

"I just remembered something I read a few

months back. Where's your toothpaste?" She started opening drawers and searching.

"The top drawer on this side." Sydney opened the drawer and handed the tube to her.

Jessie opened it and squeezed about an inch of toothpaste into the cup holding the urine. Instantly, the toothpaste changed colours and fizzed up in the pee. "That's it. You're pregnant for sure."

Sydney stared at the coloured fizzy paste. "That's supposed to mean I'm pregnant?"

"Yup."

"Guess you didn't need to waste money on pregnancy tests then. Oh, Jess. What am I going to do?"

"You're going to have a baby is what. Come on, let's clean this up and go sit down."

Minutes later they settled in the living room. "So when was your last period?"

"That's the problem. I came off the pill around the time Jax moved in because it was causing me some health issues. I have had spotting a couple of times, and the doctor said it could take a while for my system to normal out. But Jax and I took precautions."

"Guess what? Didn't work."

"How do you think Jax will take the news, Jess?"

"He'll be as shocked as you, probably as scared as you, but he loves you, and in the end he'll be proud and happy. Together you'll be great parents."

Sydney rubbed her tummy. "I'm going to be a mom."

"And you've got a few days to adjust to the idea before you have to tell Jax. And I'm going to be Auntie Jess."

❧ 15 ❧
EMERALD LAKE

The sun blinded Chelsea as she walked towards the Wildlife Centre listening to a Lady Gaga song she was plugged into. She pulled a pair of sunglasses out of her pocket and cranked up her phone. When *Gypsy* started, she sang along.

And I don't wanna be alone forever. But I can be tonight.

A month in, her studies were going well, and she loved working with Wenner. She'd left Sage at home, as she couldn't bring her inside with the animals, and tying her up outside was a bad idea, leaving her vulnerable to wildlife. A sixteen-year-old, Joanne, signed on as a volunteer. Just as well, since the centre was filling up. Spring and summer were the busiest times, apparently. A frown crossed her face as she reached the gate. *Why is it open?* She passed through and closed it behind her. As she approached the animal compound, she noticed Wenner's jeep parked by the house. *Maybe someone visited and didn't stop to close it.* Chelsea was early, and Joanne wasn't due to arrive for another hour.

Hmm…the compound is still locked. Odd. I may be early, but Wenner is usually here by now. She fished through her pocket for her keys and unlocked the door. Another

98

odd thing greeted her as she stepped into the building. The animals began to vocalize. They appeared restless and agitated. Chelsea spoke quietly to them, noting their water and food bowls were completely empty. Wenner had sent her home yesterday to complete a class assignment. If he'd handled their night feed, there would have been something left in their bowls. Something else was amiss, as well. The room was cold. They didn't need heat in the daytime, as it was approaching the end of May, but nights still chilled down. It became clear that Wenner hadn't turned the heat on last night or fed his patients. *Something's wrong.*

"Hang in there, guys. I'll be right back."

Chelsea left the building and headed to the house. She knocked on the door and called out to Wenner. When he didn't respond she tried the door. It was unlocked. The entranceway of the sprawling rancher led into an open living room. She sucked in a breath. "Uh..." The room was a mess; papers strewn around, pictures off the walls. "Wenner?" She listened. All was quiet. Chelsea followed the hallway to the kitchen. The scene in the kitchen stopped her cold in the doorway. "Omigod..." Drawers were pulled open, and broken glass covered the floor. Then she saw his legs and feet protruding from behind the end of the island.

"Wenner," she yelled.

She ran across the floor and around the island right into a pool of congealed blood. The rubber soles of her runners slipped, and she fell onto her hands and knees beside Wenner. One hand landed on a piece of steel rebar lying on the floor beside Wenner. Her palm had slid along the bar, and a protruding uneven piece of steel on the end of it had ripped into the soft tissue. Her concern for Wenner was so great that she never felt the pain in her hand. She noted his head and upper part of his body were covered with blood. She could see he had an open gash on the back of his skull. Wenner was facing the island, half on his chest and half on his right side. She felt for a pulse in his neck. *Nothing.* She pulled him back, fully on his side, and leaned across his body to place her hand inside his shirt next to his heart. *Yes. He's still alive.* She leaned back and studied his wound. *He's lost a lot of blood.* Chelsea carefully stood and reached into her pocket for her cell phone. It was at this point she felt the pain in her hand and how blood-stained her hands and clothes were. Some of it Wenner's and some her own. "Damn it, that hurts." On examination of her palm, she saw the rebar had cut through the tissue down to the bone, leaving an open two-inch wound. She moved to the counter and took a clean tea towel from the drawer where Wenner kept them. She wrapped her injured hand and dialled emergency.

"911. What's the nature of your emergency?"

"I need an ambulance and police at the Wildlife Centre at Emerald Lake. The address is 307 Aspen Lane."

"Who's hurt, ma'am?"

"I found my boss on the floor. He has a head wound. It looks like someone broke in. The house is a mess."

"Is he alert?"

"No. He's unconscious. His heartbeat is weak, and he's lost a lot of blood."

"Any idea how long he's been unconscious?"

"No, but I think it's been since last night. Please hurry."

"Okay. Hang tight. The police are on their way. Are you alone in the house, ma'am?"

Chelsea looked around the room fearfully. She never thought about whether the perpetrator might still be in the house. She dropped her voice to a whisper. "I…I think so."

"Stay where you are, and stay on the phone with me until they arrive. Okay?"

"I will."

"What's your name?"

"Chelsea Grey."

"Okay, Chelsea. Is there somewhere you can hide if you hear someone in the house in the meantime?"

"There's a bathroom off the kitchen. I could hide in the shower."

"Good. They should be there any moment."

The sound of sirens could be heard in the distance. "I hear them now."

"Stay on line with me until I hear their voices."

Chelsea heard the sirens in the yard. "They're outside. Should I go to them?"

"No. Stay where you are. Is there a table you can sit at?"

"Yes."

"Okay, Chelsea. Sit down and make sure when they enter the kitchen, they can see your hands."

Chelsea did what the operator told her to do and waited.

She'd left the front door open when she entered the house, and the sound of their boots on the front deck confirmed they were at the doorway.

"Police. We're entering the house."

"I'm in the kitchen at the end of the hallway," Chelsea yelled. In a matter of seconds, two officers entered the room with guns drawn. Both sets of eyes searched the room. They put their guns away. One moved towards Wenner and bent down. The other made his way to Chelsea and reached out for the phone in her hand.

"This is Officer Tavis. We're with Chelsea now, and officers are securing the house." He listened for a minute. "Will do. Bye."

"Are the paramedics here, too?" Chelsea asked.

"They're outside. As soon as our officers secure the house, they'll be authorized to come in." He noted her hand." You have an injury and a substantial amount of blood on you. Are you all right?"

"It's mostly Wenner's blood."

The officer sat down and pulled a pad and pen out of his pocket. Another officer entered the kitchen with the paramedics. "The house is secure. They're checking the rest of the property."

"Okay, you'd better call forensics and keep everyone out of the house." He acknowledged the paramedics who were waiting for the other officer to finish taking pictures of the crime scene. "When you can, we need a hand injury checked over here." He turned back to Chelsea. "Can you tell me what you know about what's happened?"

"I have no idea what happened. I came to work and got suspicious because Wenner hadn't fed the animals...and the gate was left open when it shouldn't have been. I came up to the house to see where he was."

"Okay. Let's begin at the start of your day. What time did you arrive, and what did you do until we arrived on scene?"

Chelsea detailed her steps for Officer Tavis. He asked some questions, especially about her injury from the rebar, and put his notebook away. One of the paramedics approached them. "We're ready to transport the victim. Let's have a look at that hand." He carefully removed the stained tea towel and examined her hand. The officer took a picture of the open wound. The paramedic placed a gauze pad over the palm of Chelsea's hand and wrapped it with a gauze bandage. "This is a nasty cut right to the bone. You're going to need stitches. Have you got an up-to-date tetanus shot?"

"No," Chelsea said.

"They'll give you one at the hospital."

"We'll get her to the hospital shortly," Officer Tavis stated.

The paramedics left with Wenner, and the other officer joined them at the table. Officer Tavis spoke to Chelsea. "This is Officer Vargas. I'm going to send her to your home to get you a change of clothes. We're going to need the ones you're wearing."

Chelsea's eyes popped. "What? Why? Am I a suspect?"

He replied in a softer tone. "Chelsea, you contaminated a crime scene when you slipped on the floor. You may have picked up DNA on your clothes. That makes them evidence. When you've changed, we'll take you to the hospital to get your hand attended to."

Chelsea shook. The impact of what she'd experienced had sunk in. Not to mention that her hand throbbed with pain. "But I...I can't leave. Someone has to feed the animals. They haven't had their meds or food since yesterday."

An officer came to the kitchen door. "We have a pretty upset teenage girl outside. She says she's working here today."

"Ask her to wait outside and I'll be out to talk to her," Officer Tavis said.

"Poor Joanne," Chelsea murmured.

"Can Joanne take care of the animals?"

"Feeding, yes. Meds no. But I don't think she'll

want to stay here by herself after all this. She must be terrified."

Officer Tavis studied her. "Alright, once you've changed, you can administer the meds with her help. We'll take her home, and you must go to the hospital. Forensics will be here for most of the day."

Officer Tavis went out to talk to Joanne, and Officer Vargas went to Chelsea's to get a change of clothes. Twenty minutes later Chelsea joined Joanne outside. The girl ran into her arms. "Oh, Chelsea. Are you all right?"

"I'm fine. It's okay, hon."

"They won't tell me anything. What's going on?"

"Wenner had an accident. No one really knows what happened. But he's on his way to the hospital. I'm sure he'll be fine." She gently pushed Joanne back with one hand and held up the injured one. "I'm a little disadvantaged this morning. Are you up to helping me with the animals? Then we'll close for the day."

"Of course. But what happened to your hand?"

"I cut myself. Nothing serious." She walked Joanne to the animal habitat. "They're all a little skittish this morning, I'm afraid. Pissed off cause they're hungry, and they sense something's wrong. So we'll have to be extra gentle and careful with them this morning."

❧ 16 ❧

KELOWNA

The smell of antiseptic made Chelsea's stomach churn. She watched the intern close the open gap in her palm. Any nervousness she felt didn't come from being stitched up or feeling any pain. The shot of lidocaine took care of that. It came from the overcautious demeanor of the student doctor. Chelsea decided to focus on the obviously inexperienced young man to take her mind away from the upset of her morning. No one was able to give her an update on Wenner, and it was futile to upset herself with worry.

"Good job," she said.

The intern looked up at her in surprise. Chelsea gave him a big smile.

He finished placing the last two stitches and put down the needle. A nearby senior doctor came over to inspect his work. He nodded and walked away. The young man visibly relaxed. "Thanks for being such a good patient," he said with a smile. He started to bandage her hand.

"It's easy when treated with competence."

The young doctor blushed and laughed aloud. "I've done quite a few of these with guidance. But you were my first patient working on my own. I tried hard to hide my jitters."

"And you did a good job. You'll be a great doctor."

"Thank you. We're done here. I'm going to put your arm in a sling; keep it on for a couple of days. We don't want you banging your hand and opening the stitches. I'll be right back."

A voice came from behind her. "Mom, are you all right?"

Chelsea turned to see Sydney hurrying across the triage floor. "I...I'm fine. How'd you know I was here?"

"The police called Nan, but she's still away, so they called me. What happened?"

Before she could reply, the intern returned and placed the sling. "Here's a prescription for some pain killers. If you have any excessive bleeding or think you've broken the stitches, come back to emergency. You can change the bandages in three days and re-place with a gauze pad. I'm giving you four pads. If you need more you can buy them at the pharmacy. Check in with your doctor in a week's time. The stitches will dissolve on their own. Definitely keep the wound covered when you're working at the wildlife centre until you're sure the skin has closed. Any questions?"

"No. Thank you, doctor."

He nodded to her and Sydney and took his leave.

"Mom, what happened?"

"I don't have all the answers. But I'll tell you what I know. Let's go. I have to find out if there is any news about Wenner." Chelsea stood. She felt a bit woozy from the pain shot they'd given her. "Whoa...just getting my footing here."

The two women left triage, and the moment they

entered the main emergency room, they were approached by two men. "Chelsea Grey?"

"Yes."

The man flashed a badge. "I'm Detective Reardon with the RCMP Major Crimes Unit, and this is my partner, Detective Dara." He glanced at her bandaged hand. "How are you feeling?"

"A little stoned at the moment, otherwise I'm fine."

"We'd like to ask you some questions. Are you up to stopping by the police station before you head home to Emerald Lake?"

Sydney looked annoyed. "Can't it wait? I'd like to take her home to rest. I can bring her in tomorrow."

Chelsea placed her hand on Sydney's shoulder. "It's okay. We'll stop in. But I want to check on Wenner before we leave."

The detective handed her a business card. "We'll see you at the station."

The two women watched them leave. "Are you sure you're up to this?" Sydney asked.

"I'm sure. Let's find out where Wenner is."

They were told he was in ICU. The women went to the nurse's station and were told he was still unconscious and there was no change. Chelsea could see him through the floor-to-ceiling glass windows of his room across from the station.

"Can I go in for a moment?"

"Are you family?"

"I'm a friend. He's estranged from his family."

"Okay, just for a minute."

Chelsea went in alone. Wenner's head was wrapped in bandages. He looked so pale. She placed a hand over his and spoke softly. "I'm here, Wenner. It's Chelsea. If you can hear me, you have to fight. Don't worry about the Centre. I'll take care of it. But we need you, so be strong. I'll come back soon."

Police headquarters were quiet when they arrived. On the drive from the hospital, Chelsea told her daughter all that she knew. They were shown to a reception area and told to wait. Detective Reardon arrived and asked Chelsea to follow him. When Sydney stood to follow, he stopped her. "You'll have to wait here, Miss Grey. Your mother won't be long."

It was apparent to Chelsea that Sydney was angry and confused. *That makes two of us.* She followed the detective into a conference room, and he motioned to a table. She sat down and he sat opposite her. He took a tape recorder out of his pocket and dictated the date, time and occupants in the room. "You're here voluntarily, and I appreciate you coming in. I have some questions for you, Chelsea, based on your testimony this morning. Okay?"

"Yes."

"What time do you usually get to work?"

"About 8:00 a.m."

"You said you arrived about 7:30 a.m. this morning. Why were you there early?"

Chelsea shrugged. "No reason. I woke up early. It was a beautiful morning and I went for a walk by the lake. I decided that I might as well continue on to work."

"How long have you been working at the Wildlife Centre?"

"One month."

"And how long have you known Wenner Gibb?"

"One month."

"And what were the circumstances under which you met?"

"I met him in the hills. I was returning from a hike with Sage, my dog, and Wenner was at the lookout overlooking the lake. We walked down together and he showed me around the Centre. He liked how I handled the animals. We had tea up at the house, and he offered me a part-time job."

"And what is the extent of your relationship?"

"He's my boss first, and we are becoming close friends."

"Intimate friends?"

Chelsea frowned. "No, just friends."

"What about his family? Do you know where they might be reached?"

"He hasn't been in touch with his family in years. He was born and raised on a farm in Saskatchewan. He has a younger brother. He left home at sixteen and never returned."

"You've admitted that you touched the rebar, so chances are when forensics come back, your fingerprints will be on it. We'd like to take your prints to identify them. Okay?"

"That's fine."

"Why did you go into the house? I mean, once in the hallway, you could see it was a crime scene? The perpetrator might still have been inside."

"I didn't think about it as a crime scene at that point. Wenner is a widower, and he's been through a rough time the past two years. I don't know, he might have had a bad moment and torn up his place. My main concern was about him."

"So you continued down the hall to the kitchen?"

"Yes…and I saw his legs on the floor, stretched out behind the edge of the island."

"And you didn't think it might be a crime scene at that point?"

"I guess. I really wasn't thinking. I mean…he was on the floor. Obviously he must be hurt. He must have fallen and hurt himself."

"After he trashed his own house?"

"Maybe…I don't know. My thoughts were on him, not on what had happened. Once I saw him, I just wanted to make sure he was okay."

"So why did you touch the rebar? When you ran around the island, it must have been obvious someone had hit Wenner across the head with the rebar."

"I slipped in the blood and my hand landed on the rebar when I hit the floor."

"I want you to think back to the moment you ran around the island. There was no pool of blood at that end of the island, so how did you slip?"

Chelsea looked confused. "Yes, there was."

"You saw his legs and you ran towards him and around his feet, and you saw him lying on the floor. There was no blood on the floor there."

A light bulb went on, and Chelsea realized what he was saying. "Oh…but I didn't run towards his feet. I ran the other way across the floor and around the far end of the island. There was a pool of blood at that end, and as I rounded the corner of the island, I ran right into it and slipped. Down I went with my right hand landing on the end of the rebar. It slid along and sliced my hand open."

"And at that point, did you realize it was a crime scene?"

"I did, but my concern was to see if Wenner had a pulse because he was either unconscious or…dead. I couldn't find a pulse, so I rolled him back and put my hand in his shirt to feel for a heartbeat. Thank God there was one."

Chelsea was starting to wane. The lidocaine was wearing off, and her hand was throbbing in pain. She asked the detective for some water and took a pill from the prescription they'd filled at the hospital pharmacy.

"What did you do next, after you determined that Mr. Gibb was still alive?"

"I stood and pulled out my cell phone. While I was talking to the operator, she asked me if I was sure I was alone in the house, that whoever had done this to Wenner wasn't still there. That was the moment I realized I could be in danger. But I could hear the sirens in the distance and tried to relax until they arrived."

"Chelsea, have you ever slept at Mr. Gibb's?"

Her head shot back. "No."

The detective stared at her for a moment and leaned across the table. "Chelsea, one of his neighbours told us you've spent a few nights at Wenner's house. So I'm going to ask you again, have you ever slept over at Wenner's house, and are the two of you intimate?"

Chelsea was pissed off now. And the pain pill was making her feel light-headed. "Okay, now I'm going to answer you again and for the last time. No, I've never slept at Wenner's house. Yes, I did stay overnight with Wenner in the animal compound for a couple of nights because we acquired a couple of bear cubs whose mother had been killed, and they needed to be bottle fed every few hours." She could have told him Wenner was gay but didn't see why she should have to. That was Wenner's personal business and not her place to tell people.

"Thank you for clearing that up. I still have a few more questions…"

Chelsea stood up and pushed her chair back. "No more questions. Unless you're planning to arrest me or something, I'm going home. I'm dizzy, I'm in pain, and I've had enough for today. And I still have to feed the animals tonight."

"Alright, you can go for now. Can we do those fingerprints before you leave?"

"As long as I don't have to wait."

❧ 17 ❧

As they started the drive home, Chelsea put her head back against the headrest. She was asleep in a matter of minutes. Sydney felt grateful that her mother could finally rest. And if she was honest, relieved that they didn't have to talk. She'd apologized for the mean words during their confrontation, but she still felt guilty. She'd avoided Jax's prodding her to call her mother and talk it out. Procrastination and fear of more confrontation had set in. *The longer you leave something unresolved, the harder it is to take a step back.* Today had been chaos, and her concern for her mother's well-being overshadowed their rift. But a reckoning was coming. Sydney felt the need to talk it out face to face.

Forty minutes later they pulled into the driveway of the cottage at Emerald Lake. Sydney studied her mother's face before she woke her. In spite of a pale face, she looked good, confirming the reports from her Nan that her mother was doing well here. She touched her arm gently. "Mom? We're home."

Chelsea stirred and opened her eyes. "Already?" She smiled at her daughter. "I guess I slept the whole way."

"You did, too. Let's get inside, and I'll make us some dinner."

The two women left the car and entered the cottage. Sydney was stunned. "Wow. Nan said you were renovating. This looks great. The last time Jax and I were here, we laughed about how entering the cottage was like stepping back into the '40s. Not anymore."

Chelsea beamed. "I'm not done yet, but it's getting there. Let's have a look in the fridge and see what we can rustle up. I'm starving."

"No, you sit down and I'll see what I can find. You need to relax and rest. You're kind of crippled anyhow."

Her mother frowned. "That's for sure." She sat down and pulled out her cell phone, checking her messages. "A text from Joanne, my helper at the Centre. Her mother won't let her work there until we know what happened to Wenner. She doesn't think it's safe. I can't say that I blame her."

Sydney leaned against the kitchen counter. "By the same token, how safe is it for you to be working there?"

"Good point. But someone has to look after the animals. I think that responsibility has fallen on my shoulders. Wenner doesn't have anyone else."

"But you only have one useful hand right now. How'll you manage?"

"Well…the bear cubs are leaving tomorrow for the Wildlife Centre in Kelowna. I won't accept…"

Sydney cut her mother off. "You have bear cubs?"

"We do. If you don't mind helping me with their feeding tonight, you can meet them. Then, you'd best be on your way home."

Sydney frowned and crossed her arms across her

chest. "There's no way I'm leaving you here alone. I'm staying for as long as you need me…" she faltered. "That is if I'm welcome."

Chelsea felt pleased that her daughter offered. "Of course you're welcome. I just thought you had clients waiting for you."

"No out-of-towners right now. I already asked Jax to cancel my daily classes."

The two women stared at each other in an awkward moment. Chelsea broke the silence. "I think I'll have a quick shower while you make us some dinner."

"Okay, but don't get your bandage wet."

Her mother retrieved a plastic bag from the pantry. "This will do the trick."

Sydney searched through the fridge. She found lasagna and placed it in the oven. Then she threw a salad together. After searching the cupboards for plates and cutlery, she set the table. Not knowing where her mother kept anything, she must have searched every cupboard and the pantry before finishing her task. A thought came to mind. *Not one ounce of alcohol anywhere. Unless she's hidden it.* Sydney laughed to herself. *And why would she hide it? She lives alone. Definitely a good sign.*

Half an hour later they sat down to eat. Chelsea struggled to cut her lasagna with her fork. Sydney pulled it towards her. "Here, let me cut it into pieces for you."

Chelsea giggled. "Too weird. I'm not used to being taken care of."

"Thank goodness you have me to help out. Nan's away for another week." Sydney's face clouded over. She put her fork down. "Look, I think it's time we cleared the air, Mom." Her eyes filled with tears. "I'm so sorry I said those awful things to you at

Nan's. I should have called you right away, but I was still angry with you and ashamed of myself…"

"It's okay. I should be thanking you. What you said to me that day pushed me to take charge of my life…and look at me now." Chelsea stared at her arm sling. "Okay…had you visited yesterday, my little speech would have been more effective."

Sydney laughed and wiped her eyes. "Still…I was mean, and that's really not who I am."

"Let yourself off the hook. You reacted out of frustration is all. You're human."

"Okay. You seem to be settling in well here. Nan told me about your online classes and your work at the Wildlife Centre."

"I love it here and my work with Wenner. I'm still not all that comfortable with people, and maybe I never will be. I don't know if you know that Wenner is gay. At first, that made me feel safe with him. No expectations from me as a woman. But as I've gotten to know him, he has sensitivity and a love of animals that matches my own. He's still grieving over the loss of his husband. We can be vulnerable together without complications."

"Makes sense. I'm happy you have a friend you can trust."

Chelsea smiled. "So am I." Her smile faded. "I hope he's okay."

Sydney reached out and squeezed her mother's hand. "We'll check in with the hospital after dinner. Let's eat before it gets cold."

THEY DROVE through the open gate. A police car was sitting on guard to keep people out. He waved them through to the animal shelter. Chelsea pointed the building out, and Sydney parked in front of the doors. She got out and stared over at the house. A yellow ribbon was in place all around the perimeter, and the forensics team was still at work. Chelsea had been told she could access the animal shelter, but the rest of the property was off limits until the police had completed their investigation of the house and land. She pulled her keys out of her pocket and turned towards the door. When they entered, the animals were quiet, a sharp contrast to the frantic chaos that greeted her that morning.

"Ooh, look at the cute rabbits," Sydney gushed. She looked around at the cages. There were partitions between them so the animals couldn't see their neighbours. Chelsea walked to the one at the end of the row and raised the blind covering the front of the cage.

"Oh my. Is that a hawk?" Sydney asked.

"Yes, a red-tailed hawk. We call her Red. She had a broken leg. Wenner removed the splint last week, and we were going to release her this week."

"She's beautiful. Where are the bear cubs?"

"They're in the room to the right. It's a larger room for animals that need larger cages. The small room on the left is the surgical room, and all the meds and feed are kept in there. We'll feed this room first. Once the cubs see us, they'll become very vocal until they are fed."

She led Sydney into the surgical room and unlocked the medicine cabinet. Chelsea made up the bowls of food with her daughter's help and added the medicines listed on the charts for each animal. They carried them into the main room and Sydney was directed how to feed them and refill their water, except for Red. Chelsea approached Red. She spoke to her in barely a whisper. "Hi, Red. Guess what? As soon as I get rid of this sling, we're going to release you back into your territory. You can rejoin your mate." She donned her glove and opened the cage. "Talon has been visiting me on a daily basis and follows me here. Did you know that? I think he knows you're here and that we've been taking good care of you." After feeding the raptor, she dropped the blind down. "Okay, let's take a look at those cubs."

True to her words, the moment they opened the door and entered the larger room, the cubs greeted them with squeals. Chelsea spoke quietly to them, and soon they began to coo.

"Omigod..." Sydney said. "They're adorable. How old are they?"

"About three and half months. Something happened to the mother. They usually stay in the den and nurse until three months before the mother brings them out in the open. But the cubs were found wandering around at about ten weeks old. When we got them, they were emaciated, and Wenner wasn't sure they would survive. We bottle fed them until they took solid food."

They gave each cub a bowl of formula for continued growth and then gave each cub a bowl of dried dog food mixed with fruit and fish.

Sydney tilted her head towards the cubs. "Are they purring like cats?"

"Yes. They purr when they eat."

"Do you have names for them, too?"

Chelsea nodded. "The smaller of the two is a female. We call her She-bear, the other one, a male, He-bear."

They sat on the floor in front of the cage and watched the cubs until they finished. Chelsea stood. "I'm done in. Let's call it a night."

"Okay," Sydney said. "How cool is this? I'm so

proud of you, Mom. You're doing a good thing here."

Chelsea felt a lump form in her throat. "Thank you, that means a lot." Her daughter couldn't possibly know what her words meant to her. She was tired, hurting, and very emotional at this moment. She quickly turned and headed to the other room. "I need to get the cubs' files and take them with us to the cottage. Since I don't have access to Wenner's office, I'll make a copy on my own printer for the attendants who are moving the cubs tomorrow."

The wound looked clean, and the stitches were intact. Sydney placed a fresh gauze pad over the injury. "Still some swelling and redness, but overall, it seems to be healing nicely."

Chelsea wiggled her fingers. The pain was still there but not as acute, and she'd cut her pain killers down to two a day. "Day three and it's much better. I don't need the sling anymore, which will make my life a lot easier." She squeezed her hand into a ball and pain shot through her palm. "My grip isn't great, but since I can't talk you into releasing Red for me, I'll manage. The leather glove will pad the palm enough for me to grip her talon."

Sydney looked stricken. "I'm sorry. I'm not as comfortable as you are handling that raptor."

"It's okay. I was nervous the first time Wenner got me to hold her."

"Do you have to do it now? Can't you wait a few more days?"

"No. Red is ready to be released. She's getting anxious, and I don't want her to reinjure herself. Given the time of year, it's very likely that when she was injured she had chicks in their nest. Talon will have looked after them and fed them. We haven't seen any young hawks in their territory, so they haven't left the nest yet. It's a big job for one parent."

"So you don't know where the nest is?"

"No. We'll release her where Wenner found her. Hawks mate for life, but if they lose their mate, they can leave their territory and hook up with another one. That's another reason we think there may be chicks. Talon hasn't left. Shall we go?"

The pair walked to the Centre and unlocked the gate. The police were done with the property, and Chelsea was happy to have it to herself. Wenner was still in a coma, and it weighed heavily on her. But she was determined to stay positive and believe he'd be okay. She intended on cleaning up his house in preparation for his return.

They entered the shelter building and spent the next thirty minutes feeding the remaining animals.

"It's quiet in here without He-bear and She-bear," Sydney said. "It'll be more so when we release Red."

Sydney looked concerned. "Are you going to be able to manage when I go home?"

"Not a problem. I'm not taking in any more patients until Wenner's home. I'm not qualified to do surgeries on my own anyway. There are other centres they can go to if necessary." Chelsea paused. "This place is so important to him. He needs to wake up and come home."

"He will…you'll see. All done here, Mom. Now what?"

Chelsea brightened up. "Time to release Red." She retrieved a small dog travel case, placing a cus-tom-made cover over the cage. She moved it onto a table with the door open. Next, she donned leather gloves. Holding a white cloth in one, she moved to

Red's cage. "Hey, girl. Today's your lucky day. You're going home to your family." She turned to Sydney. "Can you open the door for me?"

Chelsea slipped one gloved hand into the cage, speaking softly to Red as she moved her hand closer. She placed the white cloth over the hawk, making sure to cover her head and obstruct the birds view. Red relaxed. Her other gloved hand moved in quickly, and she reached forward to grasp both talons simultaneously. "Here we go, sweetheart, easy does it." She lifted the bird up, wincing as her right hand gripped tighter around the raptor's leg to carry the weight.

"Are you alright?" Sydney whispered.

"Yes. Let's do this." Chelsea eased her arms back towards the open door to the cage. She backed away slowly, clearing the cage door. She turned and moved towards the table and the travel case, whispering to Red the whole time. "Sydney, when I pull my hands back out of the cage, can you close the door and lock it?" Easing Red backwards into the smaller cage, Chelsea released her hold of the talons. She pulled one arm out of the cage. With the other, she gently pulled the cloth off Red and removed that arm from the case. Sydney closed and locked the door. Chelsea dropped the cover drop cloth over the door and removed her gloves.

"Wow. Mom, that was awesome. You so rock at this."

Chelsea beamed as she let out a deep sigh. "That was easier than I thought it would be."

"How much does she weigh?" Sydney asked.

"Between one and two kilograms." She wiggled her fingers of her sore hand. "Hurts like hell, but the bandage is clean, no damage."

"Are you up for the hike in the grasslands? I'll carry the travel case."

"I'm pumped and ready. Help me on with the backpack. We'll stop at the lookout over the lake for lunch on the way back."

The two women left the compound and walked up the trail into the grasslands. They climbed for several minutes and stopped at the lookout over the lake for some water.

"The view is breathtaking," Sydney said.

Chelsea's face clouded over. "This is where I met Wenner that first time."

Sydney studied her mother. "He's going to be fine, Mom."

"I wish he'd wake up is all."

"The doctors are deliberately keeping him unconscious until the swelling goes down. They'll wake him up soon."

Chelsea brightened up. "You're right. I'm being morose. Let's move on."

They followed the path upwards until they reached the open benches of the grasslands. Here the land was flat and stretched forever. To the right about half a kilometre away, Rattlesnake Hill loomed, an outcropping of rocks and caves. They continued forward another kilometre. Chelsea stopped. "This is where he found her."

Sydney placed the cage on the ground. "Did Wenner know how she got injured?"

"No. But her main enemy is the owl. If she has chicks, she may have been leading the owl away from the nest and gotten into a fight. That's as good a guess as any." Chelsea took off her backpack and took out her leather gloves. She bent down and unlocked the door. "Here we go, Red." She reached in and took hold of the raptor's talons and lifted her forward and out the door.

Chelsea stood and held the bird facing her. "It's your moment, big girl. Time for you to show us what you're made of." She turned her hands sideways so Red faced to her right. With a forward and upwards motion, she threw the raptor into the air, releasing her hold on the talons. Red flapped her wings instantly and flew to a nearby bush. She sat on a branch and looked around.

A sudden scream from high above broke the silence. "Look...up there." Sydney pointed above Red's head. A red-tailed hawk was circling above them. It picked up the thermals and glided slowly down. Red screeched in answer.

"It's Talon," Chelsea said.

The male raptor began a series of cries resembling a steam train whistle. Red flew up to greet the bird and they flew together up high and circled above them.

Sidney moved closer to Chelsea and linked her arm through her mother's. They stood together watching the two birds reunite. They performed a show of diving and gliding, their steam whistles blending, until they flew off together and out of view.

Mother and daughter turned to each other and smiled. "Wow, how awesome was that," Sydney said.

"That made the past month so worth it. My God, I love this work."

Sydney reached out to her mother and they hugged each other tight. "Thank you, Mom, for sharing this moment with me."

A GENTLE BREEZE cooled the air as they sat eating their lunch at the lookout. Chelsea studied her daughter's profile as she chatted about the lake view far below them. Now that she was weaned off the pain meds and the pain had settled down, she saw things more clearly. Something was different about Sydney. She saw it and sensed it.

Sydney took a bite of her egg salad sandwich and instantly gagged. She jumped up and ran behind the sagebrush and vomited. She placed her hands on her knees and took deep breaths.

"Are you alright?"

Sydney returned to her spot beside her mother. "I'm okay. Just been off for a couple of days."

Her daughter's face was white. Chelsea smiled. "How far along are you?"

Sydney looked shocked. "What?"

"You're pregnant."

Her daughter nodded her head and smiled. "Maybe six weeks or more. How'd you know?"

"A mother knows these things. You have a certain look to you. Were you going to tell me?"

"Of course, but I wanted to tell Jax first."

Chelsea's eyebrows rose. "How long have you known?"

Sydney frowned and looked away from her. "About a week."

"Oh? And you haven't told Jax? Why not?"

"Well, he was away when Jess and the doctor confirmed it. I needed a few more days to figure it out, and then I got the call about you, soooo…"

"What do you mean figure it out? You're pregnant and having a baby. Or don't you want children?"

"I've always wanted children…just not this soon.

I mean, we've only been living together for a short time. A baby is a big thing."

Chelsea took her daughter's hand in hers. "Do you love Jax?"

"I do, and he loves me. But I'm not sure how he'll take to being a father so soon. We're still adjusting to our relationship."

"Loving each other is a good start. You won't be the first couple to be surprised with a baby."

"That's what Jess said. It's just that with both of us starting new businesses…and I'll have to take time away from mine…Aargh. We aren't ready for this right now."

Chelsea studied her daughter's face. "I think it's fair to say I've been in your shoes, and I understand what you're going through. I certainly wasn't ready. I was also alone. The emotions you're going through are exaggerated by a few factors; being physically ill, hormonal changes which affect your mental state, and the shock that this life inside of you is a reality. In my case, I could have had an abortion, given you up for adoption, or raised you on my own. I chose the latter, and your Nan was there for me big time. In the end I wouldn't have done anything differently, and the moment I saw you for the first time, all my fears disappeared."

"Abortion and adoption are off the table. I'm for sure having this baby."

"Then it's time to tell Jax. If he loves you, I'm sure he'll be there for you. If he's anything like his father, he'll be a great dad. Don't wait until he notices something on his own. Secrets only add more complications. And you don't need the additional stress. There are decisions to be made here, and there's no need for you to make them alone."

"You're right. Anyway, I'm having an ultrasound

next week, and I want him to be there with me. I'll tell him as soon as I get home."

"You'll have me and Nan there to help you, too, if you want. You know that, right?"

Sydney squeezed her mother's hand. "Mom, you missed out on raising me, but you'll definitely be involved with your grandchild's life."

"That means a lot to me. Thank you."

"My nausea has passed, and I'm starving. Let's get into this lunch."

Mason Ross reached for the envelope containing the report he'd been waiting for. He tore it open and read through the pages. He stopped part-way through and flicked the pages with his fingers. *That's why I couldn't find you.* He finished reading the rest of the report and put the papers into a manila file on his desk. *The Okanagan, eh? Guess I'm going on a trip.*

He opened his laptop and Google mapped the address, switching from street map to satellite, familiarizing himself with the location he sought and the surrounding areas. His destination was about 450 kilometres away, a five-hour drive. He searched for motels in the area and found some cabins available with Internet access on Emerald Lake. One phone call reserved him a cabin of his own. With no idea how long he would need to stay in the area, he booked it for two nights with the assurance he could book longer if needed.

One suitcase was pulled out of the storage room and packed in no time. An overnight shoulder bag contained his toiletries and necessary files. Plants were watered, dishes washed, and one important telephone call made. "Hi, it's me. I'm onto something here, and I'm heading out of town." He relayed the location and resort he would be at. "I'll let you know my time schedule when I know more. Catch you later."

Mason left his apartment and placed his cases in the back of his Ford Escape. He drove across the Lion's Gate Bridge from the North Shore into downtown Vancouver. The circular driveway in front of the four-star hotel was lined with taxis and limousines, so he continued around to the parkade down the block and walked back. TED talks were happening this weekend in the city, and lots of out-of-town visitors were waiting in the lobby to check in. Mason slipped past the reception desk and entered one of the offices behind. He knocked on the door jamb and waited for the woman in charge of public relations at the hotel to acknowledge him.

Linda Ellis looked up. She leaned back in her chair with a surprised look. "Oh…so the man is still alive. Where have you been?"

"I'm working on something complicated, and I'm leaving town for a few days. I thought I'd drop in on my way out and let you know."

The woman leaned forward and folded her hands on top of the desk. "Let me get this straight. You've been back in town for a week with no calls to me, no answering my texts, and now you pop in to tell me you're leaving again. How considerate."

"Your sarcasm isn't lost on me, my dear. I'm sorry. I told you this project would be time-consuming and all-encompassing. I'll make it up to you when I get back."

Linda stood and walked towards him. She pulled him into the office and shut the door. "That's okay. I'm pretty busy myself right now." Placing her arms around his neck, she moved in close and rubbed her breasts against his chest. "But don't ignore me for too long, sport. You're the one who asked for us to be exclusive, but I'm not one to be taken advantage of. All I'm asking is you at least text me once in a while." She leaned into his face and kissed him passionately on the lips. "When will you be back?"

Mason shrugged. "I'm not sure. I promise we'll connect when I return."

"Where are you going?"

Mason sighed. "It's better you don't know."

She studied his face. "You look tired. This project, as you call it, is taking a toll on you. Can I help at all?"

"No, but thank you. You know I can't tell you about it only because the less you know, the better it is for your safety." Mason returned her kiss with a long one of his own. "I have to go."

Linda opened the door. "Okay, skedaddle. Stay safe…and call me."

"I will."

THE TRAFFIC WAS bottle-necked on the highway out of Vancouver to the Fraser Valley. Construction added to the usual all-day traffic jam out of the city. Once he crossed the Port Mann Bridge over the Fraser River, it wasn't long until he reached the farmlands of Chilliwack at the east end of the Fraser Valley. The traffic thinned and he relaxed. He made up time and reached the town of Hope in no time. He could have taken the Coquihalla Highway to the Okanagan Connector and down into the Okanagan but decided instead to travel the Hope-Princeton Highway. This secondary highway was slower but very scenic and a more relaxed pace of driving.

He was a city boy for sure, but he always enjoyed the beauty of the British Columbia Interior and mother nature in all her glory. He stopped in the small village of Hedley for coffee and continued his drive, leaving the green forests and mountainous terrain behind as he drove into the semi-arid Similkameen Valley through the village of Keremeos and along the river until he reached Emerald Lake. He found the resort easily and entered the office to check in.

A middle-aged woman looked up from a newspaper she was reading. "Hello, can I help you?"

"Yes, I'm Mason Ross. I have a reservation for one of the cabins."

'Ohh…you made good time from Vancouver." She reached under the counter for a reservation slip for him to sign.

"Yes, once away from the city, the traffic was minimal." He filled out the slip and handed it back to her with his credit card.

"It was a lovely day for the long drive."

"Very pleasant," he said.

The woman ran off a receipt, and he prepaid two nights. "The cabin is yours for longer if you still need it. So what kind of business are you in?"

Mason stared at the woman. She was only being friendly, and he realized he'd made a mistake when calling for the reservation by mentioning it was a business trip. Now he'd have to make something up. "I'm a writer on a deadline from my publisher. I'm hoping to finish my manuscript in the next couple of days. If not, I'll stay until it's done."

"How interesting. Here's your key. I'll show you the cabin."

He followed the woman out of the office and down to the lake. The cabin was rustic but clean and quite adequate. There was an open floor plan with a kitchenette in an alcove at the back of the cabin. A bathroom was beside the alcove. The front of the cabin had a living room with a wood stove, and the other side housed a queen-sized bed with a dresser.

"So do you write fiction or non-fiction?"

"Science Fiction. The cabin is fine. Thank you." He walked towards the door and put his hand on it, hoping she'd get the hint to leave. She followed him to the open door.

"So, you can bring your car down and park it beside the cabin. If you want to take out a canoe, just sign it out at the office so we know you're on the water and sign back in when you return."

He took a look at the lake from the doorway. "Thank you, I just might do that. I'll walk you back up and get my car."

The woman stepped out onto the porch, and he closed the door behind him. He wanted to get her off the subject of his lie. "You have a lovely spot here on the lake. Have you been here long?"

She appeared happy to talk about herself as they returned to the office. "Twenty years we've been here. Couldn't imagine doing anything else. We get to meet all kinds of people without even leaving home. Well, enjoy your stay, Mr. Ross. If you need anything, just ask."

❦ 20 ❧

STONEY CREEK

The lights were on in the living room, and Sydney could see Jax sitting at the dining room table working on his laptop. Her heart raced from pure love for this man and from anxiety for the news she would share with him tonight. She parked beside his truck in the driveway and retrieved her suitcase from the backseat. Before she reached the stairs to the veranda, the door flew open and Jax ran out and down the stairs. "There she is. The love of my life." He threw his arms around her and squeezed her tight. He rocked her back and forth in his arms like he always did.

Sydney laughed and rocked with him. "Hey, cowboy. Could you let a girl breathe?"

Jax released her and took her suitcase. "I missed you."

She followed him up the stairs and into the house. "Me, too."

"How's your mom? And Wenner? How were the roads down?"

Sydney couldn't help but giggle. Jax always asked questions in triplicate. "Mom is doing really well. Her hand is healing. You should see the Wildlife

Centre. So awesome, but I'll tell you about it later. Sadly, there's no change with Wenner. And no problem on the roads."

She followed Jax into the bedroom where he deposited her suitcase.

"You look tired. How about I make you a hot cup of ginger tea?"

"That would be super. I'm going to take a quick shower. I'll be right there."

Fifteen minutes later, she joined him in the dining room in a pair of yoga pants and a t-shirt. A two-cup teapot was set up on the table with her favourite mug beside it. "Thank you." She pulled out a chair and sat down. "How's your project going?"

"Almost complete. I'm just doing up the final invoices to print off tomorrow at the office."

"Okay. There's something we need to talk about when you're done."

Jax glanced up at her. "Shoot. I can multi-task."

"I'll wait 'til you're finished. I need your full attention." She stood to go into the living room taking her tea with her.

He stopped to watch her. "Sounds serious."

"Finish up and join me when you're done." Sydney curled up in the corner of the couch, adjusting the oversized pillows. She put her head back and listened to Jazz Masters playing on Galaxy. With no idea how to tell Jax about their dilemma, she chose to push it from her mind and feel the depth of the piano piece.

Ten minutes later, Jax joined her on the couch. "Okay. I'm all yours." He made a move to come closer beside her, but Sydney turned sideways and crossed her legs between them so she could see his face. She wanted to gauge his reaction.

"Do you realize we're celebrating two months of living together today?"

Jax smiled. "I wasn't counting, but I guess you're right. Two great months. Are you happy?"

"Totally, never more so. But I need to tell you something, and in all honestly, I don't know how you'll feel about it. In fact, I'm scared to tell you."

Jax looked frightened. "Are you sick? I've noticed you've been a bit pale lately." He studied her face.

Sydney grimaced. "No, not sick." She took his hand in hers. "Oh, bugger it. I'm just going to blurt it out and see where it lands." She stared at him expectantly. "Jax...I'm pregnant." His facial expression went from shock, to disbelief, to acknowledgement. "Wow!"

He spoke with a soft croak. "Pregnant? But how? We've been careful since you had to stop taking the pill."

"The doctor says it was probably a faulty condom. It happens." She studied his face.

"When? I mean, how far along are you?"

"Maybe seven weeks. We'll know for sure when I have an ultrasound."

"So you got pregnant after we moved in together?"

"Yes." She frowned, not sure why he thought of that. "Does that matter?"

"Of course it matters." His voice was stronger now, and his timbre startled her.

Sydney felt confused. "Why?"

He gave her a crooked grin. "Because the town gossips can't say I stayed with you because I got you pregnant. We were already together."

Her emotions got the better of her. "I've been worried sick about how you'd take this news, and all you're worried about is gossip? Man, I don't believe this." She tried to get up but Jax pulled her towards him and wrapped his arms around her.

"Come here. I'm messing with you to get you to relax. Bad joke, my mistake. But you look so serious and scared. You know I of all people wouldn't give a rat's ass about what people will say." Jax pushed her back and looked her right in the eyes. "It's a shock, but here it is. I love kids, and I love you. So we're going to be parents, and you will be a wonderful mother."

Sydney relaxed a little. At least he didn't run for the door. "It is serious. This changes a lot of things."

"And we'll change right along with it." Jax was smiling now. "As the seconds are rolling by, the shock is wearing off and I'm feeling…happy. See, a few more seconds have gone by…happier." He frowned. "Aren't you?"

"Secretly, I've been kind of excited. But we've been living together for such a short time, and starting a family was not in our immediate plans. I had no idea how you'd feel about this."

"Well, let me show you."

Jax stood and grabbed both her hands. He pulled her up off the couch and towards the front door. "Come with me." He opened the door and led her onto the veranda.

Sydney was giggling now. "What are you doing?"

Jax faced out towards the road. He threw his arms up and started to yell. "My lady is having a baby. I'm going to be a father." He placed one hand on his chest like an opera singer and broke out into an old song, singing the line, *'What a wonderful way of saying how much you love me'.*

Sydney broke into laughter. "Omigod…that's so cheesy."

"Yes, it is, and I love it." He pulled her into his

arms. "And I love you, Sydney Grey." They embraced in silence for a few minutes, each lost to their own thoughts.

"You know what this means, don't you?" Jax said, leading her back into the house.

"What?"

"More renos. We're going to have to build a nursery."

He escorted her to the armchair. "Sit. I'll be right back." Jax left the room. Sydney could hear him rummaging through a drawer in the bedroom. When he came back, Jax kneeled on the floor between her legs.

Sydney giggled. "What are you doing?"

"Sydney Grey, will you marry me?"

"Omigod…are you serious?"

"Never more so."

Chelsea was stunned. Her hands shot to her face. "Yes…of course, yes."

Jax took her left hand and placed a ring on her finger. "This was my mother's wedding ring. If you don't like it, we'll get you one of your own. But I want you to have it."

Chelsea raised her hand to see the wide band set with rows of diamonds, one larger diamond set in the middle. Tears filled her eyes, and she had to wipe them away to see the ring. "Oh, Jax, it's beautiful… and it fits. I don't want another ring. This one is perfect."

Jax leaned forward and kissed her with a passion that made her dizzy. He placed his forehead against hers and stared deep into her eyes. And in barely a whisper, he spoke.

"I love you, mother of my child."

SYDNEY SQUIRMED IN HER SEAT. She leaned over to Jax. "Omigod...I need to pee. How much longer do we have to wait?"

They were in the hospital waiting for her scheduled ultrasound. An hour before the test she drank the required litre of water, and now the technician was delayed. As if she heard Sydney, a door opened and a young woman called out her name. "Sydney Grey."

They went in, and Sydney was instructed to get up on the bed. She sat up partially with pillows behind, and Jax stood on the other side of the bed holding her hand.

The technician covered her with a sheet up to her lower abdomen, pulling the gown up under her breasts to expose the whole abdomen. She made adjustments on the ultrasound machine and placed some gel on Sydney's torso. "Sorry, this may be cold on your skin."

Sydney braced for the cold. They couldn't see the screen, so she focused on the girl's face, watching her every reaction as she moved the probe through the gel. So far nothing. The woman's expression was stoic.

"Here we go," the technician said. She moved the probe to the opposite side of the abdomen and focused there for some time. A few more adjustments were made to the ultrasound, and Sydney noted a rising of the technician's eyebrows, followed by a slight twitch of her mouth. Her hand moved the probe lower and focused for an even longer time there. She turned to Sydney and smiled. "I'll be right back."

Jax and Sydney looked at each other. "Is everything alright?" Sydney asked.

"Everything's fine, I'll just be a minute." The door closed behind her.

Jax walked around the bed and studied the screen. "I have no idea what I'm looking at here." He resumed his spot beside Sydney.

"Maybe she had to pee…just like me."

The door opened, and her obstetrician came in with the technician. She'd only seen her once at her office. "Hi, Sydney." She smiled at Jax and extended her hand. "I'm Dr. Andrea Gleason, Sydney's obstetrician. You must be the father."

"Jax Rhyder, nice to meet you, Dr. Gleason."

The doctor turned to the screen. "Let's have a look-see, and then I'll let you have a peek." The technician stood beside Dr. Gleason. "You're about eight weeks pregnant, which means you're having a Christmas baby."

"I noticed this week a baby bump developing. Isn't that a bit early?" Sydney said.

"I'll get to that in a minute. I just want to have a listen to the heartbeat." Dr. Gleason placed the stethoscope tips into her ears and held the chestpiece in her hands. "We'll warm this up a bit." She leaned over Sydney and moved the stethoscope around to various spots on her abdomen. "Sounds strong and healthy." She stood and removed her stethoscope. She smiled broadly at Sydney and Jax. "Okay. Are you ready to have a look?"

"Yes," Sydney said, breathlessly. Jax nodded.

The doctor made some adjustments on the screen and turned it towards them. She pointed to the centre of the screen. "This is your baby." Sydney and Jax stared at the screen in awe. The head was very visible, and they could see a semblance of a body with tiny feet and hands.

Jax gasped. "Wow. That tiny little thing is our baby?"

"Certainly is." The doctor shrunk the screen image and Sydney gasped. "What's that? An echo or something?"

Dr. Gleason pointed at the first image. "No, my dear, this is Baby A." Then she pointed to the one beside it. "That one is Baby B."

Jax suddenly came to life. "Twins? We're having twins?" He started to laugh. Sydney was speechless.

Dr. Gleason shrunk the screen even more and pointed to the image below the other two "Not exactly. This one is Baby C. And that's why you already have a baby bump. Congratulations."

The room spun out of control for a moment. Sydney stared at the screen. Three babies were definitely there. She turned to Jax whose stunned look matched her own. They turned to Dr. Gleason at the same time and cried out one word in unison.

"Triplets?"

❧ 21 ❧

EMERALD LAKE

Chloe sat on Wenner's gate watching Talon soaring overhead. Chelsea was in the Centre attending to the few animals left on site. With the police no closer to knowing what happened to Wenner, Chloe was concerned about Chelsea working alone at the Centre, and she often watched over her without her sister having knowledge of her presence. Talon flew down and landed on a fence post. He stared at her, tilting his head from side to side. "Hey there, buddy. Hunting for the family?"

The raptor sat with his head down and his feathers smooth, indicating to Chloe that he wasn't in an aggressive mood but quite relaxed with her.

"You've seen me several times now. Guess you know I'm keeping an eye on my sister. I've watched you sitting in the tree looking down over the cottage, too. She's lucky to have you. I don't have to tell you that one of your greatest attributes is your vision; you can help her develop hers on a natural plane and in a supernatural one. Chelsea needs to learn to live in harmony with other humans, and I know your hawk energy will help her with that. Thank you for being her spirit guide and spirit animal."

A guttural sound escaped from the hawk's throat in reply.

A noise behind them made Chloe and Talon look back in time to see Chelsea close the door to the Centre and lock it. They watched her get in her car and drive towards the gate. Talon flew up high, and with a screech left them and flew towards his nest. Chloe hung onto a wooden post and laughed as Chelsea swung the gate open to drive out. She waited like a child for her sister to park on the road and walk back. Chloe placed her legs and arms out and balanced with the sway of the gate, chortling with glee. Chelsea, oblivious, locked the gate.

She watched her drive down the road to her own cottage and park in the driveway. Just as Chelsea disappeared into the house, Chloe observed a black Ford Escort on the road. It passed Chelsea's place and continued towards her. The vehicle stopped and a man stepped out. He shook the lock on the gate, which wiggled the gate. *Hey, balancing here.* He stared up the driveway towards the house. With a shake of his head, he got back into his vehicle and turned around. Chloe had seen him once before driving up this same road. *Who are you? And what do you want?*

CHELSEA WASHED up and fed Sage. With a cup of tea in hand, she curled up in the armchair and began reading a book. A knock on the door caught her attention, and she put the book down. *No such luck.* A voice interrupted her thoughts.

"Don't get up. It's me." Chloe appeared in the room. "Just wanted to give you a heads up before I appeared. Look at you, all cozy with tea and a dog sleeping by your feet."

Chelsea smiled. "Thank you for not scaring the heck out of me. It's been a while, sis."

"A lot has happened, too. You seem to be handling it all."

"I am."

"How's Wenner?"

"The same. The doctors were meeting today to decide if they would bring him out of his coma soon."

"They're the experts. You know they're taking good care of him. How are the studies going?"

"Good. The Centre is down to a small group of patients. I've had a lot of time to put into my lessons, and I'm actually ahead of schedule."

"Yay you. You're doing well. Have you been going to AA?"

Chelsea frowned. "No." She put her hands up. "Not because I don't recognize I had a problem. But some of them really are addicted, you know? I don't crave alcohol or need it. They'd expect me to stand up and talk. I could support them, but no way could I talk in front of them. I was drinking to make myself feel normal...or so I thought. I may never be 'normal,' whatever that means. And I have a sponsor I can call if I need to."

"Good girl."

"I finally realized that I don't have to 'fit' in. And alcohol was deceiving me into thinking I was."

The sound of a car pulling into the driveway caught their attention. Chloe disappeared and returned seconds later. "One very handsome man is on his way to knocking on your door."

"Lucky me."

Chloe whispered. "I'm off. But I'll be back. Behave yourself."

Chelsea pulled a face and gave her a wave as she

disappeared. She went to the picture window to see who was stepping onto the porch. When she saw who it was, she ran to the door and pulled it open before he could knock.

"Chaz, what a nice surprise. Come in."

"I've been meaning to come out to see what you've done with the place." He stepped into the living room and his mouth dropped open. "Man, you've been busy. The place looks great. I'm really impressed." Sage woke up and began barking. "And you have a dog."

"It's okay, Sage. Come and meet Chaz. She arrived one rainy night as a stray and never left."

Chaz bent down and rubbed the dog's ears. "Hey, I'm a friend. Aren't you a beauty?"

"Let me take you on a tour. Time for you to see what I spent your money on."

He followed her through the cottage, admiring all that had been transformed. "I put the old furniture in the third bedroom until you could move it."

"I'll come back with a truck soon and haul it away."

Back in the living room, Chelsea nodded to the couch. "Would you like some tea?"

"Yes, thanks."

Chelsea reheated her own cup in the microwave while waiting for the kettle to boil. When she brought out their tea, Sage was on the couch with her head in Chaz's lap. "She likes you."

"She's beautiful. I was in Stoney Creek last week. Can you believe we're going to be grandparents? My God…where did the time go?"

"Exciting news, isn't it? And Nan is getting married. Did they tell you that?"

"They did. I'm really happy for your mother. She deserves this. The kids also told me about all that's happening around here. Sydney is very proud of you, you know."

Chelsea felt embarrassed but pleased. "It's been a rough year all around, but I'm getting a hang of this thing called freedom."

"I'm happy for you. It seems moving to the lake was the right thing to do. By the way, how's the hand?"

She turned her hand palm up so he could see it and ran her finger along the scar. "It's still a bit tender but healing well."

"And how's this Wenner fellow doing?"

She pursed her lips. "Still in a coma…" Before she could say more, her cell phone rang. The caller ID read Interior Health. "Hello?"

"Is this Chelsea Grey?"

"Yes, it is."

"This is ICU at the hospital. The doctor asked me to call. Wenner is awake and asking for you."

"Omigod…how's he doing?"

"The doctor will fill you in when you get here."

"I'm on my way." She hung up and stared at Chaz. "Wenner's awake." Tears came to her eyes. "I'm shaking, I'm so relieved."

"That's great news."

Chelsea stood. "He's asking for me. I think I should go to his house and get some things he might want." A feeling of dread came over her. "Could I ask you to go with me?"

"Of course. We can go in my car."

"Thank you."

They drove to the Centre, and Chelsea unlocked the gate and waved Chaz through. When they got to the house, she stood outside the police tape, remembering the day she'd found Wenner. She pulled down the tape and stepped onto the porch. She unlocked the door and they stepped inside.

Chaz let out a whistle. "What a mess."

Chelsea was drawn down the hall and into the kitchen. Chaz followed her. She stood at the end of the centre island and stared at the dried pool of blood on the floor. "I've been meaning to clean it up, but I couldn't bring myself to come into the house on my own, and I've had to let my hand heal up some."

"I, for one, don't think you should be here by yourself until they find the perpetrator."

"But I can't let Wenner come home to this."

"I'll tell you what, I'll drive you to the hospital. When we get back, I'll get a cabin at the resort. Tomorrow, we'll clean it up together. How's that sound?"

"You'd do that? But what about work?"

"Work can wait. I could use a couple of days off." Chaz took her by the hand and led her back to the hallway. "Forget that for now. Take me to the master bedroom. What do you think he needs?"

✲ 22 ✲

KELOWNA

The ICU was busy when Chelsea and Chaz entered. The nurses' station sat in the middle of the room, encircled by the patients' rooms running against the outer walls. Each room had floor-to-ceiling glass windows across the front, enabling the station to observe each patient. One of the nurses motioned them over.

"There's a small reception room over in the corner. You can wait there. The doctor is with Mr. Gibb at the moment. He'll talk to you when he's finished."

"Thank you," Chelsea said.

They didn't have to wait long. A tall, thin man in a white jacket came out of Wenner's room. He talked with the nurse and headed towards them. His dark hair fell across his forehead in disarray. He looked tired.

"Miss Grey? I'm Doctor Sensei."

"Doctor, this is Wes Rhyder." The two men shook hands. "How's Wenner doing?"

Dr. Sensei sat down beside them. "He's very lucky considering how hard a blow to the head he took. The swelling has receded. His memory appears intact, as does most of his cognitive skill. His speech pattern is normal. But his motor skills are deficient. The left side of his body was affected. His physical disability is affecting his left arm and left leg mobility, much in the same way as someone who experiences a stroke."

"Will he regain the use of the left side of his body?"

"With physical therapy, we expect in time that he'll have a full recovery. He'll start work with the physiotherapist tomorrow. He'll move into the general ward later today or tomorrow."

"How long will he remain in the hospital?"

"There's no definitive answer to that. We'll be doing ongoing assessments and tests as he progresses. We should know more within the next five days. But I'd say another couple of weeks. Since he lives in a remote area, we won't release him until he's able to pass certain criteria and is able to continue his physiotherapy at home without a therapist present. Is there anyone who can be there to assist him with cooking, dressing, etcetera?"

Chelsea looked at Chaz and back at the doctor with concern. "He has no one. I could help him out if he'll let me."

"In that case, if he wants to go home as soon as possible, he better let you. Otherwise, we'll have to send him to a short-term care facility until his mobility reaches an acceptable level." The doctor looked at his watch. "I have to run. It was nice meeting you both. I'm happy that Mr. Gibb has your friendship and your help. We'll talk again in a few days." The doctor left the unit.

"I'm going to the cafeteria for coffee while you visit with Wenner. Stay as long as you like, I'll be fine," Chaz said.

"Thank you, but I won't be long. I don't want to tire him out. I'll meet you there."

Chelsea entered the room. The first thing she noted was that the tubes and wires were gone. So was the bandage around Wenner's head. His bed was in the upright position, but Wenner's eyes were closed. She walked around the bed and pulled a chair up close. That side of his head was shaved, and she could see a few of the sutures on the wound.

Wenner opened his eyes and looked at her as she settled into her chair. "Hey, you made it."

"Nothing would keep me away. It's good to see you awake, my friend. How are you feeling?"

Wenner smiled. "Tired. This is funny, since I've been told I was asleep for ten days."

Chelsea laughed. "How does the head feel?"

"One big headache, but the drugs around here are good. How do you like the new look?" He turned his head so she could see the wound.

"It's a little bit Frankenstein at the moment. I wouldn't recommend it."

"Just call me Frankie."

"I'm glad to see you have your sense of humour...or maybe it's the drugs. You gave me quite a scare, you know."

"I'm sorry I worried you. They tell me you were the one who found me. It must have been frightening for you."

"The main thing is you're awake, and once you're ready to come home, things will be back to normal. Do you want to talk about it...the incident I mean?" Chelsea didn't want to bring up the subject unless Wenner was willing.

"I don't know who hit me. I'd come home from town with some groceries. I went into the kitchen to put the bags on the counter and was hit from behind."

She nodded. "So the house was intact when you arrived home?"

"It was fine. Why?"

"The house is a bit of a mess now, I'm afraid. You must have arrived home and interrupted him before he burglarized the place."

"The bastard."

"I have no way of knowing if anything was stolen. Chaz and I are going to clean it up tomorrow."

"Really? The two of you would do that?"

"Of course. It's not something you need to come home to."

"Home...sounds wonderful. I have no idea when they'll let me go home."

"Work hard at your physio, and when you do get released, I'll be there to help you until you're able to do things on your own again."

Wenner's face clouded over. "I can't ask you to be my nursemaid."

"Don't be ridiculous. Friends help friends when needed." Chelsea tried to look angry. "If you don't let me help you, they'll send you to a care facility with strangers. Is that what you want?"

His face reddened. "Okay, don't get uppity. I don't want to go to any facility." He relaxed. "You're a good friend."

"I am. And I don't think you'll need a nursemaid. You can wipe your own privates, thank you."

Wenner laughed. His eyes travelled to an overnight bag on the tray table. "What's in the bag?"

"Your own pajamas, some magazines, toiletries, and your cell phone and charger. Some junk food, too."

"Thank you. That was very thoughtful. How are the animals at the centre?"

"Under control. All the animals are gone that we were looking after."

"The bear cubs?"

"They were picked up and transferred to Kelowna."

"And Red?"

"My daughter and I released her. It was so awesome. Talon came to greet her, and they soared up together and headed for their nest."

Wenner shook his head. "I'm so proud of you. Sorry I missed it. Have you seen her since?"

"I hadn't, and I was starting to worry about her. I've seen Talon a number of times, but then I remembered you told me she'd stay with the young until they left the nest. And yesterday, there they were...the whole family, Talon, Red, and two young ones flying over the Centre."

"Bravo. And you said your daughter helped you? Does that mean you're talking again?"

"We are, and she's expecting a baby. I'm thrilled."

"Congratulations, grandma. Things are looking good for you. So what do you have in the Centre?"

Chelsea wrinkled her forehead. "I've turned away some because I'm obviously not as qualified as you for some things...like surgery. I was worried you'd lose your grant status because of me doing things I shouldn't. I made arrangements for any that came in to go elsewhere. As of this moment, we have a black scoter sea duck with a broken wing, a chameleon with a soft tissue infection on its tail, and three kittens."

"Kittens? Since when do we take in kittens?"

Chelsea shrugged. "Since someone threw them

over the gate in a box. At least they're litter trained. I've treated them for fleas and de-wormed them. They seem healthy enough, so I thought I'd bring them home to my place until I find them homes. I introduced them to Sage this morning, and she was so gentle with them, even cried when I took them back into the Centre. "

"Poor things, people can be such jerks. So a black scoter? Are you sure? They're so rare in the Okanagan. I mean, they breed up north in Siberia and Alaska and winter in the Pacific Northwest, usually coastal Washington state."

"The hiker who brought him in found him near Kelowna. He identified him, and I checked on the internet. Definitely a scoter."

"Wow. I'm missing something special. Be sure to take pictures. Could you put a band on him? In one of the drawers in the supply kitchen, you'll find some leg bands with branding pliers. It has different size holes in it. Measure the bird's leg first to get the right size. Each band has a number on it, record it on his file. We can register him on the online database and his whereabouts can be tagged."

"Sure. I can do that."

"What are you doing for the chameleon?"

"She has an open sore on her tail about the size of a quarter. Looks like a bite. The bleeding wouldn't stop, so I researched it and found that sprinkling pepper on it would stop the bleed. I did that. At night I cover it with antibiotic cream. I placed a heat pad under her cage and put a fluorescent light on the top of the cage. The wound is healing well. She's a bit skinny but eating the bugs and worms I've been giving her."

"What can I say? You're truly amazing. What you

don't know, you find out. Thank you so much for taking care of things."

"And now that you're awake I can ask the true expert for advice. Oh, Wenner, I can't wait until you get home and we can get back to work."

A knock on the door drew their attention, and the two Kelowna detectives that interviewed Chelsea asked if they could come in.

Detective Reardon nodded at her. "Miss Grey. Good to see you again." He introduced himself and Detective Dara to Wenner.

Chelsea turned to Wenner. "I'm going to head out. I'll come back in a couple of days." She nodded towards the night bag. "Give me a call if I forgot anything." Chelsea stood and put her chair back.

"Okay, kiddo. You're doing a great job at the Centre. I'll call you tonight."

"Get some rest; tomorrow the hard work begins." She turned to the two men standing at the foot of the bed. "He's all yours, detectives."

❊ 23 ❊

EMERALD LAKE

Chelsea studied the shelves of food in the fridge. "I'm starving. How about you? I've got leftovers in the fridge from yesterday's roast beef dinner. I can make up two plates and reheat in the microwave."

"Perfect," Chaz said.

They had driven directly back from Kelowna after visiting Wenner and had just arrived at the cottage. She gathered the food containers and reached for a couple of plates.

"While you do that, I'll look up the resort and book a cabin."

Chelsea put her utensils down and studied Chaz. She wasn't completely sure of what she'd decided, but it seemed right. "Don't bother booking a room. You can use the guest bedroom. After all, this is your place, and it seems silly for you to spend the money on a cabin for the night."

"As long as you're leasing the cottage, it's your home, not mine. I don't want to intrude on your space."

Chelsea smiled. "We're talking one night here. I can live with it."

154

"Only if you're comfortable. I don't want to put you in an awkward situation."

She leaned on her elbows on the counter. "I appreciate that, but we did go to school together. We have a history, and with our kids living together, we're family. It's okay…really."

Chaz put his phone away and rubbed his hands together. "Alright then, settled. I'll wash up and set the table."

Thirty minutes later, they were finished eating, and Chaz helped her clean up the kitchen. Chelsea poured them each a coffee, and they retreated to the porch and settled in chairs facing the lake.

"What a lovely night. Look at the water, it's the colour of jade," she said.

"I'd forgotten how beautiful the lake is. I've also forgotten how to relax. Taking some time off will force me to slow down."

Chelsea pulled her knees up under her chin and wrapped her arms around her legs. "I've reached the conclusion that you must be a workaholic."

Chaz chortled. "It shows, does it?"

"That…and it must be the reason you aren't in a steady relationship."

"Right again. When I first returned to Stoney Creek, I'd quit a promising career with a top architectural firm in Vancouver. My parents couldn't understand why I'd come back to farm country and start my own business. I had a lot to prove to them and myself. And then I had Jax to raise on my own."

"And time passes so quickly."

"It sure does. I've had a few relationships over the years, but I guess they never felt that I put them first. They were right; I didn't. And now most women I meet have teenage kids. It's hard enough to maintain a couple relationship, never mind the complications of near-adults who resent you, think they know it all and most certainly know more than you."

They laughed together. Then, Chaz's expression turned serious. "Chelsea, I'm so sorry."

It caught her off guard. "Sorry? For what?"

"For taking your father's word and not coming back to talk with you directly. Things may have turned out different for you if I had taken you with me."

"My God, Chaz. We were kids. No one could possibly have known what Arne was going to do. You have nothing to apologize for." She twisted in her chair to face him. "Let's say you did come back. I would have had a DNA test for sure, and we'd have known Sydney wasn't yours. What then? I doubt you would have understood why I was with another man so soon after you left. You were also a student in university. Your parents would have tried to talk you out of it, and they never would have accepted me and Sydney."

"That's a lot of what-ifs."

"Which is why we shouldn't second-guess the past. It is what it is. That was then, this is now."

"I hope you realize what a strong woman you are."

"Mmm...what I do know is that you were destined to raise Jax, and I'm sure you've never regretted it. And I was destined to have Sydney. Circumstance separated me from her, but I've never regretted having her. And now she and Jax are together and having our first grandchild. I doubt that would have happened if they were raised as step-brother and sister."

Chaz smiled. "There would have been complications for sure."

"I examined my own role in all of it, too. I knew

Arne looked at me in a disgusting way, and I should have said something to my father. But I didn't. Again, I'll say, we were kids. So no more guilt and no more apologies, okay?"

He nodded and stared at her. "And what about you? Do you think you will ever get over it and be able to trust in a relationship again?"

Chelsea sucked in her lips and shrugged. "That's a question I may never be able to answer. Arne damaged me in other ways, too, besides trust. Sadly, I've found that trusting people in general is hard for me. I've had people seek me out not because they want to help me or be a friend but because they have an angle that benefits them, not me."

"But if you are aware of it, you can sort them out. Your instincts are solid; follow them."

"I'm learning, but I'm still a work in progress. Moving here has been a great first step. It led me to a career and schooling, doing something I love and never knew I'd be good at. I gained a friend in Wenner, who needed a friend, too. I have family...and a friend in you. That's more than a lot of people have."

"I'm happy things are going well for you here."

"They are. And I'm finding out I enjoy my alone time and only answering to me. I'm finding the independence I was excited about at nineteen before Arne hid me away. At forty, I don't expect many men would be able to tolerate my idiosyncrasies." She stood and stretched. "Care to join me for a walk? I have to feed the critters at the Centre."

"I'd love to. Let's go."

Chelsea retrieved the keys, and they strolled down the road to the Wildlife Centre. The scoter was ready for his meal. "It could be another ten days, buddy, before I can take the tape off." After feeding the scoter, they moved on to the lizard. Chelsea fed her some worms and rubbed some antibiotic cream on her tail. "I love this girl. She reminds me of me."

"How so?" Chaz asked.

"In a few ways. People think chameleons only change colour to blend in with their surroundings for protection. But they also change colour to communicate. Like females go dark and light if they're suddenly aggressive and display bright colours when accepting and calm. They shed their skins every few months."

"And you shed your skin every few months?"

Chelsea laughed. "Mentally, you bet. It's hard to explain. It might sound dramatic, but Emerald Lake and this Centre saved my life." She stroked the head of the chameleon, checked the temperature of the heating pad and closed the cage.

"You certainly appear to belong here. I can see your confidence with the animals and how easily you fit into the surroundings."

"Thank you. Now the kittens." She returned to the kitchen and packed a backpack with some food and litter. She grabbed one of the cat cases and passed it to Chaz. "They've been treated for fleas and worms, so I'm taking them home with me. The poor little things need some love until I can find them homes."

They locked up the Centre and returned to the cottage. Sage was so excited when Chelsea released the kittens. She jumped around them but was careful not to step on them. Chelsea found a spot by the front door to set up the litter box and set up a food and water bowl in one corner of the kitchen. As they watched the kittens eat, Sage kept inching closer to the bowl. "Sage...no." Chelsea laughed. "I won't be able to leave their bowl on the floor. Dogs eat everything in sight. Not like cats. They only eat until full."

Sage went back to her doggy cushion and curled up on it. When the kittens finished eating, they found her and curled up against her side. Sage licked their heads. All four were asleep in minutes.

Chelsea locked up and decided to call it a night. "I've set some extra towels on the counter in the bathroom if you want a shower. If you need another blanket during the night, there's one on the top shelf in the closet of the guest bedroom. See you in the morning."

Chaz thanked her and headed to his room. "I think I'll shower in the morning. It's been a long day. Goodnight."

"Goodnight."

Chelsea retreated to her room and shut the door. She flipped the night table lamp on and started for the en suite. She turned and stared at the door. A battle of indecision played out in her mind. When the struggle ended, she decisively marched to the door and pushed the lock on. She retrieved the bear spray canister from her jacket pocket and placed it under her pillow. Only then did she relax.

Right. Sorry, old friend, I'm still a work in progress.

❧ 24 ❧

Chelsea grabbed half a dozen flattened boxes from the back room at the Centre and joined Chaz at the car. "I thought we could use a box for each room to gather broken and damaged items for Wenner to go through when he comes home. If we throw it out, he won't know if anything was stolen or broken."

"Good thinking," Chaz said.

They drove up to the house and entered the main hallway, where she put the boxes together with tape. "There's a mud room off the kitchen. You'll find a bucket, mop and cleaners in there. I'll start in the living room."

Chaz disappeared into the kitchen, and Chelsea stepped into the living room. Mostly there were broken vases and picture frames, and soon they were deposited into the box. End table drawers had been dumped on the floor. Chelsea replaced them in the tables and placed the items and papers back into the drawers. She hand-vacuumed the furniture and cushions strewn across the floor. It didn't take long to put the room back together again. The vertical pan-elled drapes on the living room window were damaged. Some of the old-fashioned skinny vertical panels were bent. *No fixing those.* A couple were also frayed on the edges from wear. *Time for new drapes.* A few of the panels had been torn off the track, and the plastic keepers that held them in place were broken. Chelsea picked up the ripped panels from the floor and put them in the box. The lead weights in the bottom of the panels had slipped out of their seamed pockets. She retrieved them and threw them into the box. After vacuuming the carpet, she moved on to the bedrooms. She met Chaz in the hallway.

"Living room's done," Chelsea said.

"I cleaned out the fridge and put the garbage out in the shed. Dishwasher is on. Now I'm working on the floor. Just taking a bathroom break."

Chelsea moved on. "I'll leave you to it then." She started in the two guest bedrooms first and tackled the master bedroom last. It was a large room, with one end set up as a study with a desk and an armchair in the corner. Books from a bookcase lay on the floor. *What a mess.* Once she'd sorted the en suite bathroom, she organized his drawers and closets, replacing clothing strewn on the floor. She stripped the bed and gathered what appeared to be laundry, carried it into the hallway and headed to the bathroom to gather towels. Chaz had cleaned the bathroom before he went back to the kitchen. There were clean towels hanging on the racks. *What a sweetheart.* Chelsea continued to the mudroom that housed the washer and dryer. Chaz was on his hands and knees on the other side of the kitchen island scrubbing the floor. A feeling of nausea at the thought passed over her, and she refrained from looking in his direction. "I thought I'd put the laundry on. By the time we're finished here, it'll be ready for the dryer and I can come back later to fold it."

"There's some towels sitting in the washing machine," Chaz said.

"I noticed you cleaned the bathroom. Looks great."

Once the machine was loaded and turned on, Chelsea returned to the bedroom. Nothing there had been broken. *A little less of a personal violation.* Chelsea straightened out his desktop, leaving loose papers in one pile for Wenner to sort through. Empty file folders were labelled, which in turn helped her organize the loose papers on the floor into their appropriate file. These she placed back in the desk drawer. She was almost done and ready to vacuum.

A wooden box had been opened and thrown across the room. It contained some pictures and other items. Chelsea picked up the box and gathered photos and small items thrown onto the floor. She assumed they belonged in the box. She sat cross-legged on the floor, looking at the pictures. They were childhood photos of two young boys. You could see a resemblance. They were obviously brothers. On the back was written, "Kenny and Warner." Wenner had told her his little brother called him Wenner as a toddler because he couldn't pronounce the letter r in Warner. Kenny was younger than Wenner, and it was obvious who the older brother was. He had one of those faces that even as a boy you could identify who he was. Other photos she looked at showed them with their mother, farm animals, school pictures, etcetera. For all intents and purposes, they looked happy together. However, not one picture of his father was in the box. She examined two pieces of papers that were clipped together. One was a printed copy of Wenner's birth certificate. The other was an official Government of British Columbia Certificate of Name Change. Wenner Thomas Gibb had previously been Warner Thomas Davis. *He changed his last name.* Chelsea was stunned that Wenner's pain was so great that he decided to cut his family totally out of his life. *What if his family were looking for him? What if they'd regretted how they'd treated him all those years ago?* Chelsea's mind raced in different directions. She looked at the pictures of his mother again. She was a pleasant looking woman, and in some of the pictures she stared at Wenner lovingly. *His father kicked him out of the house, not his mother. What if his mother had no say? Her pain must have been intense, as well, never knowing where her son was all these years.* She placed all the items in the wooden box, closed the lid and put it on the desk. *It's none of your business, girl. Stay out of it.*

Chaz interrupted her thoughts. "How are we doing in here? The kitchen's done."

"We need to finish vacuuming the bedrooms. We'll store the boxes in the mudroom for Wenner and transfer the laundry to the dryer. That's it."

"Okay, I'll do the vacuuming." He disappeared into the hallway.

Chelsea gathered all the boxes and finished up in the mudroom. When she returned to the kitchen, she looked this time directly at the floor behind the island. There was nothing there to remind her of what had happened.

"I think we're done."

Chelsea spun around. Chaz was leaning on the doorframe to the kitchen.

"You did a great job in here. I can't thank you enough for helping me with this. The house looks like a home again."

"My pleasure. Shall we go?"

"Yes, you must be wanting to get back to Kelowna."

"Perhaps a coffee back at the cottage and some

relaxation on the deck before I head back. What do you think?"

"Sounds like a plan."

They climbed into Chaz's vehicle, and when they reached the gate, Chelsea got out to open it. He drove through and stopped on the opposite side of the dirt road while she swung the gate closed. As Chelsea put the lock in place, a black SUV approached them from town. It pulled over beside the gate, and a man got out.

"Hello, I'm trying to find Wenner Gibb," he said, coming to her. "I understand he's been in the hospital. Can you tell me if he's back home?"

Chelsea sized the man up. He looked to be in his thirties and was definitely a stranger to the area. Trusting anyone wasn't an easy task for her, never mind a stranger. She wasn't about to talk to this man about Wenner without knowing his business with him. After all, they still didn't know who had attacked him. Chaz got out of his car and stood beside her.

She clicked the padlock shut and pushed her shoulders back. "And you are?"

The man gave her a broad smile. "I'm sorry. I should have introduced myself. I'm Mason Ross."

"How do you know Wenner?" Chelsea asked.

"I don't. Do you both work here at the Wildlife Centre?"

"I do, and Wenner is a personal friend."

"Okay. I'm an investigative reporter for the Vancouver Sun. And you are?"

"Chelsea Grey, and this is Wes Rhyder, a friend of mine." They all shook hands.

Chelsea frowned. "If you are here to write about what happened to him, I don't think he'll be up to that for a while."

"No, I didn't know about the incident until I got here. I'm working on another story. I arrived a few days back, and each time I've driven over, the place has been locked up tight. I saw the police tape and learned about his accident from the resort owner where I'm staying. Of course, the hospital wouldn't give me any information."

"I see. I can tell you Mr. Gibb was in an induced coma. They woke him up yesterday. I don't think he'll be home for a few weeks, and I'm not sure if he's up to talking with you until then."

"Of course. Can you give me any information about his accident?"

Chelsea glanced at Chaz. "I suggest you talk to Detectives Reardon and Dara at the Kelowna RCMP. Meanwhile, if you have a card, I'll show it to Wenner the next time I see him."

Mason Ross wrote the names of the detectives into a small notebook and handed her a card. "I'll do that." He said his goodbyes and returned to his car. Chelsea and Chaz watched him turn around and drive off with a wave and a horn honk.

Chelsea studied his card. "I wonder what that's all about. His card looks legit. But it's not my place to talk to him about Wenner's personal business."

"You were right to be cautious. I suggest you call the newspaper and confirm his identity, and you can probably find him on Google if he's an investigative reporter."

"Yes, I'll do both." She placed the card in her jean's pocket. "How about that coffee on the deck now?"

"Let's go. I'm so ready to chill."

❧ 25 ❧

STONEY CREEK

The winding highway led Chelsea towards Stoney Creek. Her mother had left her car at Emerald Lake, and the two were traveling together to the farm to join Sydney. Her daughter invited them to spend the night while Jax was in Kelowna on business with Chaz. They turned onto the main street. "I haven't been here since Christmas. There seems to be some sprucing up going on. Look at those gorgeous hanging flower baskets and the new branding sign." They passed the newly installed wooden sign with a painted insignia of waterways and golden fields and carved letters reading: *Welcome to Stoney Creek, where the living is easy.*

"It seems every town is trying to outdo the other with branding," Elizabeth said. "It's a complete waste of taxpayer money, if you ask me."

"Nice to see the town looking prosperous, though."

They drove across town and headed west. Chelsea tried not to look at Arne's property as they approached Sydney's farm, but she couldn't help herself.

Her mother reached out and patted her arm. "Are you all right?"

Chelsea smiled. "I am. It seems easier this time… maybe because the developers have removed the burned-out farmhouse and the trees around it." She pulled into Sydney's driveway and parked. "And you can see the property pins where they've divided the property into five-acre lots. It's not the place it was. Progress…in this case that's a good thing."

"I'm so happy to hear you say that. I couldn't bear to look over there whenever I visited Sydney because of the bad memories. Seeing the changes and the farmhouse gone has lifted some of the past for me."

Chelsea lifted her mother's hand and kissed it. "It's been quite a year, but I think we're all beginning to heal."

The two women looked into each other's eyes and smiled. They'd come a long way.

"Let's go find Syd," Chelsea said. She undid her seatbelt and opened the car door.

"Yes, let's go find our Sydney," Elizabeth said, with emphasis on the name.

"You're too funny."

"I can't help it. I never liked the shortening of her name. It's more masculine than Sydney…although I've come to like the full version. It's…cute."

Chelsea laughed. "So's her nickname." She linked her arm in her mother's. "Come on, old-fashioned. We'll get our bags later."

They found Sydney in the kitchen amidst mixing bowls, baking ingredients and vegetables.

"Smells delicious in here," Elizabeth said.

"There's an apple cobbler in the oven, and the slow cooker has a one-pot roast beef dinner on the go. I thought I'd get dinner all prepped and cooking so we could relax once you arrived. And I'm all done. Just need to the clean this mess away."

"I think she timed it so when we arrived we could do the clean-up," Chelsea said, with a wink at her mother.

"Totally," Elizabeth said with a laugh. "Why don't you sit down and let me and your mom do it?"

"Done deal," Sydney said. "I'm going to run over to the residence and put the last load of laundry in the dryer. I had a full roster this weekend of out-of-towners."

Fifteen minutes later, the women were seated on the back deck overlooking the lake, sipping lemonade and munching on cookies made with almond flour and dark chocolate.

"Mmm...granddaughter, you are definitely becoming quite the cook," Elizabeth said between bites.

"Thanks. I'm enjoying it more than ever. Of course, it's due to Bea. She's a godsend when I have clients staying over. She's taught me so much."

"I'm impressed," Elizabeth said. "You were never interested in cooking growing up. She glanced at Chelsea. "And neither was your mother."

Daughter and granddaughter laughed. "And you're a great cook too, Nan. I could have learned a lot from you if I'd put my mind to it," Sydney said.

Chelsea studied her daughter. She seemed different. She looked healthy and content. "You're looking good. Things must be going well for you and Jax."

Sydney glanced quickly between her mother and her grandmother. "Things are...moving along. Jax is wonderful. In fact, I wanted you both here today to share some news." She paused. Both women leaned forward in anticipation. Sydney took a deep breath and continued. "I had my ultrasound the other day."

Chelsea was filled with mixed emotions. She was

easing into being a mother to a grown daughter Arne had cheated her from raising, and now she was to be a grandmother. Overwhelmed was a good word for it, but still, it was exciting.

"And?" Elizabeth said.

"Everything was fine. I'm healthy, and..." Sydney paused but before she could continue, Chelsea spoke.

Chelsea took a deep breath. "So if Mom is called Nan, who'll I be?"

Sydney laughed. "I think you'll become Nana to them, and great-grandmother here will be GG."

"GG...I like it. So are you and Jax..." Elizabeth began.

Chelsea cut her mother off. "Did you just say... oh, sorry, Mom. I keep cutting everyone off. You go first."

Elizabeth giggled. "I think we're all excited. I was going to ask something that is really none of my business but...oh, I'll just say it. Are you and Jax continuing your present state of living together, or are you planning to get married?"

"It's okay, Nan. You're allowed to ask." She held up her left hand for them both to see "And yes, we will get married. This is his mother's ring. We were thinking of doing it here by the lake. Nothing elaborate. Just family and friends."

Chelsea gasped. "A wedding. I never thought I'd be around to attend your wedding."

"Me either," Sydney said. She gave her mother an affectionate look. "Mom, you started to say something earlier, what was it?"

"Umm...yes. You said I'd become Nan to 'them.' Does that mean you and Jax are planning on having more children?"

Sydney face lit up and she glowed. "I sure hope

not. That's why I wanted you here today. I'm pregnant with more than one baby."

Chelsea and Elizabeth looked at each other in shock. Elizabeth shouted. "Twins?"

Sydney laughed. "I'm afraid not. Can you believe I'm expecting triplets?" She looked from one to the other.

"Omigod," Chelsea cried out.

"Nan? Are you alright?" Sydney asked.

Chelsea looked at her mother. She had paled, and tears streamed down her face. "Mom?"

Elizabeth wiped her tears with her fingers. "Oh, sweetheart. I'm happy for you is all." She appeared to force a smile. "When are you due?"

"Around Christmas. But the doctor says if I can't give natural birth to them, we can choose a date for a caesarean." Sydney stood. "I have to take the crumble out of the oven. I'll be right back." Elizabeth stood and took her granddaughter into her arms. She hugged her so tight without a word that Sydney looked at Chelsea over her grandmother's shoulder with a crooked smile and raised eyebrows. Chelsea winked at her daughter and returned her smile. After Sydney had entered the house, Chelsea watched her mother stare out at the water. Elizabeth had wrapped her arms around herself and held herself tight.

"Mom?"

"Huh? Oh, I'm okay. Just happy and surprised." She sat down. "Three? Can you imagine the work that's going to be?"

"Oh, yes. But she has you, me and Jax to help her."

"Of course, she does." Her mother glazed over again and wrung her fingers.

"You're upset. It's okay. She's strong and healthy."

Elizabeth didn't answer.

Chelsea looked over her shoulder at the house. She could see Sydney moving around the kitchen. "Mom...I know what you're thinking."

"You can't possibly, but I'll be fine."

"Three words say I do," Chelsea said.

Her mother stared at her, a puzzled look on her face. "Three words? What three words?

Chelsea reached out and took her mother's hand. She spoke in barely a whisper.

"Chelsea...Chloe...Cameron."

Elizabeth stared at her in silence. "How did you know? When did you know?

"Since I've been at Emerald Lake, I've had visitations from a young woman from the other side. It's Chloe."

Her mother blinked a few times. "But Chloe was a baby when she passed."

"My words to her exactly. She appears before me looking like me because we were identical. She said Cameron was fraternal."

Elizabeth looked stunned. "That's right, he was. But why would she appear now after all these years?"

"She felt I needed her now because of my recent bad choices."

"And what about Cameron? Has she seen him on the other side?"

"No. Apparently, he chose to reincarnate into another life. Chloe decided to stay over there. She told me when Dad finally left us and moved on that she saw him. He was very happy that I was back with the family, and he was ready to move forward to a new realm."

Elizabeth's look softened. "I'm happy Dad got to

see her and you've met your sister. Has she been helpful to you?"

Chelsea laughed. "She has been. But she's very direct and won't let me make excuses. I don't know how long she'll stay, but I'm enjoying her while I can."

"Her personality sounds like yours. I wish I could see her."

"You're right. She's like a mirror image, and it feels like I'm seeing myself with the layers peeled back. I can't hide from myself; she won't let me." Chelsea paused. "The next time she comes, I'll let her know you'd like to see her."

Her mother's face clouded. "I'm sorry I didn't say anything, but your father forbade it. He was devastated when we lost Chloe and Cameron, and it was a closed subject. As the years passed and I thought I'd lost you too, I pushed it all behind me."

"You know, when I read my diaries there was a passage where I'd asked Dad why you and he never had more children because he might have had a son to work on the farm with him. He told me that when I was born I'd messed up your insides and you couldn't have any more kids. I was so hurt and devastated by that at the time. But now I understand his bitterness."

It was her mother's turn to reach out and touch her hand. "I'm so sorry he said that to you. I didn't know about it until I read your diaries. He was a very private man and could never show his disappointments or emotions. You caught him off-guard, and he lashed out at you."

"It's all in the past now. He made up for it all when he stayed in spirit with me all those years I was incarcerated by Arne."

Elizabeth glanced towards the house. "Perhaps

we should keep this to ourselves for the time being. I don't want Sydney to worry during her pregnancy that something may happen to her babies."

Chelsea straightened in her chair and leaned forward. "I don't agree. Sydney and her doctor should know about this, Mom. If there are any genetic reasons that caused your loss, in today's medical world, they may be able to avoid them with Sydney. You must tell her."

"I never thought of it like that." Elizabeth studied her daughter. "You really are coming into your own, aren't you? I'm proud of you, you know."

The sliding door to the patio deck opened and in a matter of seconds, Sydney rejoined them at the table. As if she knew what they'd been talking about, she turned to her Nan.

"The doctor asked me if we had multiple births in our family, and I told him I had no idea."

Elizabeth looked at Chelsea, who in turn nodded to her mother and tilted her head towards Sydney. Her mother took a deep breath. "As a matter of fact…we do." Elizabeth relayed the conversation she'd just had with Chelsea. "I'm sorry I didn't share this with you. More family secrets, but I assure you, that's the last one."

Sydney studied her grandmother. "So Chelsea and Chloe were identical? And Cameron fraternal?"

"That's right," Elizabeth said. "Do they know what you're carrying?"

"Apparently, it's rare for triplets to be identical. If they are, they have to be the same sex. If the babies share the same placenta, it's an indication they may be identical. But sometimes they can have their own placenta but share the same umbilical cord and be identical. In my case, they can only see one umbilical cord, which is an indication of identical triplets, but the doctor cautioned us that sometimes the cords intertwine and appear like one but aren't, which means fraternal babies. And placentas can bunch up together and look like a shared one. So…as close an answer as I can give is…we have some indication they may be identical, but it's not a sure bet."

"How fascinating. When I was pregnant with triplets, I knew nothing of all of this," Elizabeth said.

"They'll be monitoring me with more ultrasounds as my pregnancy progresses. They may know more later on. I'll let my doctor know about your pregnancy."

Chelsea was overwhelmed at the thought of three babies. "How's Jax taking the news?"

A raucous laugh escaped Sydney. "We were both in shock initially, to say the least. But you know, we're excited. It's an instant family, and we have a lot of people around us who are dying to help." Sydney's eyes sparkled. "Including Nan and GG."

Chelsea studied her daughter and her mother. It was a happy moment in all their lives, and she wanted to savour it.

"Omigod…" Sydney jumped up, startling the others. "The most wonderful idea just popped into my head. Nan—why don't we have a double wedding right here on the farm?"

❧ **II** ❧

What lies behind us and what lies before us
are tiny matters compared to what lies
within us

— HENRY STANLEY HASKINS

✣ 26 ✣

VANCOUVER

Toben Garrett sat back in the chair and stretched out his legs. He waited for Shen Lei to come into the room. The door opened and closed again. He sat up straight in his chair and braced himself for that silent stare he'd surely get for messing things up at Emerald Lake. Shen Lei took his place behind the ornate wooden desk. His movements were slow and deliberate. He leaned his elbows on the desk, intertwined his fingers, thrust his chin forward and rested it on his hands. Toben met his stare, opting to stay silent until spoken to. He waited, wanting to squirm in his seat, but held his position. The handsome forty-something Eurasian stared Toben down, exuding an arrogant confidence that rattled anyone who came in contact with him. You didn't want to be on the negative side of his wrath.

Chen pulled his head back and placed his hands on the top of the desk. "So…did I not make it clear that you were to avoid contact with Mr. Gibb? What happened?"

"You did. I staked him out and that night he was supposed to meet with a friend for dinner, like he always did on a Wednesday night. But he returned home early. There was no way I could get out of there without him seeing me. I picked up a piece of rebar and I hid until he went into the kitchen so I could get behind him. He never saw it coming. One blow and he was down and out."

"And that is where you fucked up. I'll let it pass that he surprised you by returning when he shouldn't have, but why in hell didn't you make it look like a robbery?"

"He's the last house on the road, and I heard some vehicles. I didn't know if it might be his friend coming to him or people heading to the lookout. Since I was finished searching the place, I panicked and high-tailed it outta there."

Again that silent stare. Shen pursed his lips. "Are you absolutely sure that he never saw you?"

"He didn't."

"And you found nothing?"

"Nothing. I searched his laptop, too."

"Tell me you didn't forget to place the bugs."

"Done, all around the house."

Shen nodded.

"For all the years you've worked for me, and for all the jobs you've done, you've never messed up. You've been my best go-to guy. For that, I'll let you off the hook this time, but just this once and only once. If it happens again, you know what to expect. Do we understand each other?"

Toben let out a sigh of relief. "We do."

"I got a call today from my contact at the paper. That reporter, Ross, is in the Okanagan. I'd wager a guess he's there to talk to Gibb. I think it's safe to say that Mr. Gibb knows nothing about our business, and since you didn't find anything, Ross is retracing his colleague's steps before we arranged his tragic accident along with Brian Proctor's. My contact wasn't able to find out what led Ross to pursue the story again. The paper wasn't aware that the other reporter was even working on it back then. It seems he and Proctor sat on it while they gathered facts."

"Then perhaps since I didn't find anything, it may be safe to say that the financial records Proctor copied from us burned up along with him in his car," Toben said.

"I don't like maybes. I want you to go back to the Okanagan and keep an eye on Ross and monitor Gibb. He's still in the hospital but will be released soon."

"Okay."

"What else should I know?"

"There's a woman. She lives at Emerald Lake and helps Gibb at the Wildlife Centre with the animals. She's been there a couple of months and lives alone. She's not a part of any of this but spends part of each day at Gibb's."

"Just make sure she doesn't become a part of it. We don't need any more complications."

Shen opened a desk drawer and took out an envelope. He passed it to Toben, who opened it and looked inside. He took out a burner phone nestled amongst bundles of cash. "Thanks, boss."

"Don't do anything but surveillance. Check in regularly, but if you learn anything new, call me right away."

TOBEN STARTED HIS CAR. Before he put it in gear, he pounded the steering wheel. "Fuck! Fuck! Fuck!"

All the years I've worked for Shen, I never fucked up once. I always managed to fly under his radar. No ruffled feathers.

He'd brag about me and my work, my loyalty, and my profes-sionalism. Now I'm in his bad books. I let myself get sloppy. One more mistake and I'm dispensable.

He backed out of his spot and headed towards his apartment to pack and head back to the Interior. "Son of a bitch."

Well, it won't happen again. And all over a stupid job that will probably amount to nothing. The problem was dealt with two years ago. Mason Ross is just chasing rainbows, but Shen...the almighty, wants reassurances. Okay, he's thor-ough...and usually I am, too. Pay attention this time, Toben. It could cost you your life.

❧ 27 ❧

KELOWNA

Wenner pulled himself out of the wheelchair while the physiotherapist supported his waist. Seven days of upper body exercises with the occupational therapist had helped him regain some limited control over his left arm and hand. But they had no strength to support his weight. These had been followed with leg exercises, warm-ups, strengthening, and stretching. This was the first time they had him standing. He leaned on the parallel bar to catch his breath while Sarah, his therapist, adjusted the brace on his left leg.

"Okay, we're going to take it really slow. Place your left hand on the bar, straighten up, and try to put some weight on your left leg, leaving the balance of your weight on your right leg. I'm right behind you."

He followed her instructions and found himself standing upright, albeit leaning lopsided to the right.

"All right. Awesome. Now put a little weight on your left hand to straighten your shoulders."

As his body straightened, his left arm shook. "I don't think I can do this. I'm going to fall."

"It's okay. That's what the brace is for. But look,

you're able to put some weight on it. Now I want you to transfer some of the weight on your right leg to the left one. Flatten your foot."

He did so, and his left leg wobbled. He panicked, thinking that he would fall. Wenner resumed his previous stance.

"That was great. Let's try it again, but this time when you transfer your weight, I want you to stay in position a little longer. Okay?"

"All right." Wenner could feel the sweat on his forehead dripping down his face. Once again, he did as Sarah told him, and this time he stayed in place. He wobbled and shook until she told him he could relax. She helped him back into the wheelchair.

"Man, all I did was stand up and I'm exhausted."

Sarah gave him a big smile. "You worked hard today, and you did an awesome job. Tomorrow we'll do it again and maybe get you to shuffle a few steps. How's that sound?"

Wenner snorted. "Pretty scary."

"We'll have you running in no time. Let's get you back to your room and we'll finish up with a few stretching exercises."

When Sarah wheeled him into his room, they found Chelsea sitting in the armchair reading a magazine.

"Hi," Wenner said.

"Hey, you're back. How'd it go?"

"He did great, stood for the first time," Sarah said.

"If you'd seen me, you would have laughed. I wobbled and shook all over the place."

"I would have clapped for you."

Sarah helped him back onto the bed and raised it up. "We have a few exercises left to do."

Chelsea stood. "Okay. Why don't I go downstairs and get us a coffee? I'll be back shortly."

"Make sure it's a double-double. I need the carbs."

Chelsea laughed and left the room.

Wenner finished his exercises, and the nurse washed his face for him. When Chelsea returned, he was propped up in bed feeling proud of himself.

He took his coffee and took a sip. "Boy, am I ready for this."

She pulled the armchair closer to the bed and sat down with her coffee. "You're looking stronger today, and you have more colour."

Wenner chuckled. "I think the colour is from my workout. But as hard as it was, it felt so good to be able to stand up after being bedridden for so long."

"You'll be home in no time. The house will be ready for you. Sarah gave me a list of medical equipment to get for home rehab. I was thinking maybe we could take down the bed in the first guest bedroom at the back of the house and set it up as a therapy room. It has the sliding doors out onto the deck and such a lovely setting looking over the grasslands."

Wenner smiled at her, with what was more a smirk.

"What?"

"I appreciate your efforts, I really do. Having a therapy room would be great, but use whatever room is easiest to set it up. The view doesn't matter."

"Of course it does. First off, that bedroom is larger so you can manoeuvre around better in or out of your wheelchair. And when you're having a bad day...not saying you will, but if you do...you can look out over the grasslands or wheel onto the deck and enjoy the beauty. It can be rejuvenating."

"You're right, and you're a good friend."

"So, I told you Sydney's pregnant."

"Yes, you did. That's so exciting."

"Mom and I were visiting her a couple of days ago, and guess what?" Chelsea looked like she'd swallowed the canary.

"What?"

"Triplets. Can you believe it?"

"Wow…she'll have her hands full with that."

Chelsea filled him in on her mother's history with triplets. They talked about family, and Wenner found himself a little envious of Chelsea's good fortune. He'd been alone for so long until Brian had come into his life, and now here he was alone again. *Knock it off. It's just the drugs making you wistful.* "Your family has much to look forward to. I'm so happy for you."

"We do. Thank you. Oh, by the way, talking about triplets—the kittens are gone. I found them homes. Poor Sage has been searching everywhere for them."

"Aw…glad you found them homes of their own, though." Wenner changed the subject. "So the detectives were back yesterday."

"Any news on who broke in?"

"None. They have no leads, no suspects, except they seemed to think you might have been involved in…" Wenner stopped. Chelsea looked stricken. "I'm sorry, I shouldn't have said anything. Of course, you weren't involved. But you're my best friend and it slipped out."

"Involved in what?"

"Because you were the last one to see me on the property and the first one to find me. And your DNA and blood was all over me and the weapon. That always makes one a suspect until they rule you out."

Chelsea turned white. "What could I possibly have to gain?"

"Well, my dear, at first they thought we might be sleeping together and you freaked out over something. I assured them we weren't. Then they asked if you might have misinterpreted my motives, insinuating I might have put the moves on you and you reacted because you are still healing from your incarceration. Then I burst their bubble by telling them they were barking up the wrong tree because I'm gay."

Chelsea half-smiled. "How'd they take that?"

"They were angry I hadn't told them sooner, and Detective Reardon muttered something about you should have told them when they questioned you."

"It's not my place to tell them your personal business."

"Well, thank you for your loyalty. Anyways, it gave me a good laugh."

28

EMERALD LAKE

T he sun sparkled across the surface of the lake, appearing like it had been sprinkled with silver glitter. Birds were singing an evening song, and a light breeze cooled the hot air. It was a perfect night, and anyone else curled up in the deck chair experiencing its magic would have been relaxed and at peace.

Not Chelsea. She felt depressed, beyond angry, and most of all labelled. Her common sense told her it was perfectly natural for the police to put her on their list of suspects. Wenner had said it this afternoon; last person to see him on his property and first person to see him after his attack.

I get it.

That wasn't what upset her. *Why can't people get beyond the fact that I was a victim?*

It was their reasoning behind their looking at her that infuriated her. That woman who was locked up for twenty years. Should she be out in society?

Yes, I have issues. Yes, I'm eccentric. And yes, I trust animals more than people. But…I'm not crazy. I'm not a threat to anyone except maybe myself. And I'm certainly not violent.

"Aargh…"

Chelsea got up and paced the deck. Sage moved out of her way and stared at her with a tilted head. She stopped and looked at the dog. "I was a victim, Sage. Why am I being punished for it?" She threw her arms up and stomped into the house. "Junk food. I want junk food."

She searched the cupboards and slammed the doors shut. *Nothing! Healthy eating just doesn't cut it when you want to reward yourself.*

She opened the last cupboard and almost closed the door but didn't. In the corner of the top shelf sat two bottles of homemade wine. One of her neighbours on the lake had left them along with a gift basket with various food items to welcome her to the area. She'd put them away out of sight and had forgotten about them. Now they were staring her in the face. *Why not? I'm home safe and not going anywhere. Maybe it'll get me out of this funk and release some steam.*

Chelsea grabbed a bottle and a wine glass and started across the floor. She stopped and turned around. A little voice said: *Don't do it.* She marched back to the cupboard, opened the door, grabbed the second bottle and headed back to the deck. *Here, in my own home, I don't have to answer to anybody but me.*

CHELSEA AWOKE TO DARKNESS. It was raining, and the rat-a-tat drumming on the tin roof overhead thundered in her brain. She shook her head to get her bearings. *What the hell? Damn, I'm freezing.* She had no idea what time it was but knew she'd been sleeping on the deck for hours. Her eyes adjusted to the darkness as the moon partially lit her surroundings. Sage was asleep at her feet. She looked at the dog and then at the table beside her where the two wine bottles and the glass sat.

"You best get inside before you catch a chill."

Chelsea's head spun back to see Chloe leaning against a deck post, staring at the table. "Don't you start with me, okay?" She stood, gathered up the bottles and her glass, then headed to the cottage door. Sage ran in ahead of her straight to her doggy bed. Chelsea closed the door and locked it. After placing the items on the counter, she turned back to Chloe, who was perched on the arm of the couch with her arms folded across her chest.

"Start with you?" her sister said. "What would I say? By the looks of things, you didn't drink any of it. What stopped you?"

Chelsea turned back to the sink, dumped the wine in the glass down the drain. As she emptied the bottles one by one, she said, "I'd like to say it was my innate ability to tap into my intellect and maturity— but it wasn't." She placed the emptied bottles under the sink and washed the wine glass, replacing it in the cupboard. Joining Chloe in the living room, she curled up in the armchair with the throw blanket.

"What was it then?"

"Talon. It was Talon. Let me tell you about my day and what led up to tonight." Chelsea filled Chloe in on her visit with Wenner and how she was upset by the detective's perception of her. "I was so angry that instead of being seen as the victim, I was seen as this crazy person who may have attacked Wenner. Then I was angry with myself for wanting to be seen by them as a victim. I mean, wasn't that the reason why I moved here? To get away from that?"

"I understand, and this move was a good one. But you can't wrap yourself in cotton batting for the rest of your life and hide away."

Chelsea winced. "I know that."

"Tell me about Talon."

"Mmm...there I was, holding that glass of wine, staring at it and daring myself to take that first sip. I heard the flap of his wings. He landed right in front of me on the lower branch of the maple tree. He just sat there, still as can be, staring at me. He held my gaze for the longest time. I felt like we were connected, and I couldn't...nor wanted...to break the link." Chelsea paused and stared at Sage sleeping peacefully in her bed. "Even Sage sat perfectly still staring at Talon."

"So what happened next?"

"Some would call it an epiphany, I guess. It was like I was on the outside of my body watching me go through my whole life, only really fast. I saw it all. The realization hit me that I was seeing me through the eyes of other people. What they wanted me to be and how they perceived I was. I tried to explain it to Chaz the other day when I told him I was like the chameleon. But it didn't come clear until tonight."

Chloe slipped off the arm of the couch and onto the cushions. "Okay?"

"I've been changing my colours to be what people want me to be. I feel like I've lost myself and almost my soul. All this past year, I've been scrambling to find myself. When I kept stumbling, the drinking took me away from it all. But that just got me into trouble."

"That's a revelation."

"I had already reached that conclusion but didn't fully understand what it meant. The most important thing I finally realized is it doesn't matter how the detectives perceive me or anyone else. That's their reality. My reality is what counts. My therapist tried to tell me that. I like me. I'm a good person. If I present myself as a strong, capable person, people will see me that way, and if they don't, that's their problem."

Chloe clapped her hands. "That's an A plus." They shared a laugh.

"When Talon flew away and I put the glass down, a sudden peace came over me, a feeling of being complete."

"About that intellect, maturity thing? You must realize that Talon may have helped open up your psyche, but you did the work, Sis. I'm so proud of you. I think you're on your way."

"Thank you."

The two women sat together in silence, each lost to their own thoughts. Chelsea remembered her recent conversation with their mother. "I told Mom about you."

Chloe's eyebrows shot up. "Really? Did she believe you?"

"Who else could have told me about us being triplets? She was shocked at first. In the end, she wished she could see you, too."

"Hmm…I'm not sure that's possible. It takes a lot of energy to come back to this realm, and conversing is even harder—which is why we carefully choose how often, why, when and for whom. But maybe I can squeeze in a short visitation." Chloe's face contorted, and her eyes expressed sadness.

"What's wrong?" Chelsea said.

"It occurs to me you don't need me here anymore. My time with you is coming to an end."

The two women stared at each other, digesting what they knew to be the inevitable.

"I wish you would stay," Chelsea said.

Chloe stood. "Well, I'm not gone yet. I shall return." With that, she was gone.

29

Wenner sat on the couch staring at the damaged panelled drapes on the living room window. It was the beginning of July, and the hospital had released him the previous day.

"Now isn't that a pathetic looking window covering. I'll go online and order a replacement. They have some new wider panels that would look much more modern."

"Would you like me to take them down and get rid of them?" Chelsea asked

"Nuh-uh. As bad as they look with missing and bent panels, the southern afternoon sun is wicked in here without draperies. They can stay up until the new ones arrive."

"You're right about the sun. Good plan."

"After that I think we'll put them away. Brian picked those out. We could cut the rod shorter and eliminate the gaps and broken panels. I think they'd be perfect for the third bedroom, which only has a mini-blind on it."

"The colour is perfect for that room. Talking about Brian, that reporter, Mason Ross, will be here soon. I'll go put the coffee on."

Mason Ross had called Wenner a couple of days ago and set up a meeting. He hadn't told him anything about his mission except that it involved Brian, his spouse. Wenner could see the meadow out front and the lake across the road, beyond his fencing. Chelsea had left the gate open, anticipating the reporter's arrival. "I think I see him now." He watched a black SUV turn into the driveway and drive towards the house.

Chelsea let him in, and they soon joined Wenner in the living room.

"You have a great property here, Mr. Gibb."

"Thank you. Call me Wenner."

Ross sat down opposite Wenner, and Chelsea joined Wenner on the couch. "I'm Mason. Thank you for seeing me, sir, so soon after your hospital release. I'm sorry for your incident."

"Thank you, Mason. As I said, Wenner, not sir. Tell me why you're here and what it has to do with Brian."

"I've been investigating a story for the paper for several months now. A couple of years ago, a fellow colleague, Emmet Zimmerman, was working on the same story, only he was doing it on the side, so no one at the paper was aware of it."

"Yes, Emmet. He died in the accident with Brian."

"That's right. Do you know how they came to meet?"

"They knew each other from college. Brian was an accountant. He ran the business side of our veterinary clinic, but he also did some freelance work for other companies. I met Emmet once just before the accident. Brian said they had some business together, something about one of his accounting clients."

"Did he tell you what their business was?"

"No, he didn't. Brian worked for prestigious companies and was always discrete about his clients and their financial business. He didn't share, and I didn't ask."

Chelsea left the room and returned with a tray of coffee, cream and sugar.

Mason sat nodding his head while he fixed his coffee. "Tell me about Brian's last couple of days. Did he seem upset or distracted at all?"

"We were here at Emerald Lake on a couple of weeks' vacation at the time. Brian was very relaxed, as we always were when here at the lake. He did spend some time working on his laptop each day. He said it was important work for a client he'd been dealing with for years and he needed to finish up. We'd been here about six days, and that night he stayed up late, saying he'd be able to finish his work and we could enjoy the rest of our vacation time."

"He never named the client?"

"No. The next morning he was vague and apologetic. He told me he'd spoken with Emmet and something important had come up. It was imperative that he drive back to Vancouver to meet with Emmet." Wenner choked up and put one hand over his mouth.

Chelsea reached out and touched his arm. "Are you all right?"

Wenner took a deep breath and let it out slowly. "Yes. It's just that I haven't talked about this out loud before. Obviously, I was angry that he was cutting short our vacation. We had a big war of words, putting it mildly."

"I'm sorry to put you through this, but it is important," Mason said.

"It's okay. Brian went to pack, and I cooled off.

He asked if I wanted to come with him and once he was done with Emmet, we could come back for a few days more. I told him I'd rather stay at the lake. Sometimes, I wonder if I had gone if he'd have done anything different that night and maybe they wouldn't have had the accident."

"Oh, Wenner," Chelsea said. "As you said, he didn't include you in his clients' business. He probably would have left you at your apartment in Vancouver and done the exact same thing."

Wenner gave them both a weak smile. "You're probably right. Anyway, we made up and he left with a promise that he'd be gone for two days and we'd have six days left to vacation. That's the last time we talked. He did text me to let me know he got back to Vancouver safe."

"Did he leave any business papers here, or did you recover anything from the car?"

"No and no. He took his briefcase and laptop with him. The car fire…" Wenner paused. "… nothing was salvageable."

"I appreciate your talking to me, Wenner. I can see how difficult it is for you."

"Tell me something. If no one at the paper knew what Emmet was working on, how did you find out about it?"

"His wife. After Emmet's death, she put all his things in boxes and stored them. She wasn't ready to go through anything. She recently sold the house and is planning to move with her kids back to Ontario where her parents live. When she sorted through his things, she came across a notebook and diary. She gave them to me. None of it made sense to her, it was reporter shorthand, some of which I was able to decipher."

"Did she know anything about what Emmet and Brian were working on?"

"No, Emmet was tight-lipped, as well."

"It must be something pretty important if you are picking up two years later where they left off."

"It is, but I can't talk about it. If the story comes out, I'll let you know. I'll also see that Brian and Emmet get recognition for it."

"I'm sorry that I haven't been much help to you."

"On the contrary, you gave me a timeline." Mason stood and reached across the table to shake Wenner's hand. "Thank you for seeing me. All the best with your rehab."

"Good luck with your story."

Chelsea walked Mason to the door. Wenner pushed himself up to a standing position. He had a brace on his leg still, but he could walk with crutches. Soon, he would progress to a cane. But not if he didn't work at his exercises. He made his way to the bedroom that Chelsea had converted to a makeshift gym. When Chelsea joined him, he was sitting in a chair doing his upper body exercises with ten-pound weights.

"He's gone," she said. "I wonder what he's working on?"

His throat tightened. He stopped his workout and slumped in his seat. "I don't want to know. Whatever the story is, it took my Brian away from me."

Chelsea gasped. "You mean you think it's something nefarious?"

"No," Wenner scoffed. "I mean if he hadn't gone back to Vancouver, the accident may never have happened."

TOBEN GARRETT DROVE to his motel. The bugs he'd planted at Gibb's house on his last visit hadn't been detected, and he'd overheard the conversation between Mason Ross and Wenner Gibb. When he was safely inside his motel room, he called Shen. "It's me."

"What's up?"

"I think we're done here. That reporter interviewed Wenner Gibb this morning. He knows nothing. Ross didn't offer any information about his investigation, but his questions to Gibb did clear up any worries you might have about what Gibb's spouse may have told him. Apparently, he kept his findings to himself."

"Okay. Good to know."

"Apparently, Zimmerman's wife is moving back to Ontario and found some notes in her husband's stuff. She passed them to Ross. That's how the paper got involved in this again."

"So no loose ends there then."

"I'd say no."

"All right. Without Proctor's findings, Mason Ross is going to hit a brick wall. I want you to stay there until you can gain access to Gibb's house and retrieve the bugs. Undetected this time. Are you hearing me?"

"Yea, I hear ya."

"Good. When you get back, your job will be following Ross. I want his house bugged next. We need to make sure he goes no further with this. Got that?"

"Got it."

"Okay, check in when you're back to Vancouver."

"Will do."

"And Toben. Good job."

Before he could answer, Shen clicked off.

❧ 30 ❧
STONEY CREEK

C helsea looked out the bedroom window at the activity in the back yard. She felt elated. It was mid-July, a beautiful warm day, and today she was witnessing the wedding of her daughter and acting as matron-of-honour for her mother's nuptials, as well. *It doesn't get much better than this.* Jax had built a wooden pathway from the back deck down onto the sandy beach in front of the lake, meeting up with a wooden platform for their wedding. It was decided that they'd leave it there permanently to picnic by the lake. A knock on the door broke into her muse. "Come in."

Elizabeth joined her daughter. They were thirty minutes away from the ceremony and stood side-by-side at the window in housecoats. Their hair and makeup were done. All that they needed to do was put on their dresses

"How pretty the decorations look," Elizabeth said.

There were five round tables set up on the back deck to seat four each for their twenty guests, and a long table for the wedding party. The colour scheme was dusty rose and beige with white and pink magnolia flowers. "I can't believe we got all this done in four weeks."

"Me either. But Sydney wanted to do it as soon as possible before her pregnancy really showed. She's already got quite a noticeable bump, but her dress design was genius. You can't see it at all."

"Time to get dressed. Can you help me on with my dress so I don't mess my hair?" Elizabeth asked.

"Of course."

A few minutes later they were both dressed. "Oh, Mom. You look lovely."

Elizabeth giggled. "And so do you. I never thought I'd ever have another wedding day. I'm as excited as a teenager."

Chelsea let out a deep sigh to keep her emotions under control. "It's going to be quite the day."

Jessie was helping Sydney in her bedroom. The grooms were already outside with their best men. They were dressed in white tuxedos with dusty rose shirts, pink magnolias pinned on their lapels. Jax had asked Chaz to stand up for him, and Jessie was there for Sydney. Chelsea was standing up for her mother, and Gord had asked a good friend, Gerry Cuomo, to do his honours.

Bea was bustling around checking last-minute details on tables. A knock sounded on the door, and Jessie popped her head in. "All ready?"

"Yes," the two women echoed. They left the room and joined Sydney in the living room.

"Oh, Syd," Chelsea cried. "You're beautiful."

Sydney was wearing an A-line sweetheart dress of layered chiffon that fell to above the knees in front and symmetrically flowed to mid-calf at the back. The sleeveless fitted bodice was ruffled and edged with beading.

"And Nan, look at you. You look so young and gorgeous," Sydney said.

Elizabeth's dress was an A-line, as well, with a V-neck topper of white lace with a cap sleeve. Under the bodice a chiffon of dusty rose flowed to mid-calf.

Sydney studied her mother's hair. Chelsea had cut her long hair to just above her shoulders. Her blond hair faded into a bottom layer of a light brown. "Love the new hair style, Mom. So sophisticated. You look much younger with a shorter bob."

Chelsea was pleased. "Thank you. I have to thank Jessie. She took me to the salon this morning to get it done. And showed me how to put on my makeup."

The maids-of-honour wore matching A-line dusty rose sundresses that fell above the knee with a fitted bodice and spaghetti straps.

They gushed over each other, and Jessie threw her arms up. "Oh, let's just say it. We're all beautiful."

Bea came rushing in. "Everyone's in place. Gerry is waiting on the deck to walk Elizabeth to the platform. And Chaz is waiting for Sydney. Chelsea, you'll walk first, followed by your mother; then Jessie you go, followed by Sydney. Got it?"

They all laughed and shouted, "Got it."

The nuptials were quick and funny. The justice of the peace stepped back and forth from one couple to the other to have them repeat their vows. Then, Sydney started with a promise. "I promise whenever I'm exhausted from three babies, I won't forget that you're my number one...baby."

Jax followed next. "I promise that I will help change poop diapers. I found an invention to prevent me from gagging." He took a clothespin out of his pocket and put it on his nose.

Elizabeth promised the big brave forest fire fighter that she would never tease him about his fear of spiders, and Gord promised her he would never ask her to cook him one of his favourite meals…liver. She pretended to gag.

They continued back and forth, laughing so hard with their guests they could barely speak. It was a stress-free and simple ceremony. The designated photographer took pictures by the lake in the magnolia tree grove, and while that happened the guests were asked to write in a book. Simple signatures as guests were taboo. Each guest was asked to write a fond memory of either the bride or groom.

They had decided on a buffet lunch, which was set up on the long dining room table behind the French doors to the deck. The afternoon passed quickly. Soon it was time for the two couples to leave. Elizabeth and Gord were travelling to Victoria on Vancouver Island, while Sydney and Jax decided to go to the Kootenays to a cabin on Christina Lake. It was only a two-hour drive to the Kootenays area, and Sydney was still having morning sickness.

Once the guests had left, Chelsea changed into jeans and a t-shirt. She helped Bea clean up the kitchen, while Chaz and some of Jax's friends worked on the outside. Tables and chairs were stacked at one end of the deck for the rental company to pick up the next day. Bea said her goodbyes and headed home. Chelsea went outside. The others were gathering garbage bags and moving flowers into the house. Wandering through the grove of Magnolia trees, the fragrant vanilla, cherry sweetness of the flowers was carried on the breeze. It took her back to her childhood and the wonderful times she'd spent playing here. Chelsea reached the single tree where she used to hide. She circled the tree lost to her memories until the carving of initials in the bark caught her attention. Her fingers traced the letters.

"Twenty-two years ago, we carved those initials, C & C. Hard to believe, isn't it?"

Chelsea spun around to see Chaz walking up to her. "We were so young, so naive," she said.

"And in puppy love."

She smiled. "That, too. Have the others left?"

"Yes, they asked me to pass their goodbyes along to you."

She nodded and stared up at the tree. "You gave me my first kiss up there on that branch. Come on, let's climb up."

She pulled herself up on a lower branch and braced her foot to give that final push up to the higher branch. Once settled, she laughed. "Not as easy as it was back then."

Chaz joined her on the branch, and they surveyed the property. "I'd forgotten about the great view you get from up here."

"Sydney told me she was sitting up here when Arne dropped his keys by the barn. Thank God she saw it, or I wouldn't be sitting here today...well, maybe in ethereal form."

"Strange, isn't it? You and I sat up here all those years ago, and then your daughter and my son sat up here all these years later. Jax told me the first time they sat on this very limb was the day he knew he was in love with Sydney."

Chelsea stared at Chaz's profile. "It's definitely weird. I mean, if we had defied our families and run off together, there would be no Sydney. Who knows if you would have adopted Jax, or maybe we would have. Wow, this is getting deep. Weddings and nostalgia do that to me."

Chaz turned to her. "Do you think it's too late for you and me?"

Chelsea squirmed. "Whoa! A lot of water has passed under that bridge."

"Too much to overcome?"

"I have no idea, Chaz. I'm not the person I was then. Hell, I'm still finding out who I am now."

"Well, I can certainly say I'm not the person I was back then, either. Today showed me that I made my business and raising Jax my whole life. I never felt like anything was missing, and I was happy. But this past year in Kelowna... the business just wasn't what I expected it to be."

"So you're saying being the big-city developer isn't as satisfying as you thought it'd be?"

"Yup, that's exactly it. As I'm getting older, acquiring things doesn't seem so important anymore. And when I think about your twenty years lost with Arne...life is too short not to do what makes you happy. I've been thinking about selling off my assets in Kelowna and returning to Stoney Creek."

"Good for you. Will you move back into your house?"

"Yes. I'm glad I didn't rent it out after Jax moved in with Sydney. I think subconsciously I knew I'd be using it again. But let's get back to topic. I know you aren't ready for a traditional type of relationship, and..."

Chelsea interjected. "Maybe never. One thing I do know is I like my life right now. I crave independence."

Chaz laughed. "Now that sounds like the Chelsea I knew all those years ago."

Chelsea put her shoulders back. "I like that. Maybe I'm finding my inner child."

"Here's what I'm thinking. Let's spend some time

together, get to know each other again and see what happens. Just friends. I'm not looking for a traditional relationship, either. I've been pretty independent, as well."

Chelsea stared at Chaz. One part of her was exhilarated, the other scared to death. "Friends I think I can do. But I need to rebuild my trust skills—so intimacy is off the table. Let me warn you that my need to feel free will take some understanding on your part."

"I'd like to think I'm a very understanding man."

They stared into each other's eyes. Chaz spoke first. "You realize that we became in-laws today? That makes us family, and that part of me you can trust."

She giggled. "Okay. We'll start as in-laws who are friends."

They sat in silence on the tree limb, watching the sun disappear behind the hills across the lake.

❧ 31 ❧

KELOWNA

Chelsea wandered through Kelowna's Waterfront Park. She had an appointment with Dr. Sauvé in an hour. The walk along the water's edge of Okanagan Lake on this beautiful day had a beckoning appeal. She sauntered along the board-walk until she reached an ice cream parlour. It was mid-August and very hot. Ice cream seemed appropriate. She stopped in to see what flavours they offered. A variety of ice cream and waffle cones made on-site had her drooling. Chelsea chose a double-scoop caramel chocolate chip concoction and paid the exorbitant price the clerk asked for. She found a table and sat, watching the passersby. *I haven't had a cone since I was a teenager. Another forgotten passion I can now enjoy.* Chelsea laughed aloud. Every bit worth the cost.

She left the parlour and walked to the doctor's office, waiting in reception until Dr. Sauvé called her in.

"Chelsea, come in."

They settled in their seats. "You look well. How are you doing?"

"Very well. Remember I told you about Wenner

last time I was here? I love working with him. It's very rewarding. And as for school, you're looking at an A student here."

"Good to hear. Congrats. Tell me, how things are on a personal level?"

"As I said last month, Emerald Lake was the best move I could have made. I'm finding it easier to be in contact with people. I think I'm stronger. If I meet someone who makes me uncomfortable, I have these little phrases I repeat to myself. If they don't work, I make my exit as soon as possible. I don't dwell on it."

"Good. Last month, you told me about your almost relapse with drinking. How goes the battle?"

"I don't want to sound cocky, but I don't see it as a battle at this point. Being a binge drinker is something I will always have to be aware of, and because of it I don't want to drink."

"No cravings?"

Chelsea thought about that before answering. "Not in six weeks, since that night I almost relapsed."

"And why do think that is?"

"Wow. Lots of things. Perhaps because I've accepted the problem and really want to control it. I'm back to my yoga workouts and meditation to de-stress."

"And this new regimen is working?"

"So far."

Dr. Sauvé shifted in her chair. "You said lots of things have affected your choices of late. What are the other things?"

"A lot has been going on that's taken me out of myself." Chelsea paused and stared out the window across the room. "Like Sydney getting pregnant, Mom and Sydney getting married, Wenner's accident. I think recognizing other people have issues to deal with, too, made me consider how I look at myself. I take myself less seriously now."

"How do you feel about the changes that have occurred in Elizabeth's and Sydney's lives?"

"Ooh…good question. I have thought about this a lot. If it had happened six months ago…I may have felt like their lives were moving on—without me —and maybe I'd have felt some resentment because my life was such a mess. But I don't feel that way. I'm very happy for them."

"That's good. What about a social life, apart from work?"

"I have Wenner. We've become good friends."

The doctor wrote more notes, put her pen down and studied her for a moment. "My one concern, in light of all the progress you've made, which pleases me no end, is that you'll become a recluse. You've created a very comfortable world for yourself at Emerald Lake, but you can't live in a cocoon. Do you understand what I mean?"

Chelsea frowned. "I understand what you're talking about but not so sure how it applies to me."

Dr. Sauvé leaned forward with her hands folded on her knees. "You're excelling at your studies, which must make you feel accomplished…but you are doing so online, no social contact. You have a wonderful job at the Wildlife Centre which seems to be your calling. And while Wenner was in the hospital, you managed it with intelligence and competence. That must have made you feel extremely capable and reliable. But there is no social contact in the workplace except with Wenner. I'm happy you have a good friend in Wenner, but he's safe."

"Because he's gay?"

"That's part of it. You don't have any trust issues there. We are social beings, Chelsea. You need to learn to trust again, women and men. Have you read your diaries yet?"

"Yes, I have."

"You were very social as a teenager, and it was important back then for your growth to interact with girls and boys. That doesn't stop when we become adults. Social interaction is important to our mental health and our growth."

"So you're saying being a loner is wrong?"

"No, choosing to be a loner is fine if it's for the right reasons. All I'm saying is be sure to examine your choices." Dr. Sauvé paused in thought. "One of the things that concerned me about you living alone in the cottage was that you would self-incarcerate yourself."

Chelsea raised her eyebrows. "Meaning?"

"Meaning that Arne incarcerated you for twenty years. You found ways to adapt to your situation that became comfortable. It's not uncommon for victims of incarceration to feel the need to lock themselves away to stay in their comfort zone."

Chelsea thought about that for a minute. "I do enjoy my own company and that of my dog, Sage. But on that note, it may make you happy to know Chaz and I have been seeing each other on occasion. We're revisiting our childhood relationship." Chelsea put her hands up in front of her. "Only as friends."

The doctor nodded. "That's a good start. Tell me…why do you find it within your level of acceptability to see Chaz and not other men?"

"I suppose it's because we have a history. We grew up together, attended the same schools and social events. I trusted him then…at least until I thought he'd abandoned me. Of course, that's not what happened. Having said that, I'm not ready for an intimate relationship, and Chaz knows that. I even let him stay in the guest bedroom last month when he helped me clean up Wenner's house." She grinned. "But I did lock the bedroom door."

"If that makes you feel safe, you should do that. It was a big step in itself having him stay over. What about female friends?"

"So far I haven't met any women I can relate to. I reconnected with my best friend from high school at the wedding. It was good to see her, but we ran out of things to talk about. Too much time has passed, and we have nothing in common."

"You've come a long way the past four months. You should be proud of where you are. I'm not trying to push rope here, but I do want you to be aware of the pitfalls. How do you feel about continuing our monthly visits?"

Chelsea sat back and thought about the doctor's question. "Mom and Sydney told me they've both ended their sessions with you, which makes me feel good for them and positive about myself. It tells me they're feeling confident in my recovery process. As for you and me, I'd like to continue. I do feel I've made progress, and I am proud of myself. But I like that you remind me to examine my motives. You push me out of my comfort zone."

Dr. Sauvé stood. "Okay, then we're done for today. I'll see you mid-September."

❦ 32 ❦

EMERALD LAKE

W enner hurried back to the Wildlife Centre. He was on a mission. Travelling as quickly as he could with his jacket wrapped around the injured bird under one arm and a cane in the other hand, he felt frustrated with his handicap. Life and death were in his hands, and he hated that his physical disability slowed him down. Once he reached the Centre, he called Chelsea. It was her day off, but he asked if she could assist him with a surgery right away. By the time she arrived, the surgical table was prepped and ready.

"Here I am," she said. "What are we doing?"

He helped her on with a surgical gown and handed her a cap for her head. "Some asshole with a pellet gun decided to have some fun. Prepare yourself. It's Talon."

Chelsea gasped. "Uh…nooo. How can anyone be so cruel?"

She washed her hands with antiseptic soap and donned a pair of plastic gloves and a face mask. Joining Wenner at the table, she watched while he examined the bird.

"I found him in the meadow on my morning

walk. He was unconscious when I found him, a weak heartbeat. I wrapped him in my jacket and came straight here. I don't feel any broken bones or see any other injuries. That suggests he wasn't shot out of the sky, but shot on the ground."

"Did you see anyone else when you hiked up?"

"No people, no vehicles. So he may have been there a while." Wenner examined the hole on the right side of his chest plate and another on the other side. "It appears it went through his body and out the other side, which is a godsend."

He placed Talon on his back and spread his wings out. "Could you hold him in this position for me, please?"

Chelsea did as he said, all the while talking softly to the bird. She knew he couldn't hear her but it was more comforting to her than him. Wenner picked up a portable x-ray and shot a number of pictures from different angles. He immediately processed them and examined them on a light board on the wall beside the surgical table. "See here? It shows the entrance wound…and this over here, is the exit wound. It appears to have cleared his lungs and other organs. A straight shot right through."

"Does that mean he has a good chance to survive?" Chelsea held her breath while waiting for him to answer.

"It certainly improves his odds because we don't have go inside and find the pellet. He's one lucky bird. But our next worry will be infection."

Wenner gave him a shot of anaesthesia. "I've added a pain medication so I can give him less anaesthesia. He'll be more comfortable when he wakes up. We have about fifteen minutes to do this." Wenner cleaned the wound openings and plucked a circle of feathers around each site. "I'm sterilizing the skin with a Nolvasan solution. Some vets use alcohol, but I prefer saline because it causes less heat loss."

Chelsea watched as Wenner stitched the wounds closed. His adeptness finished the procedure in minutes. The bird was then wrapped with a bandage, keeping his wings free. Talon was placed in a cage with a heat pad wrapped in a towel underneath. "It's important to keep him warm."

They cleaned and sterilized the surgery room and returned to Talon's cage. Wenner pulled an armchair from the corner close to the cage. "And now we wait. I can't leave him alone until he wakes up and can stand on his own."

"How about I go to the house and bring us some coffee and sandwiches?"

"I'd appreciate that. But it's your day off. After you bring the food, you can go back to your studies if you want."

"No way, Talon is special. I'm not leaving until I know he's at least survived the surgery."

When Chelsea returned, they started eating their lunch. When they heard a noise from Talon, they put their lunch down and watched the bird struggle to get on his feet. Chelsea whispered to the bird, "Hey, big guy, you've had quite a day. You're going to be just fine."

They watched as the bird managed to stand. He was huddled in the corner of the cage. "He's not exhibiting any signs indicating he's in pain. So far so good. Let's finish our lunch."

As they sat and ate, they reflected on the odds of Wenner finding Talon. "Thank goodness you did. Another predator would have found him eventually."

"You're right there." He shook his head and let out a deep sigh.

"What's wrong?"

"I don't know. Everything."

"Meaning what?" Chelsea said.

"Life stinks right now."

"I'm still in the dark here. Talk to me."

"Life—in that it's been two months of rehab and I still need a cane; the police have no idea who did this to me, so I doubt they ever will at this point. Nothing was stolen that I could find. My wallet full of money and valuables weren't taken, so what were they looking for? And will they come back?" Wenner was on a roll. "Then this reporter guy shows up asking questions about Brian's work, and ever since you asked me if I thought it was something 'nefarious,' I've been stewing about his accident and wondering if they're connected. Maybe it wasn't an accident." He paused to take a breath. "Then this happens to Talon. My work here at the centre has been my total survival and satisfaction, and some little shithead with a pellet gun decides to mess with what I've tried to protect here. Sometimes, life sucks."

Chelsea reached out to Wenner and gave him a hug. "You always seem so in control. But maybe that's the problem."

"Meaning?"

"Maybe I can help put some perspective on it all. What I mean is that you had no control over someone breaking into your house and injuring you. No control over Brian's accident or what happened to Talon. But you can control how you handle it all."

"I guess you're right. I've always been a bit of a control freak."

"As for recovery, you've progressed far better than some patients at this stage. The doctor said so. So maybe a little of that control freak has been a good thing. The headaches are gone, and your arm is back to normal. The leg is your last hurdle. Be patient."

"I know. I got frustrated trying to rush back here with Talon. It took me longer than normal, and I was afraid he'd die before I could help him."

"You did help him, and he hasn't died, in spite of your limitations. There will always be little shitheads. Thank God there's people like you doing what you do to stop them."

Wenner ran his fingers through his hair. "Sorry I exploded like that."

"I'm sorry I didn't see it coming. You've been carrying a lot." Chelsea paused. "Do you really think that about Brian's accident?"

"I don't know. The police said road conditions were bad that night with the storm. They slid off the road and over the cliff to the beach below, and the car exploded. They ruled it an accident."

"Then it probably was. As for the burglary, you said you came home early that night, and perhaps you caught him off guard. If he thought he'd killed you, he could have panicked and bolted."

Wenner gave her a weak smile. "You're probably right...about all of it. I feel better. You're a good friend."

"I'm glad I could help."

They finished their lunch and checked on Talon. The raptor was still huddled in the corner but on his feet. His eyes were closed, and he appeared to be resting.

"A good sign so far. I'm pleased. You'd best get back to those studies. Thanks for helping today. You did great with Talon."

As Chelsea locked the gate, she looked up to see Wenner standing in the driveway watching her. She smiled and waved to him. He waved back, but his facial expression bothered her. *He looks sad…and so alone.* As she walked the road back to her house, she shook her head. She'd been so self-absorbed. Of course, she knew Wenner was emotional about the break-in, and he'd experienced good and bad days with his rehab. Obviously, the arrival of Mason Ross had brought Brian back to the forefront of Wenner's thinking. It was bound to have an effect on him. She was aware of all of that but hadn't recognized that it all went much deeper. *Selfishly wrapped up in my own issues.* It hit her smack in the face. *Family joy. I'm the closest thing he has to family.*

She raced home and sat down in front of her laptop. *My studies can wait.* A Google search easily found what she'd been searching for. She'd wrestled with this for the past month or so. *Should I? But it's not my business.* She remembered his slumped shoulders when she'd left him standing in the driveway. *Do it! If it blows up in your face, so what? No one has to ever know about it.*

Chelsea wrote down the information, picked up her phone and dialled the telephone number. It rang a number of times, giving her a good reason to hang up. She didn't. Finally, a male voice answered.

"Hello?"

She froze.

"Hello?" the man said again.

Chelsea took a deep breath and spoke in a clear and determined voice.

"Hello. Is this Kenneth Davis?"

"Yes, this is he."

"Are you the brother of Wenner Davis?"

There was silence at the other end. Chelsea knew

she had the right person. She waited, afraid to say anything more and equally afraid he'd slam down the phone if she didn't.

"Are you still there?"

In what seemed like an eternity, the man spoke. "May I ask who you are?"

"Of course. My name is Chelsea Grey. I'm a good friend of your brother's."

Toben Garrett sat opposite Shen Lei, staring out the window while Shen finished his phone call. It was raining and a dismal September day.

Shen hung up and rubbed his hands together. "Now…where were we?"

"You were telling me about our contact at the newspaper."

"Ahh…yes. He told me last night that Mason Ross has been pulled off his story and given a new assignment."

"That's great news for you, Shen."

"Yes, it is. Apparently, the Editor-In-Chief said after five months on the story, Ross has found nothing to confirm there's anything to pursue."

"So what's that mean for me?"

"Well, you've been monitoring Ross for a few months and found nothing to report, either. Unless you have something to update me on, I'd say we're done worrying about him."

"Nothing I can think of."

"Then wrap things up."

"I'll take care of it tonight. He's visiting his girlfriend."

"Good. I have other work for you." Shen opened a desk drawer and pulled out an envelope. He passed it to Toben. "Final payment on the Ross job. I need to pull some things together before I pass it on to you. Take a few days off. I'll call you when it's ready.

MASON ROSS SAT on the couch beside Linda Ellis. "So I've been sidelined, and I'm pissed."

"I'm sorry, hon. It's a hard pill to swallow when you've put so much time into your investigation. But you have to admit, you haven't been able to unearth anything to substantiate your story."

"I know, and I get the position the paper's taking, but my gut tells me this could be one of the greatest scandals we've ever covered."

"I wish you could tell me what you're dealing with here. I don't know, maybe I could help in some way?"

Mason took her hand in his. "Your help is appreciated, but I can't bring you into this. Hell, I'm not in it anymore either, dammit."

Linda studied his face. "You're really cut up about this. You've lost other stories and moved on. Why is this one so upsetting?"

"Because I believe two deaths were involved, and it could have been a third."

"So you're worried about this third person. Do you think that person's in danger?"

Mason ran his hand through his hair. "He wasn't involved with any of it and doesn't know anything about the story or the people involved. He was just someone who was too close to one of the deceased. I think he's safe now."

"And what about you? Are you safe?"

He gave her a smile. "I'm sure the people involved know I was investigating them, and I'm doubly sure that they also know I'm off the story. I don't want you to worry about me. I'm fine." He took her into his arms and held her.

"Good to know. I'm glad you're done with it."

"It's not because I want to be, but there it is. We move on."

Linda pushed herself back and stared into Mason's eyes. She placed a finger on his lips. "No more business talk." She leaned forward. Her lips brushed his. "Maybe I'll get to see more of you."

Mason pushed her hair back from her eyes. "Would you like that?"

"I would."

He leaned forward and returned her kiss with more ardour, which deepened into a series of fervent ones. "I think I'd like to see more of you, too," he said, catching his breath.

Linda stood in front of him and slowly unbuttoned her blouse. She took his hands and placed them on her breasts. "How about right now?"

❧ 34 ❧

EMERALD LAKE

Wenner placed the load of laundry into the washing machine and turned it on. As he entered the kitchen, there was a knock at the door. Startled, he headed to see who it was. *I didn't hear a car on the gravel driveway; must have walked in.* He answered the door to a tall, lean man. His hair was cut short on the sides with a longer wave of dark hair that fell across his forehead to one side. Striking blue eyes stared at him from beneath the hair. Wenner took it all in, in a matter of seconds. His whole look fit the modern-day style of young men in their twenties and thirties. This man was probably well into his forties, but he easily carried the look.

"Can I help you?" he asked.

The man stared at him for a moment, and his uncertain eyes narrowed. "Uh...Wenner? I think you're him...aren't you?"

Wenner's eyebrows rose. "And if I am, who are you?"

The man gulped. "I'm Ken..."

"Well, Ken what can I do for you?"

The man's face dropped. He spoke in almost a whisper. "Wenner, it's me, Kenny...your brother."

Wenner stared at the man. He took a step back and stared some more. Realization took hold. He could now see the resemblance of this man to the teenage brother he hadn't seen in over thirty years. There was no mistaking who he was. And the blue eyes were definitely reflective of their mother's.

"Can I come in?"

"Please…" Wenner stood aside as his brother entered the hallway. He led him into the living room and gestured Kenny to sit on the couch while he sat opposite him in the armchair. "I…I'm speechless. And believe me, that's not the norm."

Kenny gave him a nervous smile. "It's good to see you. You look good."

Wenner senses were coming back to him, and his shock was replaced with puzzlement. "How ever did you find me?"

"I didn't. God knows we've tried over the years. But then we didn't know you'd changed your name."

"Then how?"

Ken seemed hesitant. "Chelsea…but please don't be upset with her. I'm so glad she called me."

"I still don't understand. She didn't know my real name. How'd she find out?"

"When she cleaned up your house while you were in the hospital, she found some papers and an ID on the floor with photos and tracked me down on the Internet."

"Did she now? A proper sleuth." He didn't know if he should be angry or not with her. Mixed emotions warred inside him.

"Chelsea called me because she was concerned for you. She told me about you losing your spouse and the attack that put you in the hospital. And she explained some of what had happened to her and how important it was to have the love and support of her family around her."

Wenner stiffened. "She's lucky to have her family." His eyes narrowed as memories of his last family encounter filled his mind. "Is that why you came?"

"Of course it is. As I said, we've tried to find you over the years. We hoped one day you'd either come home or call. We're elated you're still alive."

Elated. Wenner took a couple of deep breaths to calm his pounding heart. The shock of seeing Ken after all these years left him confused. "When did Chelsea call you?"

"About two weeks ago. She told me she tried to mind her own business, but after all that had happened to her, she knew she had to make the call. Things at home kept me from getting here sooner." Ken paused. "I could have called you, but I was afraid you wouldn't talk to me. So I waited until I could make the trip."

Wenner wrung his hands together. "Wow. This is such a shock." Chelsea had asked for the day off to study for an exam. "Did Chelsea know you were coming today?"

"She did. I walked here from her place."

Wenner chuckled. "So you're the reason she chose to take the day off."

"She seems like a good friend who cares about you a lot."

"She is that."

Ken leaned forward. "I'm really sorry about what happened to Brian. It must have been horrible for you."

Wenner studied his brother. "Thank you. It was a difficult time. So tell me about your life. Are you still living in Woodview?"

"Yes. I'm married, two kids." He chuckled.

"Though they're not kids anymore. Billy is twenty. Steph is twenty-two."

All that Wenner had pushed back into the far recesses of his mind came rushing forward. As painful as it was, he needed to know more about the lives of his family. *Are Mom and Dad still alive?* He was afraid to ask. "So did you stay on the farm with Dad?"

"Oh, God, no. I hated farming, just like you did. He was right mad about that, but he got over it. I went to college, and I'm working as a counsellor at the high school. Ginny, my wife, is a teacher. We met in college. She's my better half."

"So you're what, forty-eight?" When Ken nodded, he continued. "I'm fifty-three. That would make Mom and Dad seventy-three." He steeled his body and plunged ahead. "Are they still on the farm?"

"No, Dad sold it three years ago, and they bought a bungalow closer to town with enough land to afford the privacy they were used to on the farm."

As removed as Wenner was from his parents, a sense of relief washed over him that they were alive. "I could never imagine him retiring. What does he do with himself all day?"

"He and Mom cultivate their own fruit and vegetables during the season. In the winter, he curls and bowls."

Wenner laughed. "They still have a bowling alley in Woodview?"

"Oh yea, old man Peters is still there. His kids run it now. But don't think it's the same old Woodview you knew. It's grown considerably. We have a cross-country ski resort now, and a recreation centre with a pool, a skating rink, a curling rink, exercise room, and banquet rooms for rent."

"I'm impressed." He was happy Ken had mentioned his mother. "So how is Mom?"

"She's well, and she has her women friends, too."

"How's her health?"

"Physically, she's healthy. You must remember how she was and still is, strong as a horse in spite of her tiny body. Mentally…" Ken paused. Wenner saw Ken's lips purse and his eyebrows knit together. "She's a lot better now she knows where you are… and that you're still alive."

Wenner heard anger in his last remark. "You're angry with me."

Ken stared at him, his face stoic. "You bet I am. You left us; we didn't leave you."

"Like I had a choice. Dad told me I couldn't stay. And that town wasn't very accepting, either."

"I get why you left. But why did you change your name and disappear? She's been worried sick about you all these years. You have no idea."

"Do you even remember that day? You were there. You saw the hate in our father's eyes when I told him I was gay. Mom couldn't even look at me! And then you…huh, you just looked at me like you were ashamed and said nothing. Do you know how I felt? Any idea?" Wenner paused. "I had no choice. Home wasn't home anymore. I had to leave."

"Of course I remember, and I regret that day. Jesus, I called you a faggot. And I've hated myself for it ever since. The kids at school were saying mean things about you. I fought for you because I didn't want to believe any of it. Then you admitted you were gay. To me that meant the horrid things they said about you must be true. I was confused."

"So, let me get this straight, you came all this way to tell me how I hurt you all?"

"Of course not. I'm not fifteen anymore. I'm a counsellor, remember? I deal with gay students on a daily basis."

Wenner's head shot back. "Really?"

Ken's eyebrows shot up. "Oh yea, Woodview has a gay community, and apart from the ignorant, the town accepts them."

"And Mom and Dad?"

"You'd be surprised how far they've come."

There was a silence in the room. Suddenly, Ken laughed. "Do you remember Kathy Gregg and John Weiz?"

"Who could ever forget the 'it' couple? Head cheerleader and captain of the hockey team. The two worst gossips and champions of mean. They're the infamous a-holes that outed me."

"They got married."

"Of course they did," Wenner said.

"Well…they had three kids, two boys and one girl. And guess what? Their daughter's gay."

"You're joking. They throw her out of the house?"

"No. She went to Regina to take a hairdressing course and came home with a live-in girlfriend. They've been very accepting."

"So are you chummy with John?"

"Not really. He was your age, not mine. But his daughter comes to the house once a week to do Mom's hair. Times have changed. Even in Woodview."

"You said Mom and Dad have come a long way. I find it hard to believe Dad has changed."

"Let me say this, he understands now that your being gay is determined genetically and not a 'choice.' He accepts it's who you are and that's how you were born. He still believes because we are supposed to procreate that a husband and wife is the 'norm.'"

Wenner snorted. "So what you're saying is that

he thinks I was born a genetic defective through no fault of my own, like a child who is mentally challenged."

"Sort of. But he's also come to believe you have the right like anyone else to be happy, and if that means being with the same sex, then so be it. That's a big step for him, don't you think?"

"I guess."

Kenny stared at him. "It's the best you'll probably get from him. If it helps, he got into a few fist fights over the years, defending you to ignorant people."

Wenner mulled over what his brother had said. "Really? Now that surprises me. He was never a fighter." He paused. "I suppose he has come a ways. What about Mom?"

"She and Lucy have had many conversations about the gay community. But you can have that conversation with her yourself."

"Who's Lucy?"

"Oh, right, the gay daughter of the 'it' couple who comes to the house once a week to do her hair." Ken leaned forward. "Mom and Dad love you, Wenner. You need to give them a chance to show it."

"You said I could talk to her myself." He hesitated and drew in a breath, showing his insecurities. It was something he'd overcome years ago, and now it was back. He didn't like it. "You think she wants to talk to me?"

"She wouldn't have travelled all this way with me if she didn't."

"Whoa! Mom's here?" He glanced towards the door. "Where?"

"At Chelsea's. She wanted me to talk to you first. She was afraid you wouldn't want to see her."

Wenner leaned forward and put his hands over

his face as the room closed in around him. His brother said nothing. Wenner opened his eyes to find his brother standing in front of him. Ken put his hand out. "Come on. We'll walk back together."

Wenner let his brother pull him up and the two stood in front of each other. He opened his arms and Ken stepped into him. The two brothers held each other a long time; no words were needed, just a warm embrace and a few tears that helped to ease the years of pain and loss.

Wenner locked up the centre and they headed down the road to Chelsea's.

"So Dad didn't come?"

"No, he couldn't. I mentioned we would have come earlier but there were things going on at home? Dad had surgery to remove his gallbladder ten days ago. It was badly, infected so they couldn't remove it laparoscopically."

"Is he home now?"

"Yes, they discharged him a couple of days ago. He's staying with Ginny at our place. Mom wouldn't let him stay home alone."

They approached the cottage and followed the driveway to the other side of the house. Wenner stopped at the bottom of the stairs to the deck and took a deep breath. "I can't believe Mom's on the other side of that door."

Ken placed a hand on Wenner's shoulder. "We arrived late last night. She couldn't sleep a wink, hoping she'd be seeing you today. She's very nervous."

Wenner nodded, and they climbed the stairs. Ken knocked on the door, and a moment later, Chelsea opened it. She locked eyes with Wenner. He smiled and gave her a wink. "We'll talk later." She stepped aside as he stepped into the room.

Wenner stopped in his tracks when he saw his mother. He was twenty years old when he left, and that was thirty-three years ago. Her petite body was frail, her hair totally grey. Large blue expressive eyes told him she probably shared the same myriad of emotions as him. They gazed at each other a moment, and then she opened her arms and stepped towards him. He met her halfway, and the two embraced. The warmth of her body gave him a comfort he hadn't felt in years. It also unnerved him. His mind raced through an emotional roller coaster from love to rejection and anger to relief. He could feel his heart pounding in his chest. Her body shook so badly, he tightened his grip around her. In his peripheral vision, he saw Chelsea motioning to Ken and a moment later he was alone with his mother. Years of pent-up emotion were released in that moment, and the pair held each other tight and sobbed.

Once his mother stopped shaking and their tears subsided, he pulled back and stared into her aged face. As he did so, her eyes filled with anger. His mother pushed her head back and before he saw it coming, her hand flew forward and slapped him hard across the face.

"That's for making me worry all these years, wondering whether you were dead or alive."

Shocked by her physical outburst, his shoulders slumped and his expression turned to sadness. "I'm sorry, Mom."

Just as quickly as it had bubbled up, her anger was gone. She stroked his red cheek. "Does it hurt?"

Wenner smiled. "No. But you can sure pack a good wallop."

She took him by the hand and pulled him to the couch. "Now come and tell me about the last thirty years of your life."

35

STONEY CREEK

Sydney lowered herself onto the couch, leaned back into the cushions and flopped her legs onto the coffee table. "Aargh. I'm so done for the day."

Jessie stood with her hands on her hips. "And you're done with work. You have just become a lady of leisure."

"Whatever that means. I have never been without a schedule, a job, or commitments in my life. What am I going to do with myself all day?"

"Hey, enjoy this time. Once those babies pop, you'll be wishing for times like this."

"I can't imagine how chaotic our lives are going to be initially." Sydney stared down at her abdomen. "I still can't believe there are three of them in there. But my lower back keeps reminding me."

Jessie headed to the kitchen. "You sit there and rest. I'm going to check on the crock pot to see how your one-pot dinner's doing."

"Smells delicious. I'm starving."

Her best friend laughed. "Of course you are. No one needs to worry about your appetite."

"You've got that right. Especially since the morning sickness is gone. Though I don't know why they call it morning sickness. Mine was any time of day or night."

Jessie yelled out from the kitchen, "That's because you're carrying multiples."

Sydney heard a crunching on the gravel driveway and looked up to see Jax parking his van. "Jax is home."

A moment later, he stood beside her in the living room. "Hi, hon. How was your day?"

"A revelation." She patted the couch beside her. "Come sit with me."

Jax leaned over and gave her a kiss.

Jessie was busy setting the table in the dining room. Sydney turned to her. "Jess…what are you doing? You don't need to set the table."

"I want to. Hey, anything to make things easier for my two favourite people." She stood back and studied her efforts. She joined them in the living room. "All done. Dinner's ready whenever you want to eat." She grabbed her jacket off of a nearby chair.

"You're not staying for dinner?" Jax said.

"No, I have a date with my other favourite person, Dr. Chase Tessler."

"Thanks for taking me to my ultrasound today. And all you did around here. You're an awesome friend," Sydney said.

"That's what friends do. Have a good night, you two." As she reached the front door, she turned to Sydney. "I'll call tomorrow." And she was gone.

Sydney and Jess watched her pull out of the driveway and disappear down the road.

"So tell me about the ultrasound. I'm sorry I couldn't make this one."

"That's okay. The doctor has upped them to every two weeks now. I know you can't make them all."

Jax looked concerned. "Is that normal?"

"It is with multiples. Don't worry. But I do have elevated blood pressure, so I'm on bed rest from now on. That means I have to cancel the last of my drop-in yoga classes."

"You were reaching that point anyway."

"I was. I mean look at me. I'm only six months and I look like I'm full term. I'm a blimp." She stared at her feet on the coffee table. "Swollen belly and swollen ankles. Nothing sexy about this body."

Jax took her hand. "Hey, you're fat and beautiful. You look exactly how pregnant women are supposed to look, and you carry it like a pro."

Sydney giggled. "You nut."

"What else did the doctor say?"

"My blood work shows I have gestational diabetes. Another norm for some mothers-to-be. Apparently the placentas produce an abundance of hormones that affects my sugar levels. I'm on a Metformin. Other than that, we're all healthy, and I can look forward to getting even fatter." Sydney sighed at the thought. "My poor back."

She saw a frown cross Jax's brow. "I'm fine...really."

"Is it okay to take Metformin? It won't affect the fetuses?" he asked.

"I'm on a very low dose that they'll adjust it if necessary. It is the safest of all the diabetes medications, and it won't hurt the babies. The doctor will be monitoring everything very carefully."

"Okay. Do you need a backrub?"

"No, I'm good right now, thanks."

Jax rubbed his hands together. "Well...do I have a brainchild for you. You know the walkers that seniors use to steady their balance? I could take one of those and raise the handlebars and bring the seat up to your lower abdomen level, tilt it towards you slightly. And instead of a flat seat, curve it to fit your belly. You can rest your belly on it and wheel those little suckers around."

"What?" Sydney convulsed into laughter. "Wouldn't that be a sight."

Jax pretended to be hurt. "Hey, don't scoff at the genius. It's brilliant. And think of the stress it would take off your back."

"You may have something there." Sydney's hands went to her abdomen. "Whoa! Settle down. They've sure been restless today. Want to feel?" She pulled up her shirt, exposed her tummy and placed one of Jax's hands on a small protrusion that was very visible through the skin. "That's a foot."

"Wow. What a kick."

"Feel here, and then here." She guided his hand around her abdomen.

"See, they love my plan. They're kicking their feet in delight."

They both laughed. "Too funny. They're probably fighting for space. It's got to be crowded in there." Sydney ran a finger down Jax's cheek. "Please don't lose your humour. You make me laugh, and boy do I need to laugh."

Jax gave her a wink. "So any news on their gender?"

"Apparently, the two in front look like girls, but the one that started out beneath them has moved partially behind them. Can't tell what number three is."

"So, I guess I'll be doing all the chores around here for a while."

Sydney chortled. "Housework, lifting, and laundry are all taboo. I'm basically bedridden. My God, I'm going to be so bored."

He took her hand and kissed her fingers. "I'm sorry, hon. But I guess we have to follow the doctor's orders. I'm thinking we should offer Bea more work. She could come and take care of the cooking and cleaning and run errands for you during the week. She did offer. On weekends you'll have me here to take care of us. I can do the laundry."

"Do you think we can afford her? Without my income, we'll need to tighten our belts."

"We'll be fine."

"You know, I've been seriously considering selling off part of the farm. We're never going to farm it. Ever since Arne's land was sold to developers, they've been sniffing around and leaving cards. They're restricted to five-and ten-acre lots. It'll still keep us a little rural."

"Certainly, it would help us out with the expenses, and it would mean you wouldn't need to worry about going back to work until it's feasible. But it's your decision, hon. Think on it some more before you decide. But if we did sub-divide, what would you keep?"

"I'd like to hang onto the magnolia grove, and a couple of acres over the crest of the hill to the left of it. Maybe a couple of acres behind the barn on the right. And in the back, we'd have the lake, and I'd hold onto the two hay fields beyond the lake Arne leased off of Nan."

"For privacy, or do you have plans for that land?"

"I thought since my yoga business is on hold, I could raise sheep, not to eat, but to sell their wool."

"Good idea. You can spend some of your down time researching it."

Sydney's face lit up. "That, yes, and another idea has popped into my head. You know the journal I've been keeping about the stages of my pregnancy?"

"Yup! What about it?"

"I think I'm going to start a blog. Put it all online and have daily entries. I have some catch-up to do so I'll combine some of it until I get to the current time. Of course, I'll continue it after the babies are born, too. What do you think?"

"What a brilliant idea. I'm sure people will love to follow along."

"You really think so?"

"I do." Jax studied her with pride in his eyes. His mouth curled into a smile.

"What's that look about?"

"This is why I love you, Syd. Every time something pulls you down, you do an about-face and climb back up."

Sydney put her feet down and pushed herself into a sitting position. "Right about now I could use some help pulling this cumbersome body up so we can eat dinner. I'm famished."

36

EMERALD LAKE

I t was mid-October, and the air held a chill that brought the promise of what was to come. The Centre was empty at the moment. Wenner's mother and brother had stayed for five days and returned to Woodview with an assurance from him that he'd shut the Centre down for a few weeks to return to his old hometown and visit with his father and family. He'd followed them to Woodview three weeks later and was due home in a week's time. Chelsea planned to take in any critters she was capable of looking after, just as she had back in June. So far, nothing had come in, which gave her ample time to finish her first-semester studies. Her final exam was in November, and Chelsea felt the pressure.

Her computer clock read 3:00 p.m. She decided to take a break from her laptop and walk to Wenner's to check on the house. A brisk wind slapped her in the face, and she wondered what kind of weather the winter would bring. She'd been told the lake would freeze and people could often be seen ice fishing or skating. *Skating would be fun. I haven't done that since my teen years. The last time I went skating was with Chaz.* Chelsea chuckled. *I wonder if I could even stand up on skates now? Maybe it's like riding a bicycle. You never forget how.*

She unlocked the gate and strode up to the house. A walk inside it proved all was well. Wandering from one bedroom to the other, Chelsea sat in the guest bedroom she'd set up for Wenner's rehab. They'd returned all the exercise equipment he'd borrowed and set it back up as a guest bedroom. Watching him today, one would've never known he'd been incapacitated. Even his cane was gone. Her cell phone rang, and the call displayed Sydney's name. She sat on the bed. "Hi, sweetheart. How are you?"

"Oh, fine. Getting bored being a prisoner in my own home. I can't believe I have another six weeks of this, but I didn't call to whine. How are things with you?"

"Good. Wenner's still visiting his family, and I've got lots of study time on my hands. Did you see the doctor this week?"

"No, not since Jax took me for my last ultrasound. The babies are fine. My blood sugar is under control with the meds, but my blood pressure is still high. The doctor gave me a thumbs up, though. No additional worries."

"That's good to hear. I've been following you on your blog site. Honey, I love that you're sharing your experience with the world. Other pregnant mothers with multiples can get a lot from your posts. They're not only interesting but educational, as well. And the humour you add about how you and Jax are handling it all makes it funny and entertaining, too. Good job."

"Thanks, Mom."

"Listen, would you like me to drive down tomorrow and visit? I'd love to see you and Bea. We can have lunch, and I'll get to see what Jax has done with the babies' room."

"Aww, I'd love that. But could we make it the next day? I have a podiatrist and hairdresser coming in tomorrow; one in the morning and one in the afternoon."

"Absolutely, day after tomorrow. I'll be there about eleven. Anything else new down your way?"

"As a matter of fact, yes. I've been musing for a few months about sub-dividing the farm. It'd help us financially since I won't be contributing to our income for a long time to come."

"It's a shame to see the farm broken up, but you need to do what's best for you and Jax and the babies. Progress can be a good thing."

"Well, I've made up my mind to sell it off, but I wanted to give you a chance to pick up a few acres. I know you said last year you couldn't live across from Arne's farm, but that's gone and new acreages are being set up."

"I appreciate that, hon. Maybe I could buy a few acres for investment at least. Let me think on it, okay?"

"Take your time. I'm not in a rush to put it on the market. I know it'll go right away when I do. Developers would love to get their hands on the land. See you Friday, then?"

"You bet. Bye for now.

Chelsea tossed her cell phone on the bed and mused about how things had changed for all of them the past six months. She was staring at the window without really seeing it. She shook her head as it came into focus. *God, those are ugly curtains.* They were a thin red cotton with butterflies on them. Something out of the fifties. She smiled. She'd never had the heart to tell Wenner that the current curtains just didn't work. A past memory popped into her mind. Wenner had replaced the living room panel drapes because they were damaged by the intruder back in June. He'd held onto the rod and good panels with the intention of putting them up in this room. They held a special memory of Brian for him. Now that the room was a bedroom again, it was time they went up.

Chelsea felt excitement. She knew exactly where the box was. *Why not surprise him and put them up while he's away?* She stared at the ugly draperies. "You're coming down, suckers." She retrieved the box and the rod from the mudroom and carried them back to the bedroom, where she sorted through the panels, pulling out the good ones. There were enough to cover the window nicely. The rod was too long, but that didn't matter. Wenner had a tool she could use to cut it to size. One by one, she laid the panels on the bed. Some were missing their lead weights from their pockets on the bottom. She dug into the box and found them and went about slipping them into place. As she did so, one of the weights bounced across the floor. It caught her eye because its surface looked different than the others.

She walked over and picked it up. *Strange.* On one side of the smooth iron weight, a small digital memory card was taped in the centre. Written in pen on the tape was the name *SL Developments Inc.* Everything that had happened on that fateful day in June that Wenner had told her about raced through her thoughts. Something within told her this find was important and that it had nothing to do with Wenner but everything to do with Brian. Her mission to replace the curtains was abandoned. Chelsea slipped the weight into her jacket pocket, locked up the house and hurried home.

She got herself a cup of tea, closed her drapes and locked the door to shut out the world. Then sat down at her computer. First, she looked up memory cards. She had never seen one this small, and it certainly didn't fit any of her electronics. She tracked it down as a micro SD flash card. But she didn't have the adaptor it needed to be able to connect it to her computer or camera. Next, she looked up SL Developments Inc. They were a Vancouver-based company that dealt with high-end real estate. The owner was Shen Lei, and after doing some digging into him, she discovered he was affiliated with Asian gangs. Apparently, there was an ongoing investigation into money laundering by the British Columbia Integrated Crime Unit, and an associate of Shen Lei's had been indicted. *Holy shit.* Chelsea stared at the flash card. She knew she had to get rid of it. Perhaps she should turn it over to the detectives working on Wenner's break-in. *But how was Brian involved? And what was he doing with the card? The detectives already think I might've been involved in Wenner's incident. Maybe they'll think I'm still involved, or maybe even Wenner. Or maybe there's nothing on the card. But then why was it hidden?*

Chelsea nibbled her lip, hating her indecisiveness.

She knew what she had to do. Her gut told her this was the key Mason Ross was searching for, the key to Brian and Emmet's accident, and having it in her possession could put her life in danger. The business card for Mason Ross was in her wallet. Let him turn it over to the crime unit if it held anything important. Chelsea grabbed her cell phone and retrieved Ross's card. She stared at the number but decided she didn't want to talk on an unsecured line. She hit messaging and sent a text:

Re: Brian/Emmet. Found something you will def want.

COME NOW. VERY IMPORTANT.

All she could do now was wait. She hid the weight in a box of tampons in the bathroom. Twenty minutes later, he texted back.

Leaving tonight, see you in the morning.

SHEN LEI TAPPED his fingers on the table while he waited and counted the rings on the cell phone. Finally, Toben answered sounding vague. "Hello?"

"Did I wake you? It's barely 10:30 p.m."

"Yea! I didn't get much sleep last night. What's up?"

"I just got a call from our contact at the paper. He said something's up at Emerald Lake. Mason Ross is on his way there. He has no idea what it's about, but his editor called him at home tonight and told him he had to cover for Ross on some project tomorrow. He tried to find out what Ross was up to, but his boss ignored his questions."

"Okay. I guess I'm on my way."

"You do that and see what you can find out. And if necessary, you know what to do."

"Got it."

❦ 37 ❧

Chelsea was up early, having had little sleep. Every noise had kept her awake throughout the night. Finally, she gave up and put the coffee on. She opened the door and let Sage out, took a shower and dressed in jeans and a t-shirt. By that time, Sage was back, waiting to be let in. *What am I involved in?* Curled up on the couch, the old insecurities were creeping back, and she didn't like it. Her life had progressed well since moving to Emerald Lake. This came out of nowhere, and not having the answers scared her.

To her surprise, a knock came at the door. It was barely eight in the morning. Sage stood and growled. Chelsea peered cautiously out the window to see Mason Ross standing on her porch.

She raced to the door and threw it open. "Come in, please. Thank you for getting here so quickly."

"I arrived around two in the morning," he said as Sage sniffed around his feet. "I found a spot by the lake and slept in my car."

Chelsea pointed to the dog's bed. "Sage, go." To Mason, she waved him to the couch. "Have a seat. You could have come straight here. This thing has had my imagination working overtime, and I barely slept. Coffee?"

"Yes, please. Black is fine."

Once they'd settled on the couch with their coffee, Mason started his enquiry. "Tell me what you found and where."

She explained about Wenner being away and how she'd gone to check on his house, leading up to the curtain panels and the story behind them. "I found a micro flash card taped to one of those iron weights that hang in the pockets at the bottom of the panels."

"Have you opened it?"

"No. I don't have the digital components here to open a micro card. But it has a piece of tape over it with the name *SL Developments Inc.* written on it."

Mason's eyebrows shot up. A loud whistle escaped his lips. "Wow!"

"I did some research online, enough to know Shen Lei's a bad news bear. My gut says he might be involved in Brian and Emmet's accident. I debated turning it over to the detectives working Wenner's case. It's what his intruder was looking for, I'm sure."

"And why didn't you?"

Chelsea wrinkled her nose. "I suppose I should have…Wenner's case is still open, and they haven't ruled me out as yet as a suspect. I'm worried they'll think I was involved somehow. Sounds crazy, I know."

A look of confusion crossed Mason's face. "Why would they think you had anything to do with Wenner's incident?"

Chelsea sighed, and yet again, she explained her past history and how the detectives questioned Wenner about her stability and sanity. "Last night, after I read about the BC Integrated Crime Unit's investigation...it was like I went back in time to my incarceration with Arne. My old fears took hold. I was very confused, and I chose you instead of them."

"I'm so sorry you had to become involved with this. I knew of your story, of course, but I didn't realize who you were. Where's the card now?"

"I'll get it." She went to the bathroom and came back with the iron weight, then left him studying it while she took her cup back to the kitchen. A glance out the window left her speechless. She found herself staring down on a man, crouched low to the ground with a gun in his hand. He crept slowly towards the back deck.

Her heart leapt as she struggled not to cry out. "Mason, there's a man with a gun out there." She ran to the front window and snapped the blinds shut and then double-locked the front door.

"What? How'd they know I was coming here? Is there a back way out of here?"

"No, this is the only door. But we can climb out the bedroom window."

A pounding on the door, spurred them both into action. Sage erupted into a barking frenzy as they ran into the bedroom and Mason pushed the screen out of the window.

"Sage, come," Chelsea said as Mason pushed the screen out of the window.

Mason helped Chelsea out and lifted Sage into her arms. He followed through the window. They ran for the road. Chelsea expected Sage to follow her, but the dog ran in the opposite direction around the corner of the house and disappeared. "Sage, no. Come." She could hear Sage barking, and then a shot rang out, and she heard a distinct cry of pain from Sage. She stopped in her tracks. "Oh, no, Sage..." Mason grabbed her by the arm and pulled her to his car. "Shit, shit…I left my keys on your coffee table. The car's locked and my cell phone's plugged into my dash."

"And mine is on the charger in my bedroom." She noted a strange car parked down the road. "That must be his car."

They looked back and saw the man coming around the corner of the house.

"Follow me." Chelsea said, running into the brush on the side of the road. "We need to find somewhere to hide."

Chelsea led them into the trees that would lead them behind Wenner's property. "There's a trail back here, but we're going to have to make a run for it because it goes through open grasslands. If we can make it to Rattlesnake Bluff, there're places we can hide out in until help comes or we find another way to safety."

"Shouldn't we head towards town?"

"No. The only way into town is on the road. He'd find us for sure. The off-road terrain in that direction is full of deep ravines. Too difficult to navigate quickly. And if we try to reach a neighbour around the lake, he'd see us. We'd be putting other people in danger. If we can make it to the rock cropping at Rattlesnake Bluff, there's lots of places to hide."

They passed behind Wenner's place and reached the open field. "See the rocks over there? We'd best make a run for it."

"Okay, let's go."

They picked up their pace and began to run across the open meadow. They were almost to the rock cropping when a shot rang out and a bullet whizzed past her right side. "Dammit," Chelsea gasped. "He saw us. Follow me." They disappeared behind the rocks as Chelsea weighed their options.

As she paused to get her bearings, Mason rushed past her and began climbing to their left. He stumbled over the uneven rocks, throwing himself off balance more than once. "Here, there's a cave. We can hide."

Chelsea yelled up to him. "No, not there."

But Mason didn't listen to her and disappeared into the cave.

"Oh, shit..." She made her way through the maze of rocks and up the hill. "Mason? Where are you? Come back," she cried at the entrance to the cave.

"Chelsea, I can't move."

There was enough light to see dimly inside the opening, so she stepped into the entranceway. She put her hand to her brow and peered in, barely making out Mason who was standing rigid further back in the cave. Her ears picked up the distinct sound of a rattlesnake.

"Stay perfectly still." She backed out of the cave and searched for a stick. A noise to the right of her told her their pursuer had reached the rock cropping. She picked up a branch and re-entered the cave.

Maybe he won't see the cave and will pass on by.

She let out a snort.

Yea, fat chance!

"I'm back. Whatever you do, don't move." She let her eyes adjust to the dim light and crept towards Mason with her ears pricked until the snake came into view. It was within striking distance of Mason and had stopped its rattle for the moment. If Mason stepped slowly sideways away from it, he might be able to follow the wall towards her without riling it. If not, Chelsea braced herself to race forward and flip the snake away with the branch. Before she could explain her plan to him, all hell broke loose.

The man chasing them entered the cave and aimed his gun at Mason.

"No!" Chelsea cried as the shot rang out.

❧ 38 ❧

STONEY CREEK

Sydney eased her body into the front passenger
seat, placing a small pillow behind her lower
back. Her doctor had called and asked her to come
in a few days early for her next ultrasound; some sort
of scheduling problem. She'd cancelled her two appointments with the podiatrist and her hairdresser,
and Jax took the day off work to take her in. He
helped her on with her seatbelt. They placed the lap
belt down low across her thighs to avoid her belly
and tightened it.

"Hopefully, three more of these and we're done,"
Sydney said.

Jax eased the car onto the road and headed to
town. "Six to eight weeks, hon."

They drove through Stoney Creek and turned
onto the highway towards Kelowna. There were two
hospitals closer, but because Sydney was carrying
triplets, the birth would be handled by the Kelowna
General Hospital. It was a ninety-minute trip to
Kelowna from Stoney Creek, and it wasn't long before she closed her eyes and fell asleep.

She woke an hour later.

"You're awake. We're almost there. We just passed Peachland."

Sydney opened her eyes and stared out at Okanagan Lake as they sped past the concrete barriers separating the road from the lake.

"Maybe, on the way home…what the fuck?"

Sydney's head spun around. She looked at Jax and then out the front windshield. A car coming towards them on the two-lane stretch of highway was wavering back and forth across the white line. He was heading straight for them. Sydney screamed. Jax swerved into the opposite lane, just missing the oncoming car. A second later, a loud bang behind them filled the air. Then another oncoming car came around the bend. Jax turned the wheel to the right to renter their lane. Jerked it back again. The car following them sped up beside them. Sydney's hands shot out to the dashboard, bracing for impact. Jax jerked the wheel to the left, careening them onto the shoulder of the road. As he hit the brakes, gravel shot up in the air. The oncoming car whizzed by. A sudden jolt ripped through their car. Sydney shot forward into the exploding airbag.

A searing pain tore through her chest. She had trouble breathing. Panic took hold as she feared for the babies. The deflating bag blocked her view. She was afraid to move. Jax stirred beside her. A moment later his hands were pushing the bag away from her. She turned her head to him. Saw him looking back with abject fear on his long face.

"You… you're bleeding," Sydney gasped.

"Just a nose bleed. I'm okay. Are you alright?"

"I…I think so." She drew breath but the air just wouldn't come. "Please…remove…seatbelt. Can't breathe."

Jax reached for her seatbelt. "Damn…" He fumbled with it. His hands were shaking so hard, he struggled until it finally released. "Are you okay? Are you feeling any pain?"

"The pain in my chest is subsiding. Pain through my lower abdomen." Chelsea tried to shift in her seat but Jax placed a hand on her arm.

"No. Don't move. The babies. We'll wait for an ambulance and let them check you over. Jax searched for his cell phone and found it on the floor by Chelsea's feet.

"Okay." Chelsea could hear the stress in Jax's voice. She took deep breaths to calm her own fears.

A knock on the passenger window startled them. Jax turned the ignition to auxiliary and opened Sydney's window. "Are you folks alright?"

"I think so," Jax said.

"We've called 911. They should be here pretty quick." The man glanced down at Chelsea's very pregnant body.

"Thank you," Jax said.

Sydney could hear sirens in the distance. Her body relaxed a little, knowing they were close.

The man walked around to Jax's side of the car and motioned for him to open his window. "I don't think you'll get your front car doors open. I think your wife should stay put and let the paramedics and firemen lift her out. But you could probably climb over the seat and get out the back passenger door or stay put 'til the paramedics get here."

"I will. I'm not leaving my wife's side."

Sydney felt his hand slide over hers and hold it tight.

Moments later, the police arrived and shut the highway down in both directions as fire trucks and ambulances arrived at the scene.

A paramedic climbed in the back seat and examined Jax before he'd allow him to climb in the back and exit the car. Another paramedic leaned in the window beside Sydney. "Okay, Sydney, here's what we're going to do," he said as he took her vitals. "We'll put you on an IV of Wringer's lactate to keep you from going into shock. It's merely a precaution. We'll be using the jaws of life to pry your door open. There will be some popping noises as the devise removes the door. Don't let the noise scare you. We need you to stay still and not move."

"Okay."

The paramedic inserted the IV and stepped away to let the firemen extract the door.

Chelsea closed her eyes and braced herself for the loud sounds that were coming. With each pop she drew a deep breath and let it out slowly. *Why is it taking so long?* Pop. *Deep breath. Don't move.* Chelsea repeated the steps until the door gave way and she felt a cool breeze flow through the open doorway.

The paramedic leaned down beside the opening with a neck brace in his hand. "You did great."

"What do you want me to do?"

"All you need to do is relax and let us do our job. You're going to be fine. I'm going to fit you with a neck brace to immobilize you as much as we can. Next we'll place you in an extraction device around your torso and attach the two to immobilize your head, neck and torso." "Okay, all done. Chelsea we're going to lower the back of your seat now. I'm going to lean you forward slightly while the paramedic behind you does that. Then we'll place a backboard behind you." The other paramedic collapsed the back of the seat and positioned the backboard. The paramedic up front laid her back against the board. "We're going to pull you up onto the board by the back brace until you're lying flat. Okay?"

She was taken out the back of the vehicle and placed on a waiting bed. "Good job, Sydney. We're going to roll you over on your left side now. I want you to bend your legs, and we'll place a pillow between your knees."

As soon as Sydney was on her left side, she felt warmth spread over her thighs and through her maternity slacks. "Omigod…my water broke. It's too soon." She felt a hand on her shoulder. A paramedic came into view.

"It's okay. We'll have you at the hospital inside of ten minutes. They're waiting for us." He placed a pillow between her knees and covered her with a blanket. Straps were secured around her legs and across her upper body.

"Where's Jax? I want Jax."

Jax left the policemen who was taking his statement. "I'm here, hon. I'm coming with you in the ambulance. It's all good." He got into the front seat with the driver. They were on the road in no time, racing with sirens towards the Kelowna General Hospital.

The paramedic with Sydney spoke to her in a soft but reassuring voice. He took her vitals again. "Tell me, Sydney. Are your babies sharing an amniotic sac?"

"No, they each have their own."

"Okay. Are you feeling more fluid flowing, or has it stopped?"

"Nothing since that first whoosh."

"Any contractions? Pain?"

"Some, but they are niggling pains."

"That's good. You're going to be at the hospital in plenty of time."

Sydney pursed her lips. "But it's too soon."

"Don't you worry. Lots of multiples are born

early, and you're way past the gestation period of real concern."

Sydney felt comforted by that. A part of her wondered if the paramedic was saying what he thought she wanted to hear. But then, her doctor had told her weeks ago that she'd passed the half-way mark, and as each week passed, her percentage of success with an early birth grew higher. *Stay calm.*

The paramedic relayed her condition to the hospital, and when they arrived, a team of doctors and nurses were waiting for her. She was wheeled into a delivery room and examined. Jax joined her a few minutes later in scrubs. He stood quietly by her side, holding her hand while everyone else in the room performed a task. The braces were removed, and then her clothes were cut away and replaced with a hospital gown. Sydney tried to relax her body and her thoughts. *My babies are coming. It's out of my control.* A thorough examination was done and her vitals taken once again.

Sydney winced. The pains were coming harder and faster. "I think I'm going into labour." Her voice took on an edge of panic, and then she stared into Jax' eyes. A mask covered most of his face. She could see fear and sense his nervousness, but he whispered, "We're doing this together. It's going to be fine. I love you."

The attending physician left the room, and a few minutes later, Dr. Gleason entered wearing scrubs. She approached Sydney with a broad smile. "I guess these little dudes have a mind of their own, eh? Not what we thought was going to happen today. How's the pain level from one to ten?"

"A six."

Dr. Gleason nodded. "I'm just going to examine

you and listen to the heartbeats while the nurse sets up for an ultrasound."

Sydney concentrated on her breathing to stay calm, glad to have her obstetrician by her side. She studied the doctor's face while she administered the ultrasound for any kind of reaction, but her facial expression was stoic. Her doctor moved the wand back and forth across Sydney's abdomen, and then up and down. The babies' heartbeats resounded around the room. To Sydney, the beats seemed faster than usual, and she forced herself to stay calm and wait for Dr. Gleason to finish. When she was done, she stood beside the bed opposite from Jax.

"Here's where we're at. Baby #3, in the lower position, has lost his amniotic sac and is about to enter the birth canal. The other two are still intact. All the babies have elevated heartbeats, which is to be expected considering the shock to your body. Baby #3 is in position for birth. However, we still are unable to determine if they are sharing the same placenta or if they each have their own and they are entwined. And you have elevated blood pressure. For all of these reasons, we need to deliver your babies by Caesarean. And we need to do it now. Jax, the nurse will show you where you can wait."

"Okay." This time he looked at Sydney, with eyes full of love. But his face had paled, and his eyes glistened. He squeezed her hand tight. "It's going to be fine, hon. I'll see you soon." He leaned down and kissed her and followed the nurse across the room.

Sydney noted more medical staff had entered the room. "So many people."

"Apart from the usual surgical staff, we have one pediatrician and one nurse per baby. We're going to take good care of you and your babies." Dr. Gleason nodded to the anaesthetist. "We're going to prep you, and the anesthetist will give you a spinal block. We're placing a face mask on you to feed more oxygen to the babies. Do you have any questions?"

Sydney waited for door to close behind Jax. "Yes, and please be straight with me doctor. What are the chances of success for my babies' survival at twenty-six weeks?"

Dr. Gleason studied her face for a moment.

"Please..." Sydney whispered.

"Very high, I'd say. About eighty-five to eighty-eight percent."

EMERALD LAKE

The bullet missed, but it ricocheted around the cave from wall to wall. Chelsea crouched down with her arms wrapped around her head, hoping to avoid its path. With the shooter distracted by Chelsea, Mason charged towards him, and they wrestled over the gun. The bullet found a landing site somewhere in the cave, and Chelsea stood. All the echoed chaos and noise from the ricocheting projectile had aroused a nest of cave dwellers, and she could hear a number of agitated rattlers. She stood perfectly still while the drama played out before her.

She heard the stranger yell out, "Fuck. I've been bit." With the man distracted by the rattlesnake bite, Mason was able to knock the gun out of his hand, and it flew a couple of feet away from them. They both turned to dive towards it. Their assailant appeared to trip and fell to the ground. He instantly screamed as he was bitten yet again. He jumped up and ran out of the cave. Chelsea looked back to where the man had tripped. She saw a silhouette and realized it was Chloe. Her sister pointed to her feet. Chelsea dropped her eyes, and Chloe stuck her foot out. *She tripped him!* Chloe waved at Chelsea and disappeared.

Meanwhile, Mason reached down to pick up the gun. "Shit…I've been bit."

Chelsea spoke in a calm voice. "Mason, don't move. The snake that bit you has slithered away, but there's another coiled snake close to you. Rattlesnakes are only aggressive when they feel threatened. If we stay quiet and still, they'll uncoil and move away. Then we'll slowly step away and out of the cave."

"But what about the poison…"

"Ssssh…you're going to be fine. Believe me."

They watched in silence through the din, as the coiled snakes relaxed and rattles stopped rattling. One by one, the snakes uncoiled and began to slither towards the dark recesses of the cave.

"The entrance is clear now. Slowly inch your way towards the outside. Keep your eyes on the ground around you." She waited until Mason was at the entrance and slowly joined him.

They left the cave and followed the path between the rocks towards the grasslands. A look around their immediate vicinity told her that the assailant was long gone. She led Mason out of the rock cropping to open ground. "Where's the bite?"

Mason lifted his arm and showed her the inside of his wrist. "It bit me when I bent over to pick up the gun."

The area around the bite was already angry looking and beginning to swell. "Is that the only bite?"

Mason looked distressed. He spoke with panic in his voice. "Yes. But it hurts like a bugger. What'll we do? Am I going to die?"

"No, Mason. And I mean that. Our friend who bolted might. He had more than one bite, and he's probably running back to his vehicle, which is the worst thing you can do. First, I'm going to undo your belt. Then, you're going to sit and I'll explain some things to you." She pulled his belt from his jeans. Next, she took her jacket off and pulled off her t-shirt. She put her jacket back on and zipped it up. One hard pull on her shirt and she ripped it in two. She used one half to wrap the wrist, covering the open wound, which was still bleeding profusely.

Mason sat on a flat rock "Are you going to use my belt to make a tourniquet on my upper arm to keep the poison from spreading?"

"No, that's a myth. That will cut off the blood supply to your lower arm. Your blood has natural antibodies in it that will fight against the poison, buying you more time. If we cut off that blood supply, your body won't be able to naturally fight on your behalf. The poison will still get through and spread through your system."

She took Mason's forearm and lifted it up and laid it flat against his upper chest. "Open your fist and hold your arm and hand flat against your shoulder. We're going to use the belt as a sling to hold your arm tight against your body. We need to keep it as immobilized as possible. That will slow down the spread of the poison but allow your body to fight naturally against it. Understand?"

"Yes."

Sydney slipped the belt under his arm and pulled it around his neck, across the other shoulder, and down to meet the other end of the belt. She tightened it through the clasp to the last eyelet and secured it. "Perfect."

Sydney reached out to his other hand which held the gun. "Pass it over. You're not in any condition to use that. And I assure you, if necessary, I will." She made sure the safety was on and tucked it in the back of her jeans under her jacket.

"Now listen up, here's the facts. We have two hours to get you to a hospital before you're in serious trouble. Once we get back to my house, we'll call an ambulance. There's a station ten minutes away. So I don't want you to worry about time. We have lots of it. You need to keep your breathing at a steady beat and stay calm. The reason our attacker is going to be in trouble is because he panicked and ran. His heartbeat is pumping so fast, the poison is going to travel through his body like wildfire. With the two bites we know of, he could be dead in thirty minutes flat. So do you understand the importance of staying calm and taking our time to walk you out of here?"

"Right. I hear you."

"Good. We're not going back the way we came so we don't run into our assailant if he's still around. You don't need the aggravation of another confrontation. We'll go around the rock cropping in the other direction and cut through the grasslands to a trail. That'll take us back down to the lake. And we'll take it slow. We're only adding a few minutes to our return. Let's go."

They followed the rocks all the way around the bluff and started across the open grasslands.

"Say goodbye to Rattlesnake Bluff," Chelsea said.

"Aptly named. Now I know why you yelled at me not to go into that cave."

Mason grimaced, and she studied his face. "How are you feeling?"

"A little lightheaded, but that may be nerves."

As they walked, Chelsea panned the distant landscape, keeping vigilant in case their attacker showed up. "There are symptoms you may begin to feel. I'm going to tell you all of them so you know what to expect. You may not experience them at all. But if you do, tell me right away. There might be numbness of the face, nausea, vomiting, weakness, salivating, and sweating." Chelsea decided to leave out the worst—difficulty breathing. If he reached that stage and they hadn't gotten him help yet—it could be fatal.

"That's quite the list. You said I might not experience them at all. Is that because you expect we'll find help before I reach some of those stages?"

"Yes, I certainly do. But it also depends on whether you got a full shot of poison or a partial dose from the bite. It's all up to the snake how much poison he injects. I'm telling you this because the snake that struck out at you did so very quickly and slithered away just as quickly. He may have bit as a warning, more scared of you than you were of it. So there's the possibility that you only got a partial hit."

"I'll hang onto that."

"Remember, we have lots of time to get you help. Try not to fret."

"Doing my best. Sorry about the dog."

"Let's hope she's going to be okay. She's my best friend, and I can't lose her."

"I'm sure the neighbours heard the shots. Someone probably found her by now. They'll help her. Don't worry."

They soon hit the trail and followed it down to the lake. By the time they reached the road by Wenner's house, Mason's shirt was wringing wet, and his arm was swollen to the elbow. She led him down the road towards her cottage. "Our assailant's car is gone. He made it this far."

"As long as he's away from here."

As they got closer, she could see her driveway. "Look. The police are at the cottage."

They made their way to the driveway and around the back to the deck. An officer stood on the porch writing notes in a small pad. She recognized him as Officer Marshall from Tallulah Falls. He looked up as they approached.

"Chelsea, are you alright?"

"I am, but my friend here was bitten by a rattlesnake."

"Take him inside, and I'll call for an ambulance."

"I don't have my keys. I'll have to go in the way we left, through the bedroom window." Her eyes scoured the area. Her heart leapt into her throat when she closed in on a patch of blood at the bottom of the stairs. "Have you seen Sage? I think she was shot."

"We found her, she'll be fine. Just a graze. A neighbour took her to the vet. Here, I'll help you get him settled on the deck." After Mason was settled on the chaise lounge, the officer strode to his car and picked up the radio.

Mason reached into his pocket and pulled out the iron weight with the flash card still taped to it. "Here, you take this." He put his head back and closed his eyes.

Chelsea stared at the weight sitting in her palm. With no idea what Mason expected her to do with it, her common sense told her enough was enough. She left the deck, ran around the house to her bedroom window, pulled herself up and fell head first through to the floor. The gun tucked into the back of her jeans fell out to the floor. She'd forgotten all about it. "Good one…" Chelsea limped to her bedside table, placed the gun on top, retrieved a card out of the drawer and picked up her cell phone. *Time to do what I should've done yesterday.* Ignoring the text and voice messages, she punched the number in. When a voice answered the phone at the other end, Chelsea threw her head and shoulders back with confidence. "Detective Reardon, please."

✤ 40 ✤
KELOWNA

Jax sat in the waiting room with his head in his hands. It had been thirty minutes since they'd kicked him out of the room to do the surgery. He couldn't forget that look of fear in Sydney's eyes before he'd left her. He stood and paced the room. *Waiting. Pacing.* All the

'what ifs' ran through his mind. What if they hadn't changed her appointment? We wouldn't have been there at that moment. *Waiting. Pacing.* He worried that something would go wrong. What if one of the babies doesn't make it? What if none of them make it? Jax knew they would both be devastated. *Waiting. Pacing.* What if something happens to Sydney? He tried not think of that one. *Waiting. Pacing.*

"Jax."

He turned to see his father racing towards him. The two men embraced. "She's still in surgery, Dad."

"She'll be fine, son. You'll see."

"I'm glad you're here. I was losing it."

"Her doctor knows what she's doing. Let's stay positive."

"You're right. Did you get a hold of Chelsea?"

"Not yet. Elizabeth and Gord are on their way.

Apparently, they were shopping here in Kelowna. Good thing, since they've closed the highway. Shall I get us a coffee?"

"Yes, please. I'd love a coffee."

While Chaz went for their drinks, Elizabeth and Gord arrived. She gave Jax a hug. "Is she still in surgery?"

"Yes." He shook hands with Gord. "Thanks for coming so quickly. Have you talked to Chelsea?"

A frown crossed Elizabeth's brow. "No. I don't understand why she isn't answering our texts and calls. I know she's home looking after the Centre while Wenner's away."

Chaz returned with four coffees. He nodded to Elizabeth and Gord. "I saw you walking through the parking lot from the cafeteria." He passed the coffees around. "Here's some cream and sugar."

Ten minutes later, Dr. Gleason joined them. "Sydney is doing fine and resting comfortably. The babies are in the NICU."

A sign of relief passed through the group. Jax put his head in his hands. Chaz placed a hand on his shoulder.

"Thank God," Elizabeth whispered.

"The triplets are six weeks early, but they are well within the time frame that they have a good chance of survival. They will have to remain in the hospital until full term. The three of them are in separate incubators, but once we can take them off the IVs and know each one is stable, we'll put them together in one bed."

Jax looked up at the doctor. "What gender are they?"

Doctor Gillespie smiled. "You have three daughters, young man. And as rare as it is, they're identical triplets."

Everyone laughed and talked at once. Jax beamed. Elizabeth wiped tears from her cheeks. "How much do they weigh?" Elizabeth asked.

"Baby #1 is 2.2 pounds, Baby #2 is 2.1 pounds, and Baby #3 is 1.8 pounds and is a bit jaundiced." She looked at Jax, who tensed up. "Jaundice is normal for some newborns, especially so for pre-emies, and we're prepared for that. She may be the smallest, but let me tell you, she's the feisty one of the three."

"When can I see Sydney and my daughters?"

"Give us thirty minutes. We haven't got a room set up for Sydney yet. She's still in recovery. When we do, she'll be up on the third floor, maternity section. Check in at the desk. The babies will be in the Neo-Natal ICU section of the nursery, and the nurse on the third floor will direct you to them." She paused and looked directly at Jax. "Let me warn you, they're very small, and it's hard to see such a tiny thing hooked up to equipment and oxygen. Just remember it's all there to keep them healthy and help them grow."

"Thank you, doctor. We're so grateful you were here when Sydney came in," Jax said.

"You're very welcome. We haven't had triplets for a long time in this hospital and never identical ones. Your daughters have the hospital buzzing. I can assure you they will have lots of attention from our staff."

Thirty minutes later, they stood by the glass window looking through the Neo-Natal ICU. The incubators were labelled Baby #1 through #3 and held the tiniest infants any of them had ever seen. Jax turned to Elizabeth. "What's the blue light for on Baby #3?"

A frown formed on her brow. "Not sure, but it

may have something to do with her being jaundiced. Ask the nurse when you go in."

As Dr. Gleason warned, it was difficult to see these tiny beings hooked to tubes and wires, looking so vulnerable. Jax was filled with pride and overwhelmed with worry about their future. He reminded himself of what Dr. Gleason had said about technology. Tapping on the glass to get the nurse's attention, he motioned to the babies and then at himself. She understood that they were his and gave him a thumbs up. The nurse came out. "Let's get you gowned and introduce you to your daughters. Jax followed her in, and she helped him on with the scrub gown. He fumbled with the tie at the back. "I'm such a klutz. Can you give me a hand, please?"

The nurse gave him a big smile. "Not a problem. It's a big day for you. I'm Nurse Kelly, by the way."

"I'm Jax."

She led him to the incubators. "We placed them by the window so the hospital staff and visitors could see them. Everyone's so excited to see identical triplets."

They were all sleeping peacefully. He smiled, thinking they were probably worn out from their ordeal. They had the shock of suddenly being bumped around together in the accident. Then they were taken from their warm cocoon and exposed to the cold world, and now they were in another warm cocoon...but alone without each other. He stood at each incubator and studied them one by one. "Their heads are so much bigger than their bodies."

"That's because they're preemies. A few weeks will make all the difference to their growth."

They reached Baby #3. "Why is she under a blue light?"

"That's an HV light, treatment for her jaundice."

"Oh…yes, Dr. Gleason mentioned that."

"She'll probably only need it for a few days."

Jax moved along the line for a second time. "I can't believe they're actually here."

"A normal reaction."

"Thank you, Kelly. I'm going to go see my wife. I'll come back later."

"I'll still be on shift. You can throw your gown in the bin by the door. See you…and congratulations."

"Thank you."

As they headed to Sydney's room, Jax felt shaken. *Our lives have changed forever. I'm a father…an instant daddy to three little girls.*

"Jax?" His father's voice interrupted his thoughts.

"Yea?"

"You all right? You're looking a little pale around the gills."

"I'm fine. Just realizing I'm actually a father… and the responsibility that comes with that."

Chaz placed a hand on his son's shoulder. "I have no doubt you'll rise to the occasion. Don't forget you have a lot of family support, too."

"Thanks, Dad."

When they reached the door, the others held back while Jax went in. He entered to find her with the back of the bed half up, her eyes closed. He pulled a chair up beside her. "Hey, sweetheart. Are you awake?" Her eyes popped open. She gave him that wide Sydney smile of hers, and even though she looked drawn and pale, she looked beautiful, and he'd never loved her more.

"Hi," she whispered.

"How do you feel?"

"I'm tired and feeling pretty loopy. Have you seen the girls?"

"I have. They're so tiny, but perfect. They're beautiful, just like you."

Sydney's eyes glistened. "I wish I could see them. They told me after I've rested, they'd get me into a wheelchair and take me to them."

Jax pulled out his cell phone. "I took a video for you." Together they watched the movie that zoomed in on each one to give Sydney a good look. "Aw... I can't believe she's ours." They reached Willow, and Sydney frowned. "Why is she under a blue light?"

"She's a little jaundiced is all. She's being treated with a blue HV light. She's the smallest, but she's a fighter."

Sydney relaxed. "Listen to you, Doctor Rhyder. "

They re-watched the video. Jax leaned over and kissed Sydney. "We did good, didn't we?"

"We did."

"Your Nan and Gord and my Dad are here. Would you like to see them for a few minutes?"

"What about my mother?"

"Sorry, sweetheart. No one's been able to find her. And she's not answering her messages."

Sydney frowned. "Where is she?" A flash of anger passed through her. "I really wanted her to be here." A pout formed on her bottom lip.

Jax saw her disappointment. It passed through his mind that Chelsea had better have a good reason for being unreachable, or another family upset would occur. "I'm sure we'll reach her soon."

"Why wouldn't she see her texts and voicemail?"

"Maybe she left home for the day without it. Or lost it."

"It seems just when I start to trust her again, she lets me down." Sydney picked at the blanket edge. "What if..." She trailed off.

"What if what?"

"What if she's drinking somewhere? No one sees her on a daily basis. Maybe she hasn't been telling us the truth about her sobriety."

Jax took her hand in his and ran his fingers up and down her arm. "You, sweetheart, are expectedly emotional. It's been a helluva day. Let's not go there about your mother. Before you drive yourself crazy with the unknown, give her a chance to connect. I'm sure there's a plausible reason. None of us could have predicted the events that happened today."

"Of course, you're right. My hormones and the pain killer are making me overreact."

"How about I let the others in now?"

❊ 41 ❊

EMERALD LAKE

"Detective Reardon here."

"Detective, it's Chelsea Grey from Emerald Lake. We've had another incident. Officer Marshal is here from the Tallulah Falls station, but I believe this is related to Wenner's attack in June. I thought you should be aware of what's happened."

"Okay. Why don't you tell me?"

Chelsea explained finding the flash card and the arrival of Mason Ross and the attacker. She quickly told him about the chase through the grasslands, the snake bites, and up to the present.

"Do you know where your attacker is?"

"No, his car was gone when we got back to the cottage. I would think he'd try to reach a hospital."

"Can I talk to the officer?"

"Okay. He hasn't had a chance to talk to us yet, so he doesn't know the whole story. He went outside to call an ambulance for Mason."

"Fine, put him on. I'll be flying down. The highway is closed due to an accident."

Chelsea put on a clean shirt, went through the living room and unlocked the door. She found the officer was still on the radio. When he hung up, she handed him her cell phone and went back to the deck to check on Mason.

Officer Marshall joined them a few minutes later. "The ambulance is on its way. They're meeting an air ambulance in Penticton to fly him to the Kelowna Hospital. Apparently, Penticton has no beds and is overwhelmed in Emergency today. Detective Reardon is flying in by police helicopter because of a fatal accident on the highway."

"How sad," Chelsea said.

The ambulance arrived, and they inserted a saline IV right away into Mason's arm to lower his blood pressure. They removed the torn piece of shirt and re-wrapped his snake bite. By this time, Mason was in excruciating pain and disoriented. "Hang in there, buddy. We're meeting the air ambulance in Penticton, and the critical care paramedic on board will give you a shot of morphine for pain and an anti-venom shot." As they loaded Mason onto the ambulance. Chelsea said, "I'll call the hospital later to check on you. You're in good hands now."

"I was in good hands with you. You took good care of me."

After the ambulance left, the officer asked her to accompany him inside the cottage for questioning. She paused at the door. "Before you go in, you need to know the attacker's gun is on my bedside table. Mason wrestled it off of him, and I forgot it was in the back of my jeans."

"Good to know."

They entered the cottage, and the officer re-trieved the gun. She filled him in on what had happened that day and all that led up to it the day before. She also told him about the flash card and SL Developments and the ongoing investigation. He asked her to come to the station to sign a statement.

"Detective Reardon is bringing forensics with him to take pictures."

This time she took her keys and cell phone with her.

Chelsea sat at the police station while she waited for the typed statement. She'd given the flash card to Officer Marshall, knowing he'd hand it over to Detective Reardon.

With said card in hand, the Detective walked into the room with Officer Marshall. He read Chelsea's statement and watched her sign it. After asking Officer Marshall for a copy, he sat down with her. "We haven't located your attacker as yet. No one with snake bites has checked into any of the area hospitals or clinics. An all-points bulletin has been put out on his car."

"I wish I'd got his license plate number, but there was no time."

"If he's from the coast, he might not know where the local hospitals are."

"After he ran off, we never saw him again. If he ran all way back to his car and accelerated the poison through his system, he may have run out of time."

"We're expanding our search to pharmacies and clinics."

Detective Reardon sat back in his chair and stared at the flash card. "Why didn't you call me yesterday when you found this? Everything that happened today may have been avoided."

"Believe me, I wish I had. But today, I'm not the same person I was yesterday."

"How so?"

"Yesterday, I felt intimidated by you. I don't feel that way today."

"I don't get it. I've never intimidated you, Miss Grey."

"Not directly, no. But you know my past history, and this past year has been a struggle for me. Wenner told me how you wondered if I might have had something to do with his attack, like I was damaged goods and maybe freaked out on him for some reason. After I researched SL Developments, I was afraid you'd think I had something to do with all of this. I don't know, I guess I was feeling vulnerable."

Detective Reardon's eyebrows shot up. "After all that happened today, I'd have thought you'd still feel the same—more so."

Chelsea smiled. "No. I saved a man's life today. Mason Ross panicked just like the attacker. I knew what to do and how to get him back safely for help. It's changed me, and I'm feeling stronger than I ever have since I got my freedom back. That means basically, you can think what you want, but I know that I'm okay and I'm going to be just fine."

"For the record, I was just doing my job. Everyone's a suspect until a case is solved." He picked up the card. "I'd say by finding this, you've brought us a long way closer to solving this one. I'm glad you're safe and feeling strong. I'll be back." Before he disappeared out of the door, he turned back. "By the way, you handled yourself better than most would have. You did good today."

Left alone, Chelsea took her cell phone out of her pocket. She'd forgotten about the messages. She checked the text messages first. "Omigod..." She read them all and then listened to voicemail.

Detective Reardon returned. "The forensic team are back and you're free to go home, you'll..." He stopped and stared at her distraught face. "What's wrong?"

"The accident on the highway...I think that was my daughter. She went into labour early. They've been trying to reach me but I've been…and someone died. I need to call."

"You do that. But know it was an elderly man that died in that accident. They think he had a heart attack. I'm sure your daughter's fine. We'll give you some privacy."

"Oh, thank God." Chelsea opened her contacts, chose one and hit dial. As it rang, a distant thought drifted to mind. Of all the family members she could have called that had left messages, she'd called Chaz.

"Chelsea, hi. Where have you been all day? We're all trying to reach you."

"I'll explain later. How's Sydney and the babies?"

"They're doing fine. She had a caesarean. Three girls, identical. They're in incubators in NICU. My God, Chelsea. They're so tiny. I just got home from the hospital."

"What a relief. The last message I got only said she was in surgery. How's Jax? Was he hurt in the accident?"

"No, but sadly, the fellow that caused the accident died. So where are you now?"

"I'm in Tallulah Falls. I'll get there as soon as I can. I'll have to fly since the road may be closed for a while."

"Why didn't you get your messages right away?"

"I didn't have my phone with me and when I did, I was…tied up. Listen, I'm going to see what flight I can catch in Penticton and I'll call you back. Can you pick me up at the Kelowna airport when I arrive?"

"You bet. Let me know."

"Okay. Thanks."

She texted Elizabeth to say she'd talked to Chaz and was flying out and would see her soon. Chelsea sent a similar message to Jax. Detective Reardon knocked on the door and came in.

She sat back in her chair. "My daughter had a Caesarean...identical triplets...girls. Everyone's fine."

"Congratulations. Good to hear they're all okay."

"Wow! Hard to believe...a grandmother." She beamed at the detective. "What a day! I...umm... need to book a flight to Kelowna if the road is still closed."

"Look, you can fly back to Kelowna with us in the police chopper. Normally, that's not allowed. But you're part of this investigation. I can take you right to the hospital since I need to talk to Mason Ross."

"I need some things from home," she said as Officer Marshall came to the door.

"I'll take you." He turned to Detective Reardon. "I'll have her back inside of thirty minutes.

Chelsea stood. "Wait. What about Sage? Is she still at the vet's?"

"I'll get someone to call. But don't you worry about her. Someone will look after her while you're gone. We're keeping an officer on watch at the cottage until we find your attacker and figure out what's going on. When you return, you'll be in safe hands."

"I can't thank you enough."

❧ 42 ❧

KELOWNA

Inside of an hour, Chelsea walked into the Kelowna General Hospital with Detective Reardon. She'd called Chaz en route to tell him she was flying by helicopter and had a ride to the hospital. Again, she said she'd explain later. Sydney and Mason were on different floors, so she parted company with the detective in the elevator.

"Tell Mason I'll be popping up to see him later," Chelsea said.

"Will do. And I'll be in touch with you and Wenner soon. Take care of yourself."

Sydney's room was quiet when she opened the door and peeked in. Jax was sleeping in the armchair, and her daughter was curled up on her side, apparently asleep as well. She hated to wake them, so she snuck in, pulled another chair to the opposite side of the bed and sat. It was the first time she felt she could relax all day. She texted her mother that she was at the hospital and ignored texts coming back questioning her speedy arrival. She smiled to herself and shut her phone off. It was a story she only wanted to repeat once, so she'd wait for them all to come back to the hospital.

Jax woke up and blinked at her. "Hi. You made it."

"Finally. Are you alright?"

"I'm fine. Have you seen the babies?"

"No, I came to see Sydney first," Chelsea said. "How's she doing?"

"She's a trooper. Been sleeping pretty much since surgery. The doctor said apart from her high blood pressure, she's doing well."

"I'm so glad. Sleep is her best friend right now."

"She saw the babies as they were born, but only for a minute. They were whisked away to the NICU. After she wakes up, they said they'd take her to them. I have a video, do you want to see it?"

Chelsea beamed. "Absolutely."

Jax came around to her side and handed her his cell phone.

"Ohh...they're adorable. So little." *But will they survive?* A feeling in the pit of her stomach grew tighter. Not wanting to convey her concerns to Jax, she looked up at him and smiled. "Congratulations, Daddy."

"Thank you."

"Mom? You're here."

Chelsea turned to the bed. Sydney pushed the button on the bed and sat up.

"Hi, sweetheart. How are you feeling?"

"Exhausted but comfortable."

"I'm so grateful you're all safe. It's been quite a day."

Sydney gave her mother a blank stare. "But where were you? Why didn't you answer our calls?"

"My phone was at home. I'm so sorry."

"It would have been nice if you could've been here sooner. What'd you do today?"

Not wanting to worry them about her safety and

add to the dramatic events of their day, she hesitated with her answer and saw an accusatory look cross her daughter's face.

"I thought I could count on you. But you disappointed me once again."

Chelsea recoiled, deeply stung by Sydney's words. Before she could respond, Jax intervened. "Sydney... now's not the time."

Anger flashed across his wife's face and she pursed her lips.

Chelsea swallowed her hurt. "It's okay. We've all had an emotional day. Let me..."

Doctor Gillespie came in to examine Sydney and interrupted the moment. Chelsea was introduced by Jax.

"Jax, how about you take me to see my grandbabies?" When they got there, Elizabeth and Gord were at the window with Chaz.

"Hi, Mom."

Elizabeth spun around and gave Chelsea a hug. "Come and look."

Chelsea throat tightened. "Omigod...look at them."

The doctor joined them a few minutes later. "If you'd like to visit with Sydney for a few minutes, go ahead. I'll be back in about thirty minutes to bring her here so Mommy and Daddy can spend some time with the triplets."

The five of them returned to her room.

"How are they?" Sydney asked, an expectant look on her face.

"They're all sleeping," Jax said.

"They're beautiful," Chelsea said to her daughter.

"Dr. Gleason told me the girls are holding their own. Of course, they're going to have to stay here until they reach full term. And every hour of every day increases their chances of survival."

"That's good news," Elizabeth said. "Have you chosen their names yet?"

"Jenna, Willow and Kylie. Jax and I are going to decide who's who when we see them in a while."

They all murmured their delight at the names. Then, Elizabeth snorted. "Oh dear. I love the names...although," she paused, "I'm sure people will call them Kyle, and Will." Laughter rang out from the group.

"We all know your dislike for nicknames, Lizzie. Especially gender-neutral ones. They'll be fine," Gord said.

After the excited chatter died down, Elizabeth turned to Chelsea. "So where were you today? Once we did connect, you turned off your phone."

They were all staring at her. Chelsea felt her face go hot. Now was the time to tell them. "There was enough going on with Sydney and Jax. I didn't want to add to the drama. I told you all about Mason Ross, the investigative reporter who visited Wenner a couple of months ago? Well, yesterday, I found a flash drive at Wenner's with a business name on it. I researched the company online, and they're into some shady real estate deals involving money laundering and other things. I knew this had something to do with Mason's story and probably what Wenner's attacker was searching for in June. I contacted Mason, and he arrived this morning, but he'd been followed to my place by a gun-wielding thug who shot Sage." They all gasped. "She's going to be okay. Mason and I were chased into the grasslands, where Mason and the bad guy were bitten by rattlers. We retrieved the gun, and our attacker ran off in a panic, the worst thing to do when bitten, especially twice. I walked Mason out and got him help and spent the rest of the day at the Tallulah Falls police station. Detective Reardon flew in by chopper because your accident had the highway closed. He was kind of enough to let me fly back with him to Kelowna. Since Mason is here at the hospital, Reardon delivered me to the hospital to boot so he could interview him." Wide-eyed and with mouths open, not one of them had interrupted her. "And that's my story."

"Oh, Chelsea, are you sure you're alright?" Elizabeth said.

"I'm fine."

"What about the shooter? Did they find him yet?" Jax said.

"No. They're monitoring hospitals and clinics and searching for his car."

Elizabeth clucked. "Are you sure it's safe for you to go back?"

"There's an officer assigned to watch the cottage until they sort it all out."

. "Good on you. You realize you're a heroine?" Jax said. "You saved that Mason guy's life. How'd you know all that stuff about snake bites?"

"All part of my course training."

Chelsea glanced at Sydney. Her eyes were teary. "But you could have been hurt...or killed."

"But I wasn't. And that's exactly why I didn't want any of you to know about all this until you saw me. None of you needed the added stress. Especially you, Sydney."

"Oh, Mom. I'm so sorry I was rude earlier."

Chelsea reached out and squeezed her hand. "Hormones, hon. No worries."

Gord spoke up. "Have you heard any more about Sage?"

"The officer told me she was only grazed and not to worry. There are people who'll take care of her for me until I get home again."

Everyone had spoken but Chaz, who stood quiet, his face stoic. He came around the end of the bed and placed a hand on her shoulder. "You're staying at my place as long as you're here in Kelowna, you hear? And when you return to Emerald Lake, I'm going with you until they sort this out."

Chelsea was taken off guard. She glanced at the others. No one said a word, but she caught them looking at each with raised brows. Before she could say anything, Dr. Gleason came in to take Sydney to the NICU. *Saved by the bell, buddy.* She slipped away from under his hand and moved away from the bed.

"Gord and I'll be heading home. We'll see you all tomorrow." Elizabeth gave Sydney a kiss on the cheek.

"I'm leaving, as well. Jax, we'll see you back at the apartment." Chaz turned to Chelsea. "Are you coming?"

"Yes. Let's give the new parents some time together."

She walked back to the bed and gave her daughter a hug. Sydney held her tight, and when she released her, she said, "I'm so proud of you, Mom, and glad you're here. See you tomorrow."

"I'll be here," Chelsea said.

When they reached the elevator, Gord and Chelsea hit the up and down buttons at the same time. Gord turned and stared.

"I want to see how Mason is doing before I leave," she said.

"Do you want me to wait for you in the lobby?" Chaz asked.

"You can come up, if you'd like."

279

They stepped into the up elevator and waved to her mother and Gord. "See you tomorrow," Chelsea said.

When they were alone in the elevator, Chelsea turned on Chaz. "I appreciate your concern, I really do. But next time, I'd appreciate some heads up. You should've asked me first if I'd consider staying at your place and whether I wanted you to stay with me at Emerald Lake."

Chaz stared at her for a moment. Then smiled. "I'm sorry. I guess I stepped out of line. but it was with the best of intentions."

"That's a given, but still."

They exited the elevator in silence.

Chaz said. "So tell me…is this one of those moments we were talking about when we sat in the Magnolia Tree?"

"What moment?"

"The one where you said I would need to understand your need for independence?"

"It is."

"I get it."

"I'm sorry for lashing out. It was a knee-jerk reaction."

"Hey, I understand. I'm a big boy. I can take it."

They found Mason's room and knocked on his door. He was sitting up in bed, his wrist bandaged, an IV in his arm.

"You're looking a lot better than the last time I saw you."

"Chelsea! Hi. Yes, I'm feeling a lot better." He eyed Chaz.

"Mason this is Chaz, a friend and family member; Chaz, this is Mason Ross."

The two men fist bumped.

"Detective Reardon told me you were here.

How's your daughter doing, and the babies?"

"She's resting comfortably. The triplets are holding their own. We're optimistic they'll be okay."

"Then, congrats to you and your family." Mason looked at Chaz. "She's a heroine, you know. She saved my life."

"She is that," Chaz said.

"Oh, stop it. Being educated on snake bites is not being a heroine."

"You'll never convince me of that. You kept me calm and walked me out of there."

"If I had turned the flash card over to Reardon yesterday, none of this would've happened at all."

"Shit happens, Chelsea. What ifs are a waste of time. All I know is I probably would have run out of there like that scumbag did if it wasn't for you. Reardon said they hadn't found that asshole that shot at us yet."

"Not since I last talked to him." She glanced at his arm "I see the swelling is going down. How's the pain?"

"The meds have helped. They want me to stay in at least twenty-four hours to see how the wound is healing. There may be some loss of skin around the bite area. If not tomorrow, they'll release me the next day."

"Awesome news."

"Reardon says your dog's going to be okay. I'm happy for you."

"Yes. Another big relief."

"My girlfriend, Linda, is flying in tomorrow morning. We'll have to find some way to get to your place to pick up my car."

Chaz interjected. "Hmm…leave it with me. I can probably get your car brought here. Where are the keys?"

"I have them in my suitcase," Chelsea said. "I don't know why I brought them. Something told me to."

"Perfect. Don't worry about the car," Chaz said.

"Wow. I really appreciate that. Thank you."

Chelsea turned to Chaz. "We should go. It's been a long day for all of us." Then, to Mason, she said, "So good to see you're doing well. I'll see you tomorrow. Get some rest."

"Thanks again for everything. Night."

SYDNEY SAT in the wheelchair beside the incubators watching her daughters. "It's hard not being able to hold them. It's hard to feel like they're really mine. I was so connected to them when I was carrying them inside and now I—I feel so…empty."

"That's a perfectly normal feeling for mothers with preemies," Dr. Gleason said. "Tomorrow, we'll go over the steps you can take to overcome that separation, which will not only help you but will establish a bonding between you and the girls. That bonding has another purpose, as well, in that it'll help their brains develop."

"Okay. Right now, the only thing I have to remind me I'm a mother is a couple of really sore, milk-engorged breasts."

Dr. Gleason laughed. "When you get back to your room, the nurse will help you expel your milk. It's the best thing your babies can have right now to help them grow. It will become a routine part of your daily schedule. Knowing that should give you a purpose and allow you to feel that connection."

Jax stood beside Sydney, his face reddened by their talk. He drifted over to Baby #3's incubator and watched the uncoordinated movement of her arms and legs. "Her breathing seems so…I don't know… sporadic and jerky. Is that normal?"

"Perfectly normal. At this stage, the breath-triggering part of her brain hasn't fully developed. So there are pauses between breaths; the other two babies, as well. They will outgrow it. And the jerks are because their muscle tone isn't fully developed. It's all part of what you'll be taught about over the next two months."

Jax looked relieved. "Oh, okay."

"I'll leave you alone for a few minutes. The nurse will come in about ten minutes to take you back to your room and get you settled for the night, Sydney. I'll see you tomorrow. Goodnight."

"Thank you for everything, doctor," she said.

Sydney turned to Jax. "My God, Jax. You could hold one of them in the palm of your hand. It's so hard to believe something that small is a living thing, isn't it?"

"They're a miracle." He smiled down at Sydney. "Our miracle."

"I've been studying each of them. Baby #1 is more awake and seems to be aware of sounds around her; perhaps we can call her Jenna. The doctor told me Baby #2 sleeps a lot and is very quiet. How about Kylie for her? And Baby #3 they say is the feisty one and she's the smallest and most fragile. Willow seems like a fitting name for her." Sydney took a hold of Jax's hand and smiled up at him. "Whatcha think, Daddy?"

Jax nodded at each of the triplets, one by one, trying out their names. "What do I think?" Jax leaned down and planted a kiss on her lips. "I think you're right. I love you, Sydney Grey. And I love our beautiful girls —Jenna, Kylie, and Willow."

❧ 43 ❧

EMERALD LAKE

ONE WEEK LATER

Chelsea opened the door to Wenner. He'd arrived home that morning from visiting his family and had come straight to the cottage.

"It's good to see you, my friend." She gave him a hug. "Come in."

Sage lifted her head off her doggy bed and wagged her tail at him. She had a white plastic collar around her neck to keep from biting the stitches on her upper shoulder. They sat in the living room over coffee. Wenner looked at Sage, who had gone back to sleep. "Is she okay?"

"Never better. The stitches are dissolving, and you can see the wound is healing nicely."

"I'm so sorry I was away with all that's happened. You didn't need to be embroiled in this shady business, especially with your daughter's accident and all," Wenner said.

"Oh, nonsense. It's all working out for the good. I got a text from Mason Ross this morning. He spoke to the Integrated Crime Unit today. They promised him an exclusive when they're ready to make a public announcement. He also said the investigators would probably make a trip to Kelowna soon, and they'll want to interview us."

"Let's hope after that we can put this whole thing behind us. Have they found your assailant yet?"

Chelsea grimaced. "Not yet."

"Damn. This may sound a little mean, but I hope he's dead somewhere in a ditch."

"It's certainly a mystery and a worry that he'll come back. But Chaz and the officer outside have been a real comfort to me."

"Now I'm home, I have an officer down at my place, too."

Chelsea curled her feet under her on the couch. "Sooo...tell me about your trip home. How'd it go?"

Wenner smirked and rolled his eyes. "Okay. My dad, well, he's my dad. He thinks I was born with a genetic defect that makes me prefer men to women. But he loves me and accepts whatever makes me happy. He respects what I'm doing here and plans to make a trip out in the spring with Mom. I can't ask for any more than that. All I ever wanted was his approval, and I'll take it however he wants to give it."

"I'm happy for you. How's your Mom?"

"She's wonderful. I feel terrible about how she suffered all these years wondering about me. I told her when I saw the pain in her eyes the day I came out to her, I couldn't stand that I'd caused her pain. I had to leave. She got mad and said the pain I saw in her eyes wasn't for herself, but for me. She knew I might suffer my whole life because of people's ignorance. She was in pain for me. I cried over that one."

"Sounds like you had a great reunion."

"Oh, yes. And my niece and nephew were so much fun. I'm sorry I missed their childhoods. Uncle Wenner. Sounds weird, eh? I think what surprised me the most was how the town received my return. Very accepting and happy for my family to have me back in their lives. And…guess who apologized for bullying me at school?"

Chelsea smiled. "Let me guess…the cheerleader and the hockey captain?"

"You got it."

"I'm so happy for you, Wenner."

"Thank you for tracking them down. I don't think I would have ever had the guts to do it. Now tell me about Sydney and the babies. How are they doing?"

"Well, every day their chances are improving. They were born with an eighty-five percent chance, and now they've reached ninety. Willow, the smallest, has had some issues, but so far so good. They're opening their eyes, but their eye coordination hasn't developed yet, so they appear cross-eyed. Jax thought he had three cross-eyed daughters."

"Oh, dear God. The poor man."

"Each day brings something new, but Doctor Gillespie says they're fighters."

"Very good. How does it feel to be a grandma?"

"I can't wait until I can hold them. I missed so much of Sydney's growing up. I really want to be there for them, as much as I can be."

"You know, I think both our lives have taken a turn for the better. Sooo…what's happening with this Chaz fellow?"

Chelsea laughed. "He's a friend and, don't forget, a family member. He's only staying here until they sort out this investigation."

Wenner pulled his head back and cocked his eye. "Oh no, no, no…he's only family because you're both in-laws."

"I'm not looking for a partner any more than you

are, my friend. Nor am I ready. We've just renewed our childhood friendship is all."

"Okay. I won't pry...but if I recall, you weren't just 'friends' way back then, were you?"

Chelsea crossed her arms and her face became stoic.

"Okay. Moving on." Wenner looked puzzled. "Except where is he?"

"He went to town on some errands. But not until he knew Officer Young was outside to keep watch."

"You know, when I called Detective Reardon from Woodview, he told me the Integrated Crime Unit was looking into Brian's accident. They're thinking it may not have been one after all."

"What did he say?"

"Not much, really. Just that they had re-opened the case."

"Either way, it's a tragedy, but more so if it was a crime. Are you okay?"

"It's bringing back bad memories. I've been thinking that perhaps I've been hiding out here in Emerald Lake, clinging to the past."

Chelsea's radar went up. "Are you thinking you might want to leave Emerald Lake? What about the Centre?"

"Well, let's face it. If I develop it into the type of Wildlife Centre it should be, my property really isn't big enough."

"So you're considering giving it up? Would you go back to being a regular vet?

"I really hadn't got that far along. I do love this life. Maybe not here? Just ideas floating around in my head."

Her heart sank. She loved the Centre and working with Wenner. It would be a shame if he closed it down. "Are you considering moving home to Woodview? I can't say that I blame you."

Wenner's eyes popped. "Good God, no. Great place to visit and stay with the fam…but I couldn't go home again. Besides, I love British Columbia too much."

A sliver of an idea crept into Chelsea's head. "How about another coffee?"

"Sure, thanks."

Chelsea sat cross-legged on the edge of the coffee table right in front of Wenner. She put her cup down and leaned forward.

Wenner's head went back. "Now that's a look I haven't seen before. What's up with you?"

She was wound up. "I have an idea…it's formulating as we speak. So bear with me, don't interrupt, and listen. Okay?"

Wenner sat back in his chair and threw his hands up with a smile. "Okay. Shoot."

"First, Sydney is thinking of keeping ten acres of the farm in Stoney Creek and selling off the other forty to developers. She really hates to break up the farm, but they're going to be down to one income for a few years, and triplets cost money. The lots are restricted to five- and ten-acre plots. She asked me if I wanted to buy some of it for investment, which I've been considering. Secondly, my mother gave me half of the money she sold her house for in Kelowna; plus, I got a call from my lawyer that I have been offered a 'large' settlement from the government because the RCMP botched the investigation into my disappearance."

She paused to catch her breath. "Are you with me so far?" Wenner smiled and nodded. "Okay, thirdly, I've been checking out other centres. And you're right when you said you're no businessman."

288

Wenner feigned a look of hurt.

"You said it. Did you know you could set up education centres for the general public and school groups...that they have to pay to access? And you can 'adopt' a resident to school classes or donors who get certificates, education about their adoptee, and other benefits, and they pay for that experience? You can have general admission, yearly passes, etcetera, at certain hours of the day or week. Specialty education programs, internships and camps for kids where you take them out in the grasslands to observe raptors and other wildlife. Seasonal activities, like at Christmas with lights and wagon rides. Wenner, it's endless what you can do to make money for your Centre."

She paused to take a sip of coffee. Wenner opened his mouth to speak. Chelsea put her hand up. "Nuh uh, I'm just getting to the best part." He laughed and sipped his coffee.

"Fourthly, sell your property, throw your money in with mine. We'll buy, say, twenty acres from Sydney...or hell, all of it if we can, and build a Wildlife Rehab Centre in Stoney Creek. We'll be partners." She sat back and crossed her arms across her chest and stared at him.

"That's it? Are you finished?"

She nodded and waited.

Wenner took a deep breath. "Wow. You've done your homework. I told you I wasn't a business man. Brian took care of all of that. It's a lot to digest." He studied her face. "How long have you been thinking about this?"

"I've been studying other centres since I started my courses. Sydney offered me the land a week ago. But to answer your question, it all came together in the last ten minutes."

Wenner chortled. "You're a quick thinker." He quietly sipped his coffee, and she waited.

He nodded his head up and down. "An interesting idea."

Chelsea fidgeted. When he said nothing more, she pushed him for more. "That's it?"

"I like it."

She cocked her head sideways. "You like it. Well, okay then."

Wenner laughed. "I've never seen you so excited. I think I'm looking at a sampling of what I'm in for."

"That's a yes, right?"

"I think," Wenner paused, "… it's a brilliant idea. And I think we should check it out…partner."

Chelsea bounced off the table and fist pumped the air. "Yes."

❧ 44 ❧

Chelsea finished loading the dishwasher and turned to watch Chaz add more pellets to the fire box. A knock came to the door. She froze. Chaz moved to the window and looked out.

"It's okay." He strode to the door and opened it to Wenner and Detective Reardon. The men shook hands, and Chelsea invited them into the living room.

Detective Reardon cleared his throat. "I decided to bring you up-to-date in person rather than over the phone. We found your assailant today."

Chelsea sucked in air. Her whole body became rigid.

Wenner was more verbal. "Thank God for that, the bloody little weasel. Where'd you catch him?"

"Didn't. A couple of hikers saw his car at the bottom of a deep ravine. The sun was glinting off the metal. He's dead. He didn't get very far past Tallulah Falls It appears he may have lost consciousness and drove off the road, across the plateau and down into the ravine."

Chelsea let her body relax. She hadn't realized how taut her muscles had been. "It's over then."

"I'd say so."

"Who was he?" Wenner asked.

"Toben Garrett, a fixer for Shen Lei."

"And who is Shen Lei?" Chaz asked.

"Shen Lei is the owner of SL Developments Inc. in Vancouver and a subject of an investigation by the Integrated Crime Unit."

Chelsea's eyes popped. "The name on the flash card."

"That's right."

Wenner put his hands over his face. "Which ties them all to what Brian was working on. It's beginning to look more and more like his accident may not have been one at all."

"I'm sorry, Wenner. That could well be the case. They're still investigating that part of it," Detective Reardon said. "My part is done. Neither of you will be of interest to Shen or his organization. Since you don't know anything, you're not a threat to them. I think it's safe to say you can get on with your lives."

"Mason Ross told me the investigators are coming to Kelowna," Chelsea said.

Detective Reardon nodded. "Yes, in a few weeks." He stood. "I'll let you know when. They'll want to interview you both to close out your part in the case."

Chelsea and Wenner walked him to the door and shook his hand. "Thank you for coming all this way, detective," Chelsea said.

"You're very welcome, and thank you for your help. The two officers assigned to your homes will be returning to town. I'll be in touch."

Wenner turned to Chelsea and Chaz. "I have to get back to the Centre. I'm so glad for all of us that it's over." He shook hands with Chaz and gave

Chelsea a hug. "I'll see you at work in the morning, my dear."

Chelsea returned to the kitchen and poured two cups of coffee. She and Chaz settled in the living room.

"I guess you'll be heading home soon?" she asked.

"It's getting late in the day. If it's okay with you, I'll leave in the morning."

"Of course. It'll be nice to enjoy the evening without a shadow of fear lurking behind it."

Chaz stared at her. "You've covered your stress well. All of us in the family have been amazed at your stamina and determination, considering what you've been dealing with on a personal level."

"I appreciate that, but inside I've been scared not knowing how this Toben situation would end up. I admit it. But I learned from my twenty years of incarceration with Arne that I may not be able to change the event, but I can change how I react to it. I've tried to apply it to this situation. I think I'm stronger for it."

"You're stronger than you know. But it's over, and you can move forward."

Chelsea relaxed into the cushions. "Thank you for being my babysitter through all of this. You've been a good friend."

"My pleasure. I'm glad we've cemented our friendship."

She smirked, and Chaz appeared to pick up on it. "And what's that crooked smile for?"

"You know, trust issues are big on my dysfunction list. Remember when you stayed that night months ago to help me clean up Wenner's house?"

"I do."

"Deep down, I knew I could trust you, but I needed to test it…not you, but me. I was okay until we turned in for the night. The only way I could do it was to lock my bedroom door and keep a canister of bear spray under my pillow."

Chaz chuckled. "I knew you'd locked the door. I heard the lock turn as I went into the bathroom. But I didn't know about the bear spray. I also know you haven't locked it since I've been here this time, and I'm pretty sure it was because you knew I couldn't get into your room to help you if someone came in through your window."

"You're pretty smart, you know that?"

"Well, tonight you can lock it again. I get it."

Chelsea shook her head no. "My bringing it up was to make the point there are a hand-full of people in my world I trust—my mother, my step-father, my daughter, my son-in-law, my therapist, Wenner…and now you."

Chaz smiled. "Thank you. It's important to me that you know I'd never do anything to hurt you, and the last thing I'd ever do is enter your bedroom." His face reddened. "I mean, not without an invitation."

Chelsea stifled a laugh. Their eyes caught and held. Her face turned hot. "No promises…but I will admit that once in a while I've thought about it. Once I even dreamed about it."

Chaz cleared his throat. "Really? I won't put you on the spot and ask you to share your dream. But thinking about it is good."

"I'll keep you posted."

"No promises…but that sounds promising."

The air was full of tension, a different kind of tension than fearing for one's life. An uncomfortable sensation passed over Chelsea, leaving her uneasy. A pregnant silence fell between them. *Time to change the subject.* She jumped up from the couch.

"I don't know about you, but I'm starving. How about we head into Tallulah Falls for dinner?"

VANCOUVER

A Few Hours Later

S hen Lei threw the burner phone down on the desk. His face reddened and contorted in rage. He snorted like a bull about to charge. A knock sounded on his office door and Lyall Adams, an associate, came in and slipped into a chair opposite him. Shen glared at him but checked his temper. The man looked uncomfortable, as did all his associates and employees who witnessed his out-of-control outbursts—afraid they might be the next recipient of his anger.

"My father's not happy, Lyall. And it's all because of that fuck-up, Toben Garrett. I've managed to keep a low profile until now. Sure, there's been an ongoing investigation, but they've had nothing. Twice, Garrett has messed up, and now it's all over the news."

Lyall shifted in his seat. "At least they don't know who he is."

"Temporarily. What the fuck happened in Emerald Lake? A simple job to check out some information and clean it up if necessary. Something he's handled dozens of times over the years. Shots heard all over the neighbourhood, shooting a dog, and chasing people over the plateau—what the hell was he doing out in the desert? Now he's missing with snake bites, that reporter was in the hospital with a snake bite, too, and we still don't know if he found out anything."

"Toben must be laying low somewhere."

Shen stared at the man incredulously. His fist came down on the table. "You don't hide out when you get bitten by rattlesnakes, you idiot. You need an anti-venom shot."

"But he hasn't connected with any hospitals or clinics that they can find."

"I don't think he'd be that stupid. He'd be arrested as soon as he showed up and was treated. No, he'd be discrete and use the organization's personal doctor. But there's been no contact there, either."

"Maybe he died from the snake bites. It would certainly take care of the problem for you."

Shen stood and pushed his chair back so far it hit the wall behind him and bounced back. "And when they find him, they'll identify him, which will lead them right back here to me. What if they find some incriminating information on him?"

"So what do you plan to do?"

"Not me, you." Shen sat back down. "I want you to go to that resort Garrett was staying at on Emerald Lake. Take your fishing gear, you're on vacation. You'll be a stranger around there and you'll stand out like a sore thumb, so don't go near Wenner Gibb or that woman who works for him. Cosy up to the owners at the resort, visit the pub in Tallulah Falls, listen to the gossip around the area. See what you can learn and report back to me. Got it?"

"Got it."

Shen pulled an envelope out the drawer and handed it to Lyall. "Should you find Toben, you know what to do."

Lyall pocketed the money and stood to leave. He started across the floor towards the door.

"And Lyall?"

He stopped and turned around.

Shen stared directly into Lyall's eyes and spoke in a quiet but arrogant tone. "Don't fuck this up. I gave Garrett a second chance, and look where it got us. Hear me now and hear me good…if you mess up, no second chances."

Lyall swallowed hard. "Yes, sir." He hurried across the room, opened the door and slipped out, closing it softly behind him.

The cell phone rang, and Shen picked it up. *My contact at the newspaper.*

"Whatcha got for me?"

"I just had a revealing conversation with my editor and Mason Ross. Apparently, Brian Proctor had hidden a flash card in his house at Emerald Lake. The woman found it, and that's what Ross went there to get. None of them had access to open it, but it had a piece of tape on it that read: *SL Developments Inc.* It was turned over to the cops."

Shen pounded his fist on the desk top. "Shit."

"That's not all. They found Toben Garrett today in a ravine—dead."

"Fuck me. I'll be in touch." Shen hung up and punched in Lyall's number. "Your trip's cancelled. Toben Garrett's dead." He took the SIM card and battery out of his phone. Tossing the phone into the garbage can, he spun his chair around to stare out the window into the city streets below. *I'm screwed.* He loved this city. He'd been born in Asia but was educated in Vancouver. His father had left the business in his hands and returned to the homeland to coordinate their business interests there. A family affair that worked because he and his father had total trust and confidence in each other. His father's approval was the most important thing, and over the years, he'd never disappointed him. He felt his face grow hot as the anger bubbled up from within. *Damn, I hate to lose this life.*

His eyes moved to the safe under a credenza. He bent over and spun the dial. Shen retrieved a leather pouch and dumped the contents onto his desk. Thumbing through a number of passports with pseudonym names, he chose one. He opened it and removed the folded page sitting inside. It was labelled Shanghai Gardens Project. He read the items listed on the sheet and smiled. It was all fake. There was no such project. Not trusting the telecommunications system, each passport had a pre-planned set of instructions to be carried out by the organization's lawyer in the event that Shen felt the need to implement an escape plan. He picked up his cell phone and punched in his lawyer's phone number.

"John…Shen here. Listen, I just spoke with my father, and we've decided to go ahead with the Shanghai Gardens Project."

"Really? Let me pull the file."

Shen waited.

"Got it here in front of me. Did you have a timeline on this?"

"My father is gung-ho to get started right away. There's a lot of work to be done. How about you begin the process. I'm thinking we should get together next Wednesday."

"Sounds good. How about we meet at seven Wednesday evening for dinner at our favourite restaurant in Chinatown?"

"I'll be there."

Shen hung up and searched the list. The restaurant in Chinatown was actually a small private airport in the Fraser Valley. And the seven o'clock meeting on Wednesday evening next week was actually tonight. The Shanghai Project was set up for immediate extraction. The initial items on the list were to be handled by his lawyer right away, which included transferring funds from numerous accounts to a numbered account overseas. Shen smiled confidently. *That was easy.*

The safe was emptied into a briefcase, and Shen left his office and headed home to his condo in Yaletown.

An hour later, he moved a couple of suitcases and his briefcase into the two-car garage. He had one of those garages that was attached to his condo. An elevator brought his vehicles up to his floor. He locked his belongings in the trunk of a second car he'd never driven, purchased for the sole purchase of slipping away into the night if necessary. Shen re-entered the condo. He was rattled. Control was utmost in his business of illegalities. Now the police had what he knew to be compromising information, it was time to leave.

Shen stood by the floor-to-ceiling window, staring across False Creek to Granville Island. The distant taillights and headlights travelling along West Broadway, the boats moored in the marina, and the lit-up harbour boats navigating the bay fell flat, with him knowing that this was the last time he'd see this view.

With one last check around the condo, he locked up and climbed into his vehicle and drove into the elevator. Minutes later, he was travelling towards the highway that would take him into the Valley to the airplane that would take him out of the country.

✣ 46 ✣
KELOWNA

At thirty weeks, the babies were now out of the incubators and sharing an infant bed. Their eyes were still uncoordinated, but they were blinking, attentive to Sydney's voice, and were having longer periods of alertness. When she touched them, they responded by turning their heads. She'd spent the past four weeks visiting her babies twice a day. She stayed for hours beside them, talking and singing to them. So far, she hadn't been able to hold them, just touch their hands or cheeks. They had all gained weight but Willow was still the smallest of the three.

Jenna and Kylie were responding to her facial touch by beginning to suckle, which meant that soon they could come off of their feeding tubes and start breastfeeding. Before they could go home, each baby would have to be able to breastfeed and bottle feed. Dr. Gleason recommended both in rotation so it would be less stressful on Sydney and the girls. If she was breastfeeding on both breasts at the same time, Jax or anyone else in the household could bottle-feed the third. They each would also have to reach a weight of four pounds twelve ounces to prove they were suckling well. Willow was ahead of the other two in one aspect—she was raising her hand to her mouth, comforting herself.

This afternoon, Sydney was especially excited. When she'd visited this morning, the nurse told her she had something special in store for her. The nurse joined her with a big smile. "I knew you'd be here for this. How would you like to wash them and change their nappies.?"

Sydney was beside herself. "Are you kidding? Yes, yes, and yes."

"When you wash them, don't rub the cloth over their skin. As a newbie, their skin is sensitive and a rubbing motion can irritate them. Just like when you touch their cheeks and don't rub your fingers down their skin."

Sydney did as she was told. "That's it," the nurse said. "Dab the wet cloth up and down; same with the drying cloth."

For the first time in the month since the babies were born, Sydney felt like a mother. "I've felt so detached, like they weren't mine. It was so depressing," she said to the nurse. "Like I was one of you, except you got to care for them and all I could do was talk to them and touch them with my finger."

"It's very normal for you to feel that way. But it won't be long now and you'll be able to hold them."

"I can't wait."

"At the very least, now when you visit, you can do this part. It'll be great bonding for you and your daughters."

After she finished washing each one, Sydney settled in a chair and talked to them. Sometimes, she'd catch the eyes of one and she would stay quiet and stare with all the love she could, hoping it transferred from her eyes into the soul of her child. Her daughters weren't developed enough to focus on her voice and her eyes at the same time. Sydney's heart swelled during these moments. She shut the world out and experienced the joy of sharing her maternal love with her girls through a silent bond. Her connection with Jenna was the strongest, as she was awake the most and much more alert than her sisters. Kylie, the most laid back, spent more time sleeping than the other two. Today, it was Willow that she bonded with. Her weight gain had been the most dramatic, and she was almost the same size as her sisters. *What a little fighter you are.* Sydney found she couldn't hold Willow's gaze for as long as the other two, but if she swayed her head with Willow's eye movements she could lock into her gaze. After a time, Willow's movements slowed and her eyes closed. *Nap time.* Sydney watched Willow's body relax. *Aw...little angel.* Her breathing was slow and shallow. Suddenly, Willow's nostrils flared and she took in a deep breath. It startled Sydney, and she stared at her daughter's chest. *Why isn't your chest going up and down?* She knew it was normal for preemies to have periodic breathing episodes but this seemed longer than usual. Sydney's heart began to pound. She glanced up at Willow's face and saw the distinct change of colour from rosy pink to a bluish shade. "Omigod..." she screamed. "Kelly, Kelly...Willow's stopped breathing." Nurse Sara came running, took one look at Willow and nodded to nurse Kelly who hit the intercom. "Dr. Waters, Dr. Gleason, NICU team, stat, Dr. Waters, Dr. Gleason, NICU team, stat."

"No, no, no," Sydney sobbed. "What's happening?"

Sara picked Willow up and ran across the room. With her back to her, Sydney couldn't see what she was doing with her. Kelly approached Sydney, who

303

was hysterical. "Sydney, let's go into the private reception room and let the team take care of Willow."

Sydney couldn't move. Her legs were wobbly, and a pounding in her ears pulsated through her skull. "No, I'm not leaving," she screamed.

Dr. Waters and Dr. Gleason arrived with a number of other people. Dr. Waters and the team headed straight to Willow. Dr. Gleason approached Sydney. "Sydney, the nurse will take you into the reception room. I'll join you as soon as I can."

"No, Willow needs me," she cried out. Sydney tried to push past the nurse to get close to Willow, but Dr. Gleason stepped in front of her. She placed her hands on her shoulders. "Sydney, you're upsetting the other babies, and you're in our way. Let us do our job and help Willow."

The doctor nodded to Kelly, who linked her arm through Sydney's. Dr. Gleason joined the rest of the team across the room. Sydney senses returned enough to hear the cries of the other babies. The maternal side of her didn't want to leave, but the rational side told her to let the nurse lead her back to the NICU reception room. Kelly closed the door and sat in a chair while Sydney paced around the room. Her demeanor was calmer, but her mind was still manic.

"She has to be okay. She has to be."

"Why don't you sit, hon. You'll wear yourself out. Willow's in good hands."

Sydney sat on the couch and stared out the window. *What if she dies? No—don't even think it!*

"Is there someone you can call to be with you?" Kelly asked.

"They're all outside of Kelowna. I don't want to upset them until Dr. Gleason comes back." She paused and stared at her phone. "There's my father-in-law." She picked up her cell phone and punched his number. As soon as she heard his voice, she lost it. "Chaz?" Her throat constricted, and tears spilled down her cheeks. Sydney took a moment to inhale deep breaths and keep her emotions in check.

"Sydney? What's wrong?"

"Chaz? Willow…Willow stopped breathing. Can you come?"

❧ 47 ❧

Chaz raced down the hospital corridor to the NICU waiting room. When he entered, he found Sydney standing by the window, her head leaning against the frame. The young nurse nodded at him.

He rushed to his daughter-in-law's side. "Sydney?"

"Oh, Chaz." She slipped into his arms and hung on tight. "We haven't heard anything yet."

He led her to the couch and sat down beside her. The nurse stood. "I'll leave you two together and get back to work. I'm sure Dr. Gleason will be here soon."

"Thank you for staying with me, Kelly."

"You're so welcome." Nurse Kelly left the room.

"Do you want to tell me what happened?" Chaz asked. He moved into the arm chair and faced Sydney.

Sydney took a deep breath and sighed. "It was such a great afternoon. I got to bathe the girls and change their diapers. Jenna and Kylie fell asleep. I was bonding with Willow and she stopped breathing.

Her colour went blue. I panicked, became hysterical, and the next thing I knew the nursery was full of people. My histrionics woke up most of the other babies, and they were crying. Total chaos."

Dr. Gleason opened the door and came into the room. Sydney looked up at her, and time stood still. Her heart leapt into her throat, and the ringing in her ears began again as she tried to read her expression.

The doctor gave her a reassuring smile. "Willow is stable."

"What a relief," Chaz said.

Sydney covered her mouth with her hands to stifle the sobs she felt bubbling up inside. She rocked back and forth on the couch until she had control. "Thank God."

Doctor Gillespie sat on a chair. "Her heart didn't stop. It's very strong. It was her lungs. As a preemie, they still haven't become strong enough to stay inflated on their own when she has periodic breathing episodes."

"Is she back in the incubator?" Sydney asked.

"No. But she'll be in her own bed for the time being. We've placed a two-prong oxygen tube in her nose to force oxygen into her lungs. If she experiences a periodic breathing episode, the oxygen will keep her lungs inflated. We're feeding her caffeine to stimulate her nervous system and placed an apnea monitor on her. It monitors her breathing and heartbeat, and an alarm sounds if there's any sudden change."

Sydney frowned. "What about Jenna and Kylie? What if it happens to them?"

"The reason it took me so long to get back to you is because we wanted to check them out, too. Their lungs have developed at a faster pace and are stronger than Willow's. But should there be any issues, they'll be treated in the same manner as their sister."

Sydney's shoulders dropped in relief, and her taut muscles relaxed.

"The girls are doing fine, Sydney. I suggest you go home and get some rest. You've had a stressful time of it."

"I need to expel my milk first. And I'd like to see the girls before I go."

"Of course, I'll get Kelly to help you."

Chaz stood. "I'll wait for you outside by the window to the NICU."

Sydney nodded. "Okay." She turned to Dr. Gleason. "Thank you, Doctor. I'm so sorry, I caused a scene in there."

"Emotions and fears run high in these situations. No apology needed."

After Sydney expelled her milk, she went into the nursery. All three girls were asleep. They had placed Willow's bed beside her sisters' shared bed. It was difficult to see Willow hooked up to wires again and on oxygen. But Sydney was comforted by the fact that Willow's colouring was back to a rosy pink. She glanced up at the window to see Chaz watching her and the girls. He gave her a wide smile, a wink, and a thumbs up.

SYDNEY JOINED Chaz in the hallway.

"You ready to go home?"

She nodded and followed him to the elevator. Home was her father-in-law's condo, which had become a temporary home since being discharged from the hospital, when Chaz had offered them the use of his condo. Jax, who'd returned to Stoney Creek to run his business, was leaving his work in the hands of his capable staff every three or four days to travel back to Kelowna and spend a couple of days with Sydney and the girls. Chaz had remained in Emerald Creek with Chelsea until the day they'd found Toben Garrett in the ravine.

Sydney was enjoying spending time with her father-in-law and getting to know him. Plus, he told her funny stories about Jax as a child that Jax would never have told her.

Fifteen minutes later, they entered the condo. "How about some tea?" Chaz asked.

"I'd love some." She sat at the table and relaxed on her elbows. "Jax texted me when I was extracting my milk. He's on his way. In fact, he should be here soon. I texted him to come straight here and not stop at the hospital first. He doesn't know about Willow. I didn't want to upset him while he was on the road."

Chaz's cell buzzed. Sydney went to the washroom to wash her face while he checked his phone. When she came back, he was pouring the tea.

"That was a text from your mother. She and Wenner are in town. They were asked to drive in for a meeting with Detective Reardon and the Integrated Crime Unit from Vancouver. They'll be here around dinner time."

"Now that complicates things. I'd best text her about Willow in case she goes to the hospital before coming here." She sent a simple text to her mother that there had been an incident that afternoon with Willow but not to worry. She was on oxygen and being monitored. Everything was fine. "Maybe we can order in. What do you think? Chinese?"

"Great idea."

She watched Chaz work in the kitchen. She couldn't help but smile.

He caught her looking at him. "What are you grinning about?"

She laughed. "I was thinking how much I've enjoyed spending time with you here in Kelowna. Wasn't it just eighteen months ago that I literally ran into you at that restaurant in Stoney Creek? You freaked me out. I thought you were a stalker. Then I found out you were Jax's father and thought, 'His father's stalking me?' Then we thought you might be my father and I'd committed incest with my brother." She raised her hands and one shoulder. "And…here we are."

Chaz laughed. "One big loving family. I'm glad it turned out I wasn't your father. As your father-in-law, I'm just as proud of you. I think of you like you're my daughter."

"Thank you. Jax told me you're planning to move back to Stoney Creek."

"Yes. I realized I don't want to become the developer king of the Okanagan. I miss Stoney Creek and being closer to family."

"What about the projects you're working on?"

"The prelims are done for all of them. I know a developer that would love to buy me out. My company has been his biggest competitor. We're at the negotiating table right now. It'll probably take a couple of months to complete."

"Jax is really happy about you moving back. He says you offered to cut his company loose if he wants or become partners, Rhyder & Rhyder—you doing commercial projects and him residential."

"I told him to think about it. He has lots of time to decide."

"It's all he thinks about…and talks about. I think

it's safe to say he's already made his mind up. You didn't hear that from me. It's up to him to tell you his decision." Sydney leaned across the table and whispered, "But I think father and son will make a great team."

Chaz laughed. "You're an imp."

"On that note…" Sydney leaned on her elbows. "What's going on with you and my mother?"

"Nothing. We're friends from childhood. Remember?"

"Renewing an old friendship, are you?"

"That's right." He placed her tea in front of her. He titled his head and raised one brow, a warning not to go there.

Sydney ignored the look and continued. "Hmm…but you were more than friends back then, as I heard told."

Chaz sat down. "My dearest daughter-in-law, there are some things I'm not going to discuss with you…and that's one of them. But I will say your mother has come a long way in the past sixteen months. But she needs to go a lot further before she'll trust in an intimate relationship. Even then, she may only be able to go so far."

"I know. I just want her to be happy. And if she ever does involve herself with anyone, I hope it's you. I know you have the utmost respect for her and would never hurt her."

"Thank you. I just don't want you to have this romantic image of your mother falling in love, with a wedding, and a knight in shining armour carrying her off into the sunset. I doubt that will ever happen."

"You may be right."

"Chelsea lost a lot of years, and she wants to live

the rest of her life by her own choosing. Her independence is very important to her."

"I hear you. But…I have a feeling you'd be willing to help her achieve what she's looking for. Am I right?"

Chaz grinned. "Mind your own business and drink your tea."

❊ 48 ❊
KELOWNA

Chelsea and Wenner sat in the conference room waiting for Detective Reardon to join them and the two men from the Integrated Crime Unit in Vancouver. They'd been interviewed about their interactions with Mason Ross and Toben Garrett, and now they were to be briefed on the status of the case.

Detective Reardon joined them. "Sorry you had to wait." He nodded at Chelsea and Wenner. "Good to see you both."

The lead of the Crime Unit, Jack Williams, addressed Chelsea. "We have to tell you that the flash drive proved to be the catalyst that blew this case wide open. We were fast reaching a point of having nothing to work with until you found it. The card gave us the evidence we needed to charge Shen Lei with money laundering, bank fraud, wire fraud, and a multitude of other criminal charges. We can't thank you enough."

Chelsea nodded. She was happy everything that happened that fateful day wasn't for naught.

Jack turned to Wenner. "You know the case into your spouse's accident was re-opened. I'm sorry to have to tell you it wasn't an accident. We have a man in custody who's given us evidence Toben Garrett ran Brian and Emmet off the road. Brian had been doing some freelance bookkeeping for an associate of Shen Lei. Somehow, he came across the records for SL Developments. He knew these records depicted a double set of books, involving the crimes I laid out to Chelsea."

Wenner looked stricken. Chelsea reached out and took his hand. He stared at Jack Williams. "He never let on anything to me. I do know he was stressed when he left to go back to Vancouver and meet Emmet. I thought it was because we'd fought about him ruining our holidays. I was so selfish."

"I'm sure he didn't tell you to keep you safe," Jack Williams said.

"How did they find out Brian had the information?" Wenner asked.

"Our witness was a plant at the newspaper. He knew what Emmet was working on and reported to Shen directly. The newspaper didn't know about the story, but Shen's contact figured it out. Toben Garrett was an enforcer who worked for Shen. We think the flash drive is a copy and that the original was damaged in the accident. Moving forward to the present, Mason Ross told us he believed there was a mole at the newspaper because only his editor knew he was coming to meet Chelsea that day. And the only one his editor told was the plant because he needed him to cover another story while Mason travelled to meet Chelsea. We set a trap and caught him. I'm so sorry for your loss, Mr. Gibb."

"Thank you. There is some solace that at least his death stood for something."

"Shen Lei was tipped off after Garrett was found. We've since learned that he fled the country back to Asia. I doubt Canada will be able to get

China to extradite Shen Lei, given the current strained relations between our countries. If we ever do have him in custody, we won't need your testimony in court. This meeting ties up our loose ends with your involvement in the case."

Chelsea looked at Wenner. She could see the relief in his eyes that she felt. "That's good to hear," Chelsea said. Wenner nodded.

The two Crime Unit investigators stood up. "We're done here. Thank you for coming in." Detective Reardon walked them out and returned to sit with Wenner and Chelsea. "We're closing our case into your incidents at Emerald Lake as well. We know Toben Garrett was sent by Shen Lei to see what Mason Ross was up to. He was supposed to search your house, Wenner, but you returned home early that night, and he had no choice but try to make it look like a burglary, except he didn't steal anything."

"We thought after he hit me from behind that he panicked and ran without taking anything," Wenner said.

"At the time, it was the only thing that made sense." The detective looked at Chelsea. "You played an important role in all of this, Chelsea. The department wants to thank you, as well."

"I'm just glad it's over with and we're all safe."

The detective stood and held the door open for them. "I wish the best for both of you."

They said goodbye and left the building. Chelsea studied Wenner. "Are you all right?"

"I'm fine."

She looked at her watch. "We're due at Chaz's in an hour. You want to come to the hospital to see the babies with me?"

"How about I drop you off and run a couple of

errands? I'll come back to pick you up and pop in to see them."

"Sounds good."

On their way to the hospital, Chelsea checked her messages. "Oh dear, there was an issue of some kind with Willow today. But Sydney says not to worry, she's fine."

"How old are the girls now?"

"Thirty weeks."

"They've come a long way. When do they expect they can go home?"

"In another four weeks. Hopefully, they'll be home for Christmas."

Wenner pulled up at the front entrance to the hospital. "I'll be back in about forty minutes."

Chelsea wrapped her coat around her and hurried through the brisk wind into the entrance. She went to the cafeteria to get a cup of coffee and stepped into the elevator with a young woman who appeared to be staff. The girl smiled and said hello. Chelsea returned her smile and nodded. The employee exited on the same floor and stood beside her at the window of the NICU. Chelsea studied Willow, saddened to see her separated from her sisters and hooked up to a monitor. But Sydney said she was fine. *I'll go with that.* They were slow to gain weight, but you could definitely see that all three had filled out. They had grown in length during the past month.

The young woman interrupted her thoughts. "Aren't they beautiful?" she asked.

"They truly are."

"I work part-time in admissions and stop by whenever I'm on shift to see them. We have a fund set up to raise money for Sydney and the babies when they go home. And we've been collecting baby clothes, diapers, and the like to present to her on the day they're released."

"How thoughtful and generous of you all. Please thank everyone for me."

"It's the least we can do to help her. Identical triplets don't come along every day. We've all been so excited about the girls."

"We're all looking forward to the day they can go home."

"I bet. And it's a secret, so please don't say anything to her."

Chelsea grinned. "I won't."

The girl smiled back. She appeared to hesitate and then spoke. "You're Chelsea Grey, aren't you?"

Oh, here we go.

"I am." Chelsea braced herself. Please don't go there. *That part of my life is over and done with.* She looked directly into the girl's eyes waiting for the look of pity, determined she wouldn't slip into the role of the victim.

The young woman put her shoulders back and put out her hand. "I'm Madison Hayes, you can call me Madie."

Chelsea shook her hand. "Nice to meet you, Madie."

"You work at the Wildlife Centre with Wenner Gibb, right?"

"I do."

"Well, I work part-time at the one here in Kelowna."

"I haven't visited it yet. It's much larger and more established than ours. Do you enjoy the work?"

"I love it. I was wondering if you're hiring? The Kelowna Centre only has part-time workers, except for the veterinarians. I'm looking to work full-time at a facility. I'm very qualified."

Oh! Wasn't I being presumptuous? She's only looking for a job. Chelsea laughed silently at herself. "Unfortunately, you've caught us at the wrong time. We're moving the facility to Stoney Creek."

Instead of looking disappointed, Madie brightened. "That's dope. Well then, will you be hiring when you open? I'd love to be a part of a new start-up. I have four years of college; business courses and animal husbandry. I love working in the Education Centre, running tours."

Chelsea loved the girl's enthusiasm. It reminded her of herself in her teens. "How old are you, Madie?"

"Twenty-two."

"Well, it's a bit premature for us to be talking about staffing, but you sound well qualified. Why don't you send me a resume?"

"Really?"

Chelsea rummaged through her shoulder bag. "Here's a card with the address. Would you be willing to relocate?"

"Absolutely."

"We won't be setting up until spring, with hopefully an opening date in June. But you never know; with so many details to take care of, we may need some help before then."

"I'm available anytime."

"Good."

"Can I ask why you're moving it?"

"We have an opportunity to expand the facility, and in order to do that we need more land. And we want to focus on the educational aspects, too, with programs and tours."

"Which is right up my alley."

Chelsea chortled. "So it seems."

"Wow. I'm really excited about this. I hope we can get together in the future and talk about it."

"It probably won't be until the New Year, but I will connect with you at some point."

A voice rang out from down the hall. "I made it. Parking was ridiculous," Wenner said, marching to them.

"This is Madie," Chelsea said. "Madie, Wenner Gibb."

The two of them shook hands. "Nice to meet you, Mr. Gibb."

"It's Wenner. Glad to meet you, too, Madie."

Madie glanced at her watch. "Oops, I'm late." She turned back to Chelsea. "I'll send you my resume right away. I hope to hear from you." She gave Wenner a nod and a wave.

"What was that all about?" Wenner asked, as he watched her hurry off down the corridor and disappear around a corner.

Chelsea laughed. "She wants a job at our new facility. She works part-time at the Kelowna Centre."

"A bit premature, I'd say."

"That's what I told her. But I like her attitude, and from the sounds of it, she's qualified. I told her to forward her resume."

But she'd already lost his attention. He stood at the window staring at the three girls. "Omigod...look at those little darlings."

❊ 49 ❊
KELOWNA

It was early December and almost three weeks since the upset with Willow's lungs. The triplets had reached their thirty-third week. Sydney sat in a private room off the NICU waiting for Nurse Kelly to bring her Jenna. A combination of excitement and nerves had her stomach in knots. Today, she would begin her first breastfeeding with two of her daughters. Willow wasn't developed enough yet, but she was off the oxygen and back with her sisters in a shared bed. Although she appeared to be outgrowing her apnea, the monitor was still being used during sleeping times, and Sydney had been taught how to set it up. All three had developed muscle tone, could move their heads from side to side and bend their arms and legs with smoother fluidity.

For the past two weeks, Sydney had been able to hold her daughters when they were fed through their feeding tubes to develop a bond between the girls and their mother at feeding time. Sydney had also worked with a lactation consultant provided by the hospital for teaching mothers how to increase their milk flow and help preemie babies breastfeed well.

Nurse Kelly arrived with Jenna and placed her

into Sydney's arms. Nancy, the consultant, arrived, and Kelly left them alone. "Okay, little momma, you ready for this?"

Sydney took a deep breath. "As ready as I'll ever be."

"First, let yourself relax. If Jenna feels your tension, she'll have trouble feeding. And don't have great expectations. Remember, mothers can have trouble breastfeeding with full-term babies, never mind preemies."

"I'm so glad you're here to help me."

"All right. First thing you'll do is put your pinky finger in Jenna's mouth and press on her tongue a couple of times, pull out your finger and do it a second time." The second time, Jenna latched down on her finger and began to suck.

"Perfect. Now pull out your pinky and lower your nipple to her bottom lip. Tap a couple of times and her mouth should open wider. When it does, I'll place her jaw underneath in the right position."

She did as she was told, and when Jenna opened her mouth, Nancy placed her jaw in position. Sydney slipped her nipple into Jenna's mouth, and her daughter latched on and started to suck.

Sydney's eyes popped. "It's working. She's feeding." She sat still, afraid if she moved, it would stop the process.

"Relax, hon. You're tensing up. Sit back and get into a comfortable position. Jenna is latched on perfectly. She'll come with you."

Sydney was elated. She settled into the chair, and the tightness in her stomach lessened. "I've waited so long for this."

"It's been a journey. We brought Jenna first because she seems the most developed of the three girls. I'm so happy your first time worked out so well."

As Jenna fed, she stared into her mother's eyes and Sydney's heart soared, filling her with a love that almost overwhelmed her.

After a few minutes, Jenna fell asleep and Nancy took her back to the nursery, returning with Kylie. "Now let me warn you, it may not go as easy with Kylie. So don't get discouraged. We'll switch breasts this time around."

Sydney placed Kylie in position for the opposite breast and repeated the steps she'd been taught with Kylie. True to Nancy's words, Kylie wouldn't latch on.

"Okay, let's relax, and I'll leave you to bond with your daughter. I'll be back in a few minutes and we'll try again."

Alone with Kylie, Sydney tried to hide her feelings of disappointment. The problem with Kylie was that she was still the one who slept the most, and she kept closing her eyes to nap. "Wake up, little one. Let's show Nancy that we can do this."

Sydney placed her pinky in Kylie's mouth and tapped on her tongue. Her daughter latched onto her finger and began to suckle. "Omigod, you're doing it." Gently pulling her finger lose, she placed her nipple into Kylie's open mouth and adjusted her daughter's chin and lower lip. Kylie began to feed. The first time she swallowed, Kylie started to choke and let go of Sydney's breast. "On, no." Sydney lifted her up onto her shoulder and patted her back.

Nancy returned at that moment, and Sydney felt guilty.

"She latched on and started to feed, but she started choking. I should've waited for you to return."

"Not at all. Good for you to take up the challenge on your own. Swallowing for the first time is a new experience for her. She startled herself is all. She's settled down now so let's try again."

Sydney repeated the process with Kylie again, and this time she latched on and swallowed without choking. Before long, she fell asleep and her mouth loosened.

"A great start, hon. Be proud. I'll take Kylie back to her bed."

Sydney sat smiling, feeling good about finally achieving the ultimate role as a mother. When Nancy returned, she sat down with her. "You must be prepared that feeding your girls will be a full-time job. Once you're home with the girls, they'll need eight to twelve feedings a day each, depending on how much they take in with one feeding, and they may not all need feeding at the same time."

Sydney's brow wrinkled. "How do I know if they're getting enough milk? Especially Kylie, who sleeps a lot."

"You'll know by how many feedings they want, first off. But don't forget you'll be rotating them on the bottle. We'll introduce them to a bottle next week. In a couple of days, we'll see if Willow is ready to begin breastfeeding. Understand that they all may lose a couple of pounds transitioning from tube feedings to the breast and bottle. Not to worry."

"Okay."

"It'll be a while before you will have any sort of steady schedule. I suggest that you get your rest when the girls are sleeping. You need to make sure you eat well. Do you have lots of help initially when you all go home?"

"Yes. We have a live-in housekeeper during the

week, and Jax, my mom and grandmother will all be helping."

"You're lucky to have a strong support system. Any questions?"

"Not at the moment."

"Then we're done for the time being. Kelly will let me know when the girls are ready for their next feed, and I'll come back. One last thing. The girls probably will be going home in a couple of weeks' time. A couple of nights before they go, we'd like you and Jax to stay the night here. We set this room up with cots. Jax will be shown how to help you and bottle feed one of the girls while you feed the other two. We find that new fathers of multiples do better with transition if they get some support here before you all go home. Will that work for you both?"

"Absolutely. I know Jax would appreciate the support."

After Nancy left, Sydney entered the nursery. She stood and watched her daughters sleep. Her world had changed so quickly and drastically in the past two months. *But I wouldn't change a thing. Now I'm truly a mother.* Her heart soared, and a wide smile spread across her face.

God help us!

I t was Christmas Eve day, and Chelsea, Chaz, Elizabeth and Gord were gathered at the farmhouse. It was discharge day. The triplets were coming home. Sydney and Jax had spent the past few days in Kelowna prepping for their trip home with the girls. Jax had traded his jeep for a family van, and everyone at the farm was excited.

The day before in Kelowna, Sydney had signed the final papers transferring the ownership of a forty-acre parcel of land to Chelsea and Wenner. Wenner's property in Emerald Creek had sold at the beginning of November with the new owners wanting a December 15th closing date, as they were determined to be in by Christmas. Wenner had moved into the cottage with Chelsea until they were ready to make the move in the spring to Stoney Creek. After the paperwork was finished, Wenner left for the Kelowna Airport to fly home to spend Christmas with family. Chelsea had never seen him so happy.

The women had prepped dinner, and there was nothing left to do but enjoy the day while they waited.

Chelsea looked out the window at the frozen lake

and the foot of snow covering the ground. Memories of her childhood were at the forefront of her mind. Skating on the lake, the making of snowmen and snow angels, and building snow forts. Jax had shovelled a path from the deck to the lake and another one to the left of the deck and through the magnolia grove.

She donned her jacket, scarf and gloves, searched for her boots amongst the pile in the mud room, and left the house. She followed the path into the magnolia grove and continued on to her favourite tree. Moving around the trunk, she found the heart with the letters C & C carved into the bark. So much had happened since that innocent moment she and Chaz had carved their initials here.

Good and bad, love and hate, peace and violence —life; a family once divided—now united. *If this tree could talk, what a tale it would tell.*

"Are you going to stare at that spot all day or notice me up here sitting on your favourite limb and talk to me?"

Chelsea gasped. "Chloe? There you go again. Heart attack going on here."

"Oh, stop, I know you're happy to see me."

Chelsea smiled. "I thought you were gone forever. I didn't expect to see you again."

"What? And miss this important family day? I had to see the babies. In case you've forgotten, they are my great-nieces."

"By the way, thanks for showing up at the cave and tripping Toben Garrett. You were an important part to that day ending on a positive."

"Talon and I had been watching over you for weeks. But somehow I think you would have managed fine without us. You really got it together that day. I'm so proud of you."

"Thanks, Chloe."

Chloe looked over the landscape and towards the lake. "So this is what I missed. It really is beautiful. You've come full-circle, Sis, and something tells me you're going to thrive back here on the farm."

"I think so, too."

Chloe stared up the pathway. "I think someone is joining you. Time to say goodbye, my dear sister."

Chelsea spun around to see her mother entering the magnolia grove. "Before you go, this is your moment to meet our mother."

Her sister watched the woman approach. Chloe gasped.

"Say hello, Chloe."

Elizabeth cocked her head to one side. "Are you talking to yourself?"

"No, she's talking to me."

Elizabeth glanced up at the tree with a start. Her mouth dropped open as her hand went to her chest. Her eyes moved to Chelsea's, and she pointed to Chloe. "Is...is that her?"

Chelsea smiled and nodded. Her mother stared at Chloe.

"Hello, Lizzie. It's nice to meet you."

Her mother began to shake. "Well...how weird is this?"

"It seems that way. But it's really two parallel realms connecting together at the same time. I want you to know I admire that you stood by Chelsea. You're a good person."

Elizabeth shook her head. "I think your being here to help Chelsea through her struggles these past months did more good than anything. From what Chelsea says, you didn't pull any punches. That was something I couldn't bring myself to do."

"Well, it seems we sisters are very similar in personality." Chloe looked around the property. "I wish I'd been able to stay and grow up here. But it wasn't to be. You have a beautiful family, Lizzie, and I wish all of you the very best. But I'm happy I got to meet you both. It's not too often that we get to meet our earth mother and siblings." Chloe sighed. "Now I must take my obnoxious self and thrust my way into someone else's life."

"Stay true to form, Sis. You do great work. Thank you," Chelsea said.

Elizabeth didn't know what to say. She raised her hand and waved. "Goodbye."

Chloe disappeared.

"I'm so glad you got to see her," Chelsea said.

Her mother's eyes glistened. "Now, how weird was that? But I'm glad I saw her, as short as it was."

Chelsea came to stand beside her mother. She linked her arm through hers. "I hope this tree never dies. It's a spiritual tree. It holds so much of our family's history. It's been a part of my life, Chaz's, Sydney's, Jax's and now Chloe's."

Elizabeth squeezed Chelsea's arm. "With this tree, we've come full circle, haven't we?"

Chelsea's eyes popped. "More than one person has said that to me recently."

"I came out to tell you they're all home."

"Then let's go. I want to see my grandbabies."

They entered the house and all was quiet. *Where was everyone?* They searched the kitchen and living room. *No one.*

Chelsea giggled. "I think I know where they are." She led the way down the hall to the doorway of the nursery. Gord, Sydney, Jax, and Chaz were standing around the three basinets, silently observing the newest additions to their family. Oblivious to them all, except for Chelsea, Chloe wandered behind them peering down at each of the girls. She looked up at Chelsea, gave her a thumbs up and disappeared. The two women crept into the room. Elizabeth joined Gord, and Chelsea went to stand beside Chaz.

Gord spoke in a whisper. "Lucky thing they sent them home with their name tags. I sure can't tell them apart."

"They'll soon outgrow their wrist bands," Sydney whispered, with a chuckle. "But I can usually tell them apart. They're developing distinct personalities. Willow may have been the smallest in the beginning, but she's the feisty one. Very demanding. I'm going to paint her pinky fingernail red; a power colour. Jenna's the most alert to what's happening around her and she loves funky jazz music; purple for her pinky. And Kylie's very quiet, sleeps the best, a real little lady; her pinky gets pearl pink."

Elizabeth teared up. "Aw…"

Without giving it a thought, Chelsea slipped her hand into Chaz's, and he tightened his grip. Emotion overtook her as she glanced around the room at her family. *This will be the best Christmas in over twenty years.* Her throat tightened. Love, pride and gratefulness all rolled into one took a grip, and she knew this was a moment she'd never forget. A happiness she'd never known bubbled up inside until she thought she'd burst. A wide smile broke across her face. She caught Sydney nudging her grandmother and tilting her head towards her and Chaz. Their gaze went down to her hand entwined with Chaz's. Grandmother and granddaughter gave each other knowing grins.

Chelsea rolled her eyes. *Oh please…we're just holding hands!*

EPILOGUE

WOMEN'S VICTIM SURVIVORS CONFERENCE, UNIVERSITY OF BRITISH COLUMBIA, KELOWNA CAMPUS

SIX MONTHS LATER

C helsea sat on the stage facing the audience. Her nerves were taut, her mouth dry. She listened to Dr. Sauvé talk about her work with abused women. Her hands were folded together in her lap to keep her from wringing them. This attempt to appear calm and professional did nothing to quiet the storm brewing within her stomach and lungs, not to mention the drum beat pounding in her head. She tuned the room out until the sound of applause brought her back. Dr. Sauvé had finished her presentation and stood at the podium in silence waiting for the clapping to cease.

"I'd like to introduce the next speaker. She is a woman who not only was a victim in every sense of the word, but is a true survivor. Please help me welcome Miss Chelsea Grey."

Chelsea stood and made her way to the podium. To say she was overwhelmed at the response from the audience was an understatement. The standing ovation and noise level assaulted not only her ears but her inner being. The room spun, and she held on to the sides of the podium to support her shaking legs and keep her balance. *What am I doing here?* She remembered the night last year when she attended an Alcoholics Anonymous meeting with about ten people. *No way could I talk to that group.* Her eyes scanned the hall and the hundreds of people who were settling in their seats to listen to her speak. Reporters were snapping pictures, and a film crew was taping. She glanced at Dr. Sauvé, frozen in fear. The doctor placed a hand on her shoulder and squeezed. As she left her alone at the podium, she whispered in her ear. "Deep breaths. You'll do great."

Chelsea cleared her throat and started. "Good afternoon. I'd like to thank the university and Chairman Westman for inviting me here today. Being a part of this conference is truly an honour." Her voice echoed back at her, and she could hear how shaky she sounded. She forced a cough and pulled the microphone closer, determined to sound more confident. "I'm here to share a story of abduction, incarceration, abuse—and survival. I must tell you that this is the first time I've spoken to anyone about these events other than my therapist. There are members of my family here today who will be hearing me talk of some my experiences for the first time. Sharing my story with all of you is a little daunting, and I ask that you forgive me should I pause or lose my way." Chelsea took a sip of water from the glass placed for her on the podium.

Someone in the audience yelled, "We're with you, Chelsea." The audience applauded in agreement.

She smiled and began. "When I was a teenager, I was very outgoing—and rebellious, as teenage girls can be. I loved Cindy Lauper, dyed my hair pink and was filled with a sense of adventure that had me day-dreaming for the time when I could leave the family farm and head to the big city. The summer I gradu-ated from high school, I learned I was pregnant, and to quote Robert Burns, 'The best-laid plans of mice and men often go awry.' And so I stayed on the farm, and on my nineteenth birthday, I gave birth to my daughter, Sydney. One year later, I made plans to leave the farm with my daughter. Through social ser-vices, I registered for a medical program in Kelowna, which included an apartment and a daycare for Sydney at the school. I hadn't told my parents I was leaving because my father had insisted if I went to the city, Sydney must stay with them on the farm. I disagreed, and not wanting to argue the point fur-ther, I chose to leave on a day they were away on a shopping trip. The morning of my departure, I awoke with an excitement and expectation that my life was about to begin for the positive. Little did I know I'd never reach Kelowna. A neighbouring farmer came looking for my father. Arne had been obsessed with me for years, a fact I wasn't aware of until that fateful morning. Realizing I was about to leave the farm, he panicked and attacked me. He tied me up and took me to an outbuilding on his farm and locked me in. He took Sydney to his wife, Mary, at the main farmhouse, telling her I'd left to go to school, and could she babysit Sydney for the day until my parents returned that afternoon. And so began an incarceration that would last twenty years.

I spent the next months in that outbuilding in the middle of a field, too far away for my screams to be heard. I tried to dig my way out, screamed until I was hoarse, physically fought with my attacker, who always won, and I escaped twice, only to be caught and beaten for my efforts. His threats to kill me if I didn't comply fell on deaf ears. I'd have rather died than stayed locked up in that dirty one-room building with a dirt floor and two buckets—one to wash in and the other to serve as a toilet. It reached the point that my body was in a constant state of cuts, bruises and always in pain, and in the end, Arne still had his way with me. But he never left unscathed without scratches or bruises for his attempts, which he explained away to Mary as a hard-working farmer's lament.

One day he sat me down and told me we needed to reach a truce. He told me if I didn't become compliant, he'd see to it that Sydney had an accident, and after that, he'd kill my mother. There are many forms of violence. Arne had tried physical and sexual abuse to tame me, and it hadn't worked. It was time for mental abuse. He left me alone for a number of days to think about it. Fearful he'd kill my family, I made the decision to become compliant. Not for me —for them. He'd broken me. Knowing he had control, he worked it to his advantage and never stopped reminding me of what would happen if I fought him again or ever did escape. Time passed.

I hated myself for giving in to him, but if I ever doubted his promises to kill my family, he proved his determination to protect what he believed was his... me. One day, Mary followed him to the outbuilding, suspicious of his many trips to the far field of the farm. When she discovered me, I'll never forget the look on her face of disbelief, hurt, and then anger. She told Arne she was calling the police and turned to run back to the house. He caught her quickly enough and injected her with a vial of potassium chloride. She died within minutes. The drug dissipated into her blood stream and passed out of her body. Coroner's report: fatal heart attack. This single event showed me what Arne was capable of. His control over me was complete."

Chelsea paused. Reliving Mary's death had shaken her, and her voice became shaky again. She sipped some water and took a deep breath. With a glance into the front row, she saw her mother wiping her eyes with a tissue. Determined not to lose control, she straightened her shoulders and focused on the back of the auditorium.

"A week after Mary's funeral, Arne moved me into the house. He'd always discouraged visitors, and no one ever came to the farm. When I wasn't upstairs to do housework, cleaning or succumbing to his personal needs, Arne padlocked me in a room in the basement. There was no window, but at least it had a proper bed, a carpeted floor, a sink and toilet...and it was warm. I had a radio and a television with local channels. He became my lifeline to the outside world. Brought me clothes, toiletries, and books from the library. Months would pass and he'd be nice to me, as long as I was compliant. I became what he wanted and was dependent on him for my well-being. A few years passed, and it was always in the back of my mind that if he ever let his guard down, perhaps I could get the upper hand over him and escape. But Arne was always vigilant; he watched me cook and never let me handle knives or scissors.

Early one Sunday morning, my father walked to the farm to ask for Arne's help with a broken tractor part. He knew Arne was home, and when he didn't answer the door, Dad walked around the house and looked in the kitchen window to see me making breakfast."

Chelsea heard her mother groan and forced her eyes away from her direction. Her throat constricted and she paused. Her face contorted as tears wet her eyes and she swallowed hard. *Stay strong. No crying.* She held on and continued.

"For a second time, I experienced the look of horror on his face…like Mary's. He ran towards the front of the house, but Arne was waiting for him. He injected my father with potassium chloride. I slipped away behind his back and ran up the driveway. Arne caught me, dragged me back and…and…" Chelsea stared into a light at the back of the hall and focused on its brightness. She took a deep breath. "He forced me to watch my father die. Locked in the basement room, he took my father home and dumped him on the front porch like a sack of potatoes. When he returned to the house, he beat me for running.

His threats intensified against my mother and Sydney, and I gave up hope of ever being free. I accepted my fate. A total of twenty years passed, and one day, the locks came off, and the door opened, and a young woman entered the room. My daughter, Sydney, was my saviour until Arne returned. He threw her across the room, knocking her out. I escaped upstairs to the kitchen in the hopes I could get help for us both, but he caught me. We struggled by the stove, knocking over a pot of stew simmering on the stove. Arne's shirt caught on fire. He let me go to pull it off and threw it in the sink, which lit up the window curtains. I ran again, and he caught me near the open front door and dragged me back into the kitchen. Freedom was so close. With his hands around my neck, he began choking me. My mother arrived, another saviour, and hit him with a cast-iron fry pan. That day, the farmhouse burned down, Arne died, and I was free at last."

Chelsea drank some more water. She felt a sense of relief that the worst part of the story was over.

Her chest muscles relaxed, and for the first time since she'd begun to speak, she felt strong. The tight grip she'd had on the edge of the podium had left her arms numb. She let go and folded her hands together on the flat surface in front of the microphone. With a new confidence, Chelsea continued.

"Now, you'd think I'd be ecstatic to taste freedom again and have my life back. But when you lose your sense of self and your sense of worth, you also lose your identity. Having absolute power after having your mind broken and your will stripped is a fearful thing. You lose your ability to trust in others and along with that your ability to trust in your own choices. I locked myself away for three months at the farm with my mother and daughter. When my mother returned to her home in Kelowna, I went with her, still afraid to venture out. For the first six months after I was freed, I had intensive therapy, and I talked, talked, and talked some more as I went through the stages of shock, anxiety, guilt, depression, and finally anger.

After all of that, I still didn't feel free. Then I discovered alcohol, pills, nightclubs, and people who wanted to party, not talk about my incarceration. At first, I thought this was freedom. It took me away from my feelings of angst and vulnerabilities. But that was short-lived, and I realized I was on a path of destruction. What I needed to do was remove myself from people who pitied me and constantly wanted to know my story. How could I get over being a victim if people looked at me and treated me like I was one? I retreated alone to a cottage on Emerald Lake. I found work with injured animals and began online studies, gave up the party life, and slowly rediscovered who I am. I learned to develop a relationship with my daughter, from the only one I'd known when she was an infant to one with her as a young woman. I was lucky to have a mother who never gave up on me and helped me rediscover the lost teenage girl who'd been full of adventure and excited to meet the challenges of life. The one truth that set me free was realizing that other people had issues to deal with, too. I wasn't unique. And that some people will always look at me as a victim. That has nothing to do with me. I won't be defined by what other people think...good or bad. It's not my business. I continued to check in with my therapist, and now, two years since I was freed, I'm still a work in progress but no longer think of myself as a victim. I'm ready to share my experience with others who have been victims and with those who are still subjected to abuse.

I came here today to share my story because it's so important that educators, doctors, and social workers understand what a victim experiences and how a support network is crucial to the healing process. But education programs are equally important for young girls and women, so perhaps they can avoid becoming a victim. The Me Too Movement has brought into the foreground what people for years already knew was happening but felt powerless to stop and were afraid to talk about. But it's only the beginning.

"A few facts. In Canada, approximately every six days, a woman is murdered by an intimate partner. On any given night, three hundred women and children are turned away from shelters because they are full. Full! There are approximately thirty-five hundred women and twenty-eight hundred children sleeping in a shelter to avoid abuse. And seventy percent of abuse cases are never reported. We have much, much more work to do.

I'm humbled to be speaking before people who

337

not only work hard every day to protect women and children but care so deeply. Speaking here today not only fills me with pride but contributes to my own healing journey. I thank you for allowing me to be part of this important conference and share my story. I'm Chelsea Grey, and I'm a survivor."

Chelsea stepped to the side of the podium. The audience applause resounded. Another standing ovation. She glanced to the front row at her family. Her mother, unable to stop crying, wiped at her cheeks. Gord stood beside her clapping enthusiastically. Sydney was teary-eyed but smiling broadly. Jax clapped loudly and whistled, making Chelsea laugh. And Chaz beamed at her with pride.

The resonance of their applause vibrated within her body. She actually felt its warmth and embraced the sensation. She nodded at the audience and turned towards Dr. Sauvé, who stood behind her. The two embraced. The doctor pushed her back, and the two stared into each other's eyes.

"You did it. How does it feel?" Dr. Sauvé asked.

With glistening eyes, Chelsea gave her a wide smile.

"Like I'm free at last. The Chameleon Games are over."

THE END

Chameleon Games
ISBN: 978-4-86750-383-6
Mass Market

Published by
Next Chapter
1-60-20 Minami-Otsuka
170-0005 Toshima-Ku, Tokyo
+818035793528

4th June 2021

Lightning Source UK Ltd.
Milton Keynes UK
UKHW041024170621
385669UK00001B/71